So Near
So Far

C. NORTHCOTE
PARKINSON

RICHARD DELANCEY NOVELS, NO. 5

MCBOOKS PRESS, INC.
ITHACA, NEW YORK

For Charles

Published by McBooks Press, Inc. 2003
Copyright © 1981 by C. Northcote Parkinson
First published in the United Kingdom by John Murray Ltd, 1981

Cover painting: *Sir J. T. Duckworth's Action off St. Domingo,
February 6th, 1806,* engraved by Thomas Sutherland after a painting by
Thomas Whitcombe, for J. Jenkins *Naval Achievements,* 1817.
The Stapleton Collection/Photo courtesy of Bridgeman Art Library.

Library of Congress Cataloging-in-Publication Data

Parkinson, C. Northcote (Cyril Northcote), 1909-
  So near so far / by C. Northcote Parkinson.
    p. cm. — (The Richard Delancey novels ; no. 5)
  ISBN 1-59013-037-5 (alk. paper)
  1. Delancey, Richard (Fictitious character)—Fiction. 2. Great
Britain—History, Naval—19th century—Fiction. 3. Napoleonic Wars,
1800-1815—Fiction. I. Title.
  PR6066.A6955S6 2003
  823'.914—dc21
                                    2002155775

Distributed to the trade by National Book Network, Inc.,
15200 NBN Way, Blue Ridge Summit, PA 17214
800-462-6420

Printed in the United States of America
9 8 7 6 5 4 3 2

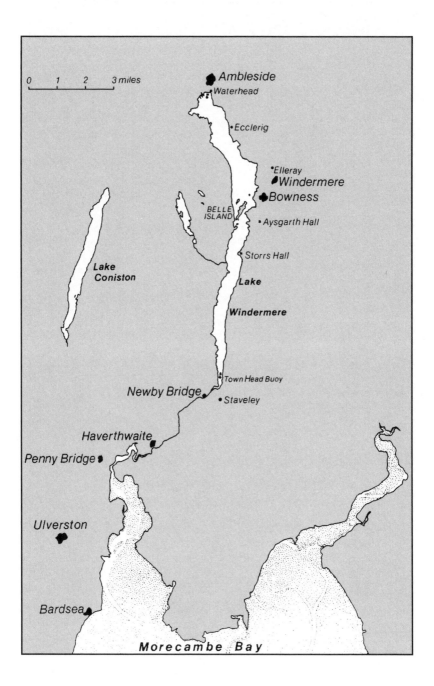

0   1   2   3 miles

Ambleside
•Waterhead

•Ecclerig

•Elleray
Windermere
Bowness

BELLE
ISLAND

• Aysgarth Hall

Lake
Coniston

Storrs Hall

Lake

Windermere

Town Head Buoy
Newby Bridge
• Staveley

Haverthwaite
Penny Bridge

Ulverston

Bardsea

Morecambe Bay

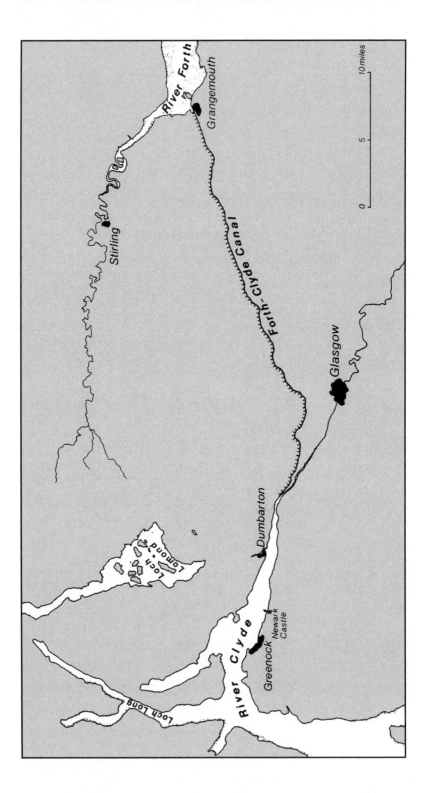

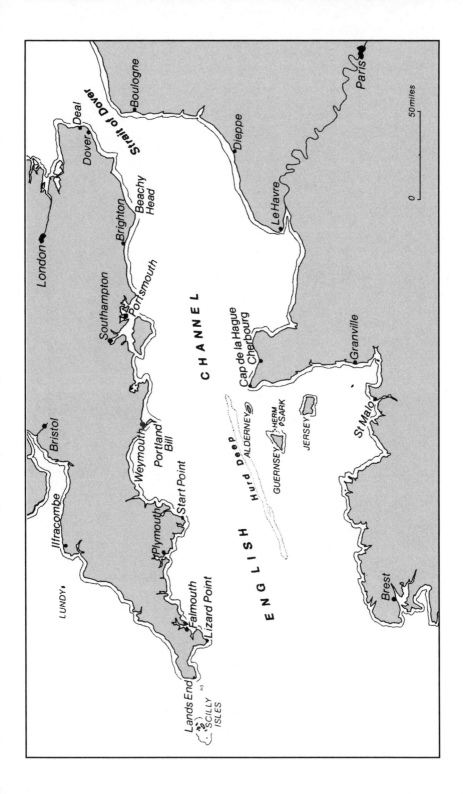

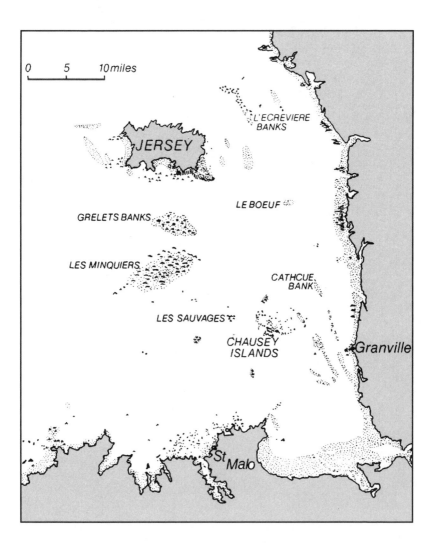

0   5   10 miles

JERSEY

L'ECREVIERE
BANKS

LE BOEUF

GRELETS BANKS

LES MINQUIERS

CATHCUE
BANK

LES SAUVAGES

CHAUSEY
ISLANDS

Granville

St Malo

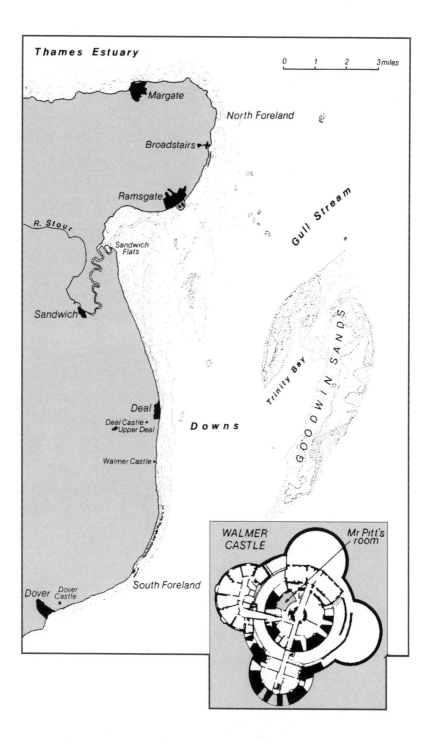

Thames Estuary

0   1   2   3 miles

Margate

North Foreland

Broadstairs

Ramsgate

Gull Stream

R. Stour

Sandwich
Flats

Sandwich

Downs

Deal

Deal Castle
Upper Deal

Walmer Castle

Trinity Bay

GOODWIN SANDS

WALMER
CASTLE

Mr Pitt's
room

Dover   Dover
Castle

South Foreland

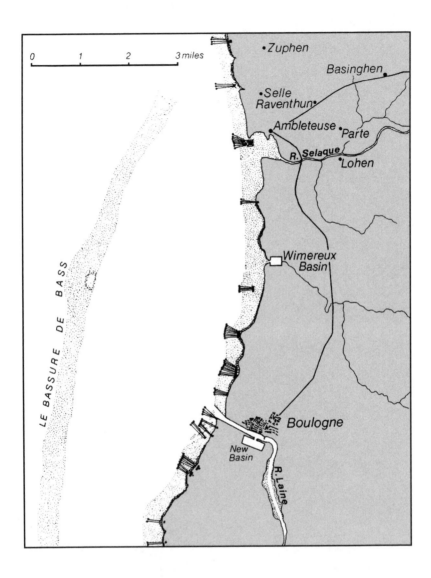

0   1   2   3 miles

• Zuphen

Basinghen •

• Selle
Raventhun •

Ambleteuse •   • Parte

R. Selaque

• Lohen

Wimereux
Basin

LE BASSURE DE BASS

Boulogne

New
Basin

R. Laine

Chapter One

THE "DAPHNÉ"

"**A**GE AND LENGTH of service bring with them certain privileges. I claim one of them in proposing that we presently drink the health of our host, Captain Richard Delancey."

It was Captain Savage who was on his feet and fairly launched on a speech. With some reluctance, those who had been about to drink put their glasses down again.

"Before we drink I shall explain in a few words why Delancey has won our admiration. From the stern window we can glimpse his prize, the French merchantman *Bonaparte,* captured the day before yesterday and brought into harbour almost undamaged save in her rigging. The war ended yesterday in the Channel and the *Bonaparte,* had she been taken a day later, would have been released again. She was captured in the nick of time and we all have some idea of her value. Ashore here in Guernsey all the old seamen are telling each other that Dick Delancey has been fortunate again, as lucky as he was that time when he took the *Bonne Citoyenne.* There was, believe me, but a small element of luck on either occasion and a far larger element of forethought, courage, and skill."

There was applause at this point, after which Savage continued: "Few other men would have known what to do when the master of the French ship threatened to blow up the *Bonaparte* with the *Merlin* close alongside her. To fight against

11

a brave opponent must require resolution but Delancey's task was more difficult than that. His adversary was a madman! As I have just said, Delancey is thought to be lucky and I will concede that he was fortunate on this occasion in one respect. Two French coasting vessels were brought in yesterday by the *Swordfish*, private man-of-war, and were released at once as vessels taken in time of peace. Seizing his opportunity, Delancey sent all his prisoners on board her and soon afterwards saw that ship sail for Cherbourg. He was relieved, I fancy, when the madman Charbonnier was fairly out of his sight! Not the least remarkable aspect of this, Delancey's last exploit, is that the *Merlin* came into port with only five seamen slightly wounded and the sloop herself undamaged save for the foreyard broken and the spritsail yard shot away; just damage enough to explain a few days spent here in St Peter Port. Although he is not a post captain yet he is young enough to end as an Admiral. That he will reach flag rank I am confident and I shall tell you why. Many another man might have captured the *Bonaparte* only after bloodshed and damage on either side, with gain of prize money to be set against loss of life. But that is not Delancey's way—"

Delancey's interest was wandering by this time. Why must the old man go on and on? His prediction was nonsense, anyway. The war had ended and there might be no further conflict for twenty years. So the chances were against his ever having another command. He would be ashore on a meagre pension, a landowner in a small way but with barely enough money, perhaps, to complete the repair of his ruined manor house. He would have time to marry but would make no great match, having little to offer. His sensible course would be to marry for money, given the chance, but his own inclination would lead

him towards some wild gamine, some young red-haired mis-
chief-maker, perhaps an actress like that girl he had seen briefly
back in 1794. But war was his only trade. How was he to make
a living in the years to come? He had the respect of other seamen but reputation is of little use without income. What was
the *Bonaparte* actually worth? If ship and cargo sold for £20,000,
legal costs and commission would reduce that to about
£16,000, of which £6,000 would come to him. That would be
more than enough to set him up as some kind of merchant but
he doubted whether he possessed a head for business; and the
Bonaparte might not be worth as much. No one knew yet
whether the goods in the lower hold had been spoilt by sea
water. . . . He was called back to the present by the sound of
applause. Old Savage was about to finish.

"Well, gentlemen, if Sir James Saumarez is the greatest
Guernseyman of the present age—and I hear of none nearly
his equal—I venture to predict that Captain Delancey will count
as the second before he finally comes ashore. So I ask you all
to raise your glasses and drink the health of Richard Delancey!"

Delancey thanked Savage for his compliments and all present for their kindness. Those really deserving of praise were
the officers and men of H. M. Ship *Merlin* and he proposed their
health accordingly. Looking round the cabin afterwards, he
realised how lucky he had been in his followers afloat and his
friends ashore. Mather was the perfect first lieutenant, Stirling
a very valuable officer, and the young gentlemen, Langford,
Northmore, and Topley, were all extremely useful and promising. As for the Guernseymen, Savage himself, Le Poidevin, De
Guerin, and the rest, he was now one of their heroes. Even
Nicole Andros now claimed him as a cousin and Le Pelley's

admiration was outspoken. The man oddly missing was Sam Carter who had sailed the day before on some unspecified errand. Delancey remembered, with an effort, that a visit to France was now perfectly legal. There could be no doubt that Sam would be resuming his regular smuggling trade which the war had tended to interrupt. The *Dove* might be gone for a few days but the *Merlin* might be in port for as long, with repairs to be completed and ropes to be spliced. He hoped, therefore, that he might see Sam again before he had to sail for Plymouth. Delancey, meanwhile, must call on Lady Saumarez and on the Bailiff, read the newspapers and hear the gossip. He would also find time to see how the builders had progressed with the restoration of Anneville Manor, some parts of which should by now be habitable. He had the pleasant feeling of being on holiday. There would follow the task of paying the ship off and hauling down his pennant for what might be the last time. Then he must decide how to make his living. More immediately, however, he had to say goodbye to his guests, showing a special deference to Captain Savage's seniority.

At Anneville Delancey was pleasantly surprised to find that the old building was no longer a mere ruin. The roof was watertight, the floors were finished, the windows complete. Such had been the recent progress that he felt able to order the furniture, the mattresses, and bedding. Were he to marry, his wife could expect no life of luxury. She would, nevertheless, have a house in which to live, with garden, stables and pasture for her horse. He dared not order the curtaining and carpet, supposing that his bride would wish to choose the pattern for herself. Yes, he had something to offer these days: his courtesy rank of "Captain," his feudal position as Seigneur, his prestige as a minor landowner. He should have income enough to support a family in moderate style; lacking a carriage, to be sure (there were no metalled roads in the island) but able to keep half a dozen servants. For as poor a boy as he had been, Delancey had done well. The pity was that the peace had come so soon, while his fortune was still to make.

Three days later Sam Carter reappeared in St Peter Port and Delancey invited him to dine at the Golden Lion. Sam, it soon appeared, had news from Cherbourg.

"This man Charbonnier, the madman who captained the *Bonaparte*, has obtained the command of a privateer called *La Daphné*—"

"What, in time of peace?"

"So I hear tell. He gives out the story that you captured the *Bonaparte* after peace had been signed."

"Of course I did, but the capture took place before peace applied to the Channel."

"He swears that you cheated over that. He plans to recapture the *Bonaparte* now and is hiring men who dare make the attempt."

"Does he plan to attack St Peter Port?"

"No, Dick. He thinks that the *Merlin* will sail for Plymouth while you send the *Bonaparte* into Portsmouth with a prize crew. Should he manage to intercept the *Bonaparte* he will have men enough to overpower any detachment you can spare from the *Merlin*."

"The man is demented and talks so loudly of his intentions that we hear of them in Guernsey!"

"He is a madman, sure enough."

"And he can persuade other madmen to follow him?"

"Seemingly. The Cherbourg privateersmen will all be out of work."

"But all I need to do is escort the *Bonaparte* to Portsmouth and then continue my voyage to Plymouth. But wait—what if I capture the *Daphné?*"

"A second prize while Charbonnier tries to rob you of the first!"

"No, on second thoughts, that cock won't fight, Sam. The *Daphné* could be no legal prize, not when taken in time of peace."

"What then would be her fate?"

"I should suppose that Charbonnier's attempt would count as an act of piracy. As a madman he would 'scape hanging but the *Daphné*, pirate vessel, would go to the Crown."

"Much good that would do us! Suppose, however, that the *Daphné* were deserted by her crew and brought into harbour by the seamen who found her, they could claim salvage, couldn't they?"

"I couldn't but you could! I see what you mean, Sam. If all the Frenchmen board the *Bonaparte*—but that cannot be. Charbonnier is bound to leave some men on board the *Daphné*—a helmsman and one or two more."

"Very true, Dick. I might still find the ship deserted though."

"Nothing more likely. Now tell me, Sam, has Charbonnier someone in St Peter Port to report on my movements?"

"No doubt of it."

"Very well, then. My first move will be to put a strong prize crew on board the *Bonaparte* including all my marines. I shall do this after dark, seen by nobody. Next day the *Merlin* will sail for Plymouth. It will be common knowledge that the *Bonaparte* is to sail two days later for Portsmouth, manned by barely enough men to take her out of the Russel. Is that allowing time enough?"

"Make it three days later, Dick. Make certain that Charbonnier hears about it in time."

"Agreed. Three days later the ill-manned *Bonaparte* puts to sea, followed presently by the *Dove,* well manned and well armed. You will need to recruit some privateersmen, Sam."

"They are going cheap. They'll have no share in the venture—just their pay."

"When the *Daphné* closes the *Bonaparte* from to windward, you will be still further to windward, with sails struck. It will be a dark, moonless night. When Charbonnier boards the *Bonaparte,* you board the *Daphné.* The men you find aboard her will be set adrift in one of her boats."

"What if Charbonnier uses all his boats?"

"Take one extra with you—anything you can find as a bargain in St Peter Port. By then the *Merlin* will appear and the *Daphné* will part company, sailing up Channel. You will sight her for the first time somewhere off Dieppe and take her into the Downs. Report your arrival to my prize agent, Mr Lawrence, who has an office in Leadenhall Street."

"Will the owners turn up at Chatham, demanding the return of their ship less the salvage payable?"

"How can they? It would be a confession of piracy or at least of aiding pirates and being accomplices in crime. For their loss they will have no remedy at law and can do little but blame each other for listening to Charbonnier in the first place. No, I think that the ship's full value will go to you, and I hear that she was refitted quite recently."

"Half the money will go to you, Dick, and you will really deserve the whole of it."

"Half is enough, Sam, and it will come to me as the gift of a friend, having its origin in your generosity alone. To be open with you, I confess that I shall need it. Heaven knows when I shall receive my share of the *Bonaparte* and I have ordered the furniture for my house at Anneville. It is amazing what joiners expect to be paid these days."

The two friends parted in complete agreement but Delancey had an uneasy feeling that it had all been too easy. He had been presented with a simple problem, an addition sum in which two was to be added to two. He had come up with the expected answer of four but could not suppose that it was really as simple as that. There must be some aspect of the situation he had overlooked. Where was the trap into which he was to fall? To make matters worse, his opponent was mad. The plan he was to thwart must be a lunatic plan, one which Charbonnier had concealed from both his owners and his men. While pondering the problem, Delancey made a rash decision of his own. He resolved to sail in the *Bonaparte*. In doing so, he would break the sacred rule which tied a naval captain to his ship. He would be going against his conscience and his common sense, following only an instinct that he must make some move which his opponent would not expect. He admitted to himself that he was being too much influenced by his own financial needs. As against that, with the war ended, he would have no further chance of making money. He had been too ambitious, perhaps, in buying the manorial rights in Fief Anneville but he had really no alternative. With one more useful capture, the half-share in *Daphné*, he would have enough to live on. But was the tale he had been told the story he was intended to believe? And what, in that event, was the real story? It would be a clever move, surely, to sidestep at the outset, like the castle move in chess. But that would not be enough in itself and might even have been foreseen. He felt at a disadvantage, Charbonnier being able to anticipate his sensible moves while he himself could not foresee what form mere lunacy would take.

On board the *Bonaparte,* to which Delancey had shifted his gear after dark, Mather received his final orders:

"I have taken many of our best men but have left you with seamen enough to handle the *Merlin.* You will sail tomorrow forenoon, setting a course for Plymouth. By evening you will double back under easy sail and place *Merlin* to windward of the course I shall follow towards Portsmouth. I have marked on the chart the position I expect to have reached before the *Daphné* stages her attack. All this is guesswork but I do not suppose that the marked position is wildly wrong. I cannot believe that *Daphné* will be well manned but Charbonnier has the advantage of knowing the *Bonaparte* extremely well. If all goes as I expect, there will be no cannon fired on either side. What fighting we do will be with boarding pike and cutlass, with pistols as necessary, and a belaying pin to finish the argument. Should we fail in our efforts, which seems unlikely, you must rescue us. Whatever the event, leave the *Daphné* alone. Let her escape. Is that clear?"

"Aye, aye, sir. Should I make it seem that you are on board the *Merlin?* If Langford were to wear your uniform when we sail? He is about your height . . ."

"Use every deception possible. For my part, I shall keep out of sight until we put to sea and Stirling will keep most of his men below hatches. His visible crew will number twelve as seen from the quayside."

"I shall do my part, sir. Let's hope we make an end of Charbonnier this time."

"I don't mean to take him alive; nor do I want many other prisoners. As someone said—Cromwell, perhaps—'Stone dead hath no fellow.' We must put an end to this nonsense. Of war against lunatics I have already had enough."

When the *Merlin* left harbour next morning quite a few people saw that her captain was on the quarterdeck. Mr Stirling, moreover, who was ashore the previous night, was loud in his complaints about the weakness of his prize crew. "How am I to bring a large ship into Portsmouth with a dozen men and those the worst we have?" Below decks in the *Bonaparte* Delancey issued his orders to Stirling, Northmore, and Topley:

"We are to sail for Portsmouth the day after tomorrow. It is my belief that we shall be attacked by a privateer called the *Daphné* commanded by the former master of this ship, intent on recapturing her before she is brought into an English port."

"Can he do that, sir, in time of peace?" Northmore protested. "Surely the capture would be disallowed?"

"One would think so, Mr Northmore, but Charbonnier may have an answer to that. He may plan to bring the ship into an Italian port under a false name. All that is surmise. That he means to recapture the *Bonaparte* I am very reliably informed. I plan to surprise him. While he has reason to expect a weak prize crew, he will actually meet with strong resistance. I am merely guessing when I suppose that he may have thirty men in his boarding party. Given that sort of strength, he will find himself outnumbered by experienced and vigilant opponents. Mr Stirling, you will command this ship. I am on board merely as a passenger. Make your own plan for dealing with the privateersmen but remember that we don't want to have any prisoners. Charbonnier, who will probably lead the attack, should be killed on sight. One other thing—don't fire any cannon nor even any muskets if you can help it. The French should be cut down, bayonetted, knocked on the head. I suggest you let them on board before you reveal your strength. Is that all sufficiently clear? Mr Stirling?"

"*Is* Charbonnier a madman, sir?"

"Undoubtedly, Mr Stirling. His whole plan is mere lunacy."

"Shall we capture the *Daphné,* sir?" asked Northmore.

"No," replied Delancey. "We cannot take a prize in time of peace. Let her escape."

"What if the privateer opens fire on us?" asked Topley. "Are we to reply?"

"She won't open fire."

"Should muskets be loaded, sir?" asked Northmore.

"No. Any further questions? Very well, Mr Stirling, take command of the prize. I shall be in the Captain's cabin if you want me and I invite all officers to dine with me this afternoon."

In making Stirling assume the command, Delancey had acted again on instinct. He felt that Charbonnier had some other trick up his sleeve. He wanted to think about it and decide how it should be countered. In taking no part in the action he was giving Stirling some useful experience but neither he nor anyone else was going to gain credit from the sort of skirmish which no government would want to know about. Was it just possible that Charbonnier had obtained the co-operation of another privateer, one that was better armed and manned than the *Daphné?* Would Stirling find himself outnumbered after all? Over dinner he heard something about Stirling's plan, which seemed very sensible.

When the time came for the expected attack the night was dark, the sea nearly calm, and the westerly breeze no more than moderate. The presence of the privateer was more sensed than seen for she showed no light and made no sound. She was there all right and edged down from to windward, a shadow among shadows but with purposeful movement. There was no sound of her boats being lowered (she must have been towing them) and the helmsman could fairly start with surprise when the first of them came alongside.

The leader of the first boatload was evidently young and without experience, placed at the head of men who were not the desperadoes for which the scene was set. Petty criminals they may have been but buccaneers they certainly were not. When suddenly lit by the flare they looked more woebegone than menacing. Before they could panic they were joined by a second boatload, this reinforcement being enough to encourage them to face their opponents. After a few minutes of conflict they were attacked in the rear by the marines. They must have known by then that their position was hopeless. The ship they had boarded was not the defenceless merchantman they had been led to expect. While they wavered, Stirling charged them at the head of his best seamen. He was a ferocious fighter by temperament and he had been told to offer no quarter. Making straight for the French leader he hit him a powerful blow with the butt of the musket he had seized and then finished him off with the bayonet into his throat. An instant later he knocked aside the cutlass brandished by a French petty officer and kicked the man in the stomach, going on from there to bayonet another man who was probably about to surrender. Several of the enemy who had held back made for the boats, only to discover that they were sinking. Stirling's assault continued, the privateersmen putting up only a feeble resistance. Northmore killed two of them with his cutlass and Topley may well have accounted for three. This ruthless conduct was at least partly due to the fact that the *Bonaparte* was the *Merlin's* prize, fairly captured in battle, and that the French were trying to retake a ship that had surrendered. It was, as Delancey afterwards pointed out, "expressly against the law of arms, as arrant a piece of knavery, mark you now, as can be offer't." It was knavery for which the French were to pay in full. Eventually the fighting died away as the last of the Frenchmen were cut down and as one at least was tossed overboard. The fighting fury vanished quickly and several of the severely wounded were spared. When four men came alongside in a boat, moreover, begging for quarter, they were allowed on board and treated quite well. As for the privateer herself, she had disappeared as silently as she had come and Stirling knew that there was no question of pursuit. He set his men to swabbing the bloodstained deck.

Leaving Stirling to defend the ship, Delancey had made his way down to the lantern-lit passage which led to the *Bonaparte's* magazine. He was armed with two loaded pistols and a jug of water. Sitting down on an upturned tub, he wondered whether he had made a fool of himself as never before. As like as not he would have to remain there, doing nothing, until the fighting was over. Seamen would soon be asking—they would be asking now, some of them—how the captain had come to lose his nerve. He had, however, reached a certain conclusion and he could see no other course open to him. It was his task to sit and wait. He could not order anyone else to do it because there was no one he could trust to do the right thing at the right moment. A muffled noise overhead told him that the boarding party had arrived, the poor deluded creatures. Against proper men-of-war's men they should not last five minutes. They were serving Charbonnier's purpose, for all that, or this at least was Delancey's guess. Another minute or two would suffice to prove him right or wrong. For the third or fourth time he looked to the priming of his pistols. He shifted his position slightly and started a silent recitation of "Toll for the Brave," which he had once learnt by heart, probably as a punishment. He wished that the whole nonsense were over and done with.

When things happened, they happened quickly. There was a sound of footsteps descending the hatchway. There was a pause for less than a minute, after which the footsteps broke into a run. Suddenly, Charbonnier appeared, holding a lighted hand grenade (he had paused, no doubt, while lighting it) and looking the maniac that he was. Seeing Delancey he snarled his hatred and prepared to throw his grenade at the closed door of the magazine. At that instant Delancey fired his first pistol, hitting Charbonnier in the stomach. The Frenchman reeled backward, dropping the grenade, while Delancey fired his second pistol, the shot blowing out the madman's brains. In an instant Delancey threw water over the grenade's fuse and trod out whatever spark was left. His part in the action was over and he went on deck where he found that little remained to do. The *Merlin* now appeared from to windward and he returned to her, giving orders for most of his men to follow. The ships soon afterwards parted company and the *Merlin* set a course for Plymouth.

At dinner the following day, to which Delancey invited his officers, he gave his own explanation of the recent skirmish:

"This man Charbonnier had probably been losing his sanity for years. He went quite mad when we captured the *Bonaparte,* hiding in the magazine and threatening to blow both ships to eternity if we did not steer for Cherbourg. He became obsessed with the idea of a great explosion to end everything. He wanted the explosion more than he wanted to capture the *Merlin.* As you all know, we knocked him on the head and put him in irons, finally sending him back to France. Still clinging to his obsession, he managed to persuade her owners to lend him the *Daphné,* probably for a short period like two weeks."

"But what was his plan, sir?" asked Mather. "Did he mean to repeat his former trick, seizing the magazine and blackmailing us into obeying his orders?"

"No," replied Delancey. "Whatever he told the owners was a lie. Whatever he told the crew was probably a different lie. His real and suicidal purpose was to blow up the ship, end his life, and have his revenge on us at the same time. He lighted his fuse, remember, before he even saw me. He had no slow match either. The grenade was to go off in about six seconds and his intention was to throw it into the magazine."

"But the door was locked," Mather objected. "Would the grenade have touched off the magazine when exploded outside?"

"An even chance," said Delancey, "but it would have a better than even chance of breaking the door hinges or lock. Had he run back out of immediate danger, throwing himself on the deck, he could have finished the job with his pistols. That was no doubt his intention."

"But how did he reach the magazine?" asked Topley. "Did he follow the boarding party?"

"No," replied Delancey. "He entered through one of the stern windows. What I did not expect was the grenade. I had water at hand to damp the priming of his pistols. Anyway, it served my purpose. Once more it was a case of touch and go."

Chapter Two

DRURY LANE

D ELANCEY'S AGENT, Mr Lawrence, had been at sea as a purser, serving in India and becoming agent for several regiments in the Indian Army. That was why he and his partners kept an office in Leadenhall Street. As navy agents they had another but smaller room in St Martin's Lane. It was at his main office in the City that Delancey and Mather had their appointment one afternoon, their plan being to dine together, call briefly at the Admiralty, and end by going to the theatre. Lawrence was no stranger to Delancey but Mather, meeting him for the first time, saw a rather short, rotund, and owl-like businessman with grey hair and spectacles, attended by a tall and weary clerk, surrounded by a litter of paper and having as background many shelves laden with leather-backed ledgers.

"Good to see you, Captain," Mr Lawrence began, looking up from his newspaper. "And this gentleman was your first lieutenant, I think, in the *Merlin?* Happy to make your acquaintance, sir. Do be seated, gentlemen. Lawkins, fetch me the correspondence about the prize *Bonaparte.*" As the agent's clerk looked for the relevant papers Lawrence returned to his newspaper and to the item of news which he had been studying when his visitors arrived:

"Did you see this astonishing story about a ship found abandoned off Dieppe? She was brought into the Downs by the master of a Guernsey coasting vessel—quite possibly by some seaman who is known to you, by George—but without a soul on board when she was boarded. Did you ever hear of anything so extraordinary?"

"Perhaps she was leaking and had been abandoned in panic by her crew?"

"No such thing, sir. She was watertight and in good order, armed, provisioned, and under sail. French-built, seemingly, the ship had no papers, no log, and no name. One of her boats was missing but she was otherwise complete. The Guernseyman can obtain salvage to her full value unless the owners come forward to claim the vessel."

"Her having no name would seem to make it hard for the owners to identify her."

"Which may explain why the name was painted over or chiselled off. Ah, here is the correspondence with the clerk of the Admiralty Court—thank you, Lawkins—together with a shipbuilder's valuation and a manifest of the cargo. I'm afraid that the peace will bring about a fall in the price of brandy but the general goods should find a good market. Yes, you were fortunate, Captain, with the *Bonaparte*. There can be no doubt as to the Court's verdict—I have checked that with Counsel—"

A long and technical discussion followed and Delancey gained the general impression that his share of the prize money should come to a very useful total. Bewildered by talk of high finance, Delancey and Mather eventually said goodbye to their agent and dined presently at a tavern near Charing Cross. After calling at the Admiralty, where he had some business to transact, taking an hour or so, Delancey led the way into the Strand and began a leisurely stroll eastwards. He had been enjoying his stay in London and had widened his circle of friends there. On this particular evening he had been asked to join a party at the theatre and had been authorised by his host, Major Mark Willoughby, to bring a friend with him. Mather had been the obvious choice and the evening's amusement was a fitting conclusion to a day of business.

"The play we are to attend," explained Delancey, "is at Drury Lane. It is called *The Scheming Lieutenant,* a three-act farce in a naval setting."

"And not the first one, by God," replied Mather. "As for scheming—well, you, sir, have been accused of it."

They were walking slowly towards the playhouse where the curtain was due to rise at half-past six. To the casual observer these two officers, both in civilian clothes, offered a certain contrast. Delancey, the taller of them, was dark-haired with dark blue eyes, his figure sturdy, his manner confident and direct. He might be "Captain" only by courtesy, his real rank being Master and Commander, but he looked the part of a senior officer.

"What exactly is the story you have heard?" asked Delancey after a minute's pause.

"Well, sir, the story goes that you are betrothed to the Honourable Mrs Farren, the former Diana Rice, younger sister of Mrs Markham and of Lord Dynevor. She is known to be wealthy and Captain Markham—well, he is at the First Sea Lord's elbow. It is said that you should be posted any day and can choose your frigate if war should come."

"Fiddlesticks, Mather, you shouldn't believe all the gossip you hear. I am not betrothed to anyone."

"No, sir? But you have often been seen with the lady, surely?"

Delancey knew that this was true enough, that his attentions had been well received and that he could not break off the friendship without giving offence to Lord Dynevor and the

Markhams. He had first met Mrs Farren at a dinner party given
by his American cousins and their mutual interest was at once
apparent. Delancey admired her good looks, fine complexion,
and perfect breeding. She, on her side, had been a widow for
the last six years and was a little past the age at which her
friends expected her to marry again. They had become friends
and it was a friendship which her relatives had finally approved.
Delancey was admittedly no great match for her, as all her circle had agreed, but she was past her prime and perhaps a little
thinner than the reigning beauties of the day. Her
brother-in-law, John Markham (*the* John Markham) was a very
senior Captain, Member of Parliament for Portsmouth, and a
key member of the Board of Admiralty. Delancey's future seemed
assured.

"Yes," replied Delancey, "I have been much in her company
of late. She is a lady I hold in the highest esteem."

"Is she to be one, sir, of this evening's party?"

"Good God, no! I should explain that she took to evangelical religion after her late husband's death. She strongly
disapproves of horse-racing, gambling, betting, and the stage.
Her late husband was killed while riding in a steeplechase."

"And she thinks, I suppose, that all actresses follow the
moral example of Nell Gwyn?"

"She certainly regards them as prostitutes and little better,
indeed, than her family's political opponents. A very high stan-
dard of virtue is characteristic of the circle in which she moves."

They walked on, jostled by other pedestrians, and Delancey
wondered again whether he was doing the right thing. He
remembered every magic moment of that first meeting. He had
been long at sea and he had suddenly found himself next to

this dark-haired lady with her delicate features, slim hands, and that subtle perfume. She coloured slightly at his compliments and made some passing reference to the Battle of Algeçiras— just enough to show that she had followed his career. His admiration for her was real enough but he could not fail to see what he gained from her friendship. For all he knew he might himself end with a seat in Parliament for a dockyard constituency. But could he live with Diana's standards of piety? He had never pretended to share her beliefs yet he felt, nevertheless, that he was expected to conform to them. But Mather was speaking:

"It is always difficult, sir, to represent a ship's deck on the stage. I remember once seeing a performance of Shakespeare's play *The Tempest*—well done, too, in a general way—but what a feeble mess they made of Act I, Scene I! What, however, is the stage manager to do? His task is impossible and I expect that we shall see the same sort of failure this evening."

The party which foregathered at the theatre entrance numbered six in all, the other guests being Colonel Wilding, Captain Benham of the 7th Foot, and a solitary civilian, Mr Wansford. After the necessary introductions and greetings they took their seats, Delancey finding himself between Willoughby and Benham. The curtain rose before they had done more than glance at the programme. It was not in any way a masterpiece of drama and stagecraft for the characters were predictable, the plot lacked originality, the humour was merely boisterous, and the story's end could be easily foreseen.

Delancey, for his part, made little effort to hear the dialogue or follow the plot. He saw only one person on stage and that was the young actress who played the part of Susan Staywell.

When she was off stage he merely waited for her return. She was extremely pretty but his admiration was confused by the feeling—no, by the certainty—that he had seen her before. Their previous meeting could not have been recent, for he had been at sea for years. Perhaps he had merely seen her in some other play, but how seldom had he been in London! She was no novice, it would seem, for she acted with an assurance, a neatness of movement, a studied charm which could derive only from years of experience. Fiona Sinclair was her name as printed in the programme. He certainly could not remember that name but he knew, of course, that stage names are often assumed. For the whole of Act I he puzzled his brain without result. He must see her and talk to her but it was vital that they should not meet as strangers. There must have been men enough seeking to make her acquaintance and she would know very well how to brush them off. Where had he seen her before? Light suddenly dawned in the course of Act II. By all the social conventions of the day her costume as cabin boy was unthinkably indecent, not because her shirt was open at the front, as it chanced to be, but because her white linen trousers were a size too small and revealed the curves of all that they were meant to conceal. She was barefoot, too, and her feet were unbelievably shapely and white. It was this provocative appearance which suddenly brought back total recollection. She had played a similar part in a play called *The Poor Sailor* presented at the theatre in Guernsey back in about 1794. She and another girl, both clad as seamen for theatrical purposes, had appeared on the quayside in St Peter Port in a frolic done for a bet.

Watching her on stage, and seeing no one else—not even Mrs Siddons herself—he realised that her part in Act II was quite needless. There was no real point in her masquerading as a cabin boy, no object in her boarding the cutter. Her part had been written in solely to display her breath-taking figure. How old would she be? She looked about eighteen but that would seem to have been her age nearly seven years ago. She must now be twenty-four at least . . . and now it was the end of the play. The Tories had won the Boughtborough election to the accompaniment of loud jeers from the Whig members of the audience. Colonel and Mrs Staywell had given their consent to the marriage of their only daughter to Lieutenant Mainbrace. Sir John Sitting had agreed to secure the Lieutenant's promotion, having plenty of influence to ensure this. All came forward to take their bow and then the audience began to leave.

"Shall we go backstage?" Delancey heard himself saying. "I must beg the stage manager to amend some of his mistakes in seamanship. The scene in Act II could be easily improved and the seamen might appear to work with a purpose." The others agreed with some reluctance and Delancey led the way to the stage door. They were finally admitted, after a bribe to the doorman, and found themselves moving with difficulty among a tangle of scenery, furniture, and props. Some members of the cast were still on stage, discussing some point with the stage manager, Mr Ward. When they paused for breath, Delancey begged to introduce himself as a naval officer. "Pray forgive my seeming officious, but there are some ways in which your business on stage could be made more true to life. Might I call sometime tomorrow so as to offer what help I can?"

"Really, sir," said Mr Ward, "I am vastly obliged to you. We shall be rehearsing another play during the morning but will be on stage again at two and will be glad indeed of your professional advice. The stage will be rigged as for Act II and all will be present who appear in the Act."

"Very well, sir," replied Delancey, "I shall be happy to wait on you then. The changes I'll advise are all quite small in themselves but should serve to make the scene more authentic."

"I shall hope then to see more naval men in the audience."

Delancey and his friends were just about to take their leave when there was the sound of running feet and Fiona Sinclair fairly scampered on stage, still dressed as a cabin boy. The sight of the visitors checked whatever it was she had to say and she blushed prettily while Mr Ward performed the introductions.

"I beg to present Captain Delancey, Miss Sinclair, together with other distinguished officers who have been good enough to patronise the evening's play."

"I need no introduction, Mr Ward," said Delancey. "Miss Sinclair and I are old friends—I hope at least that she will remember me from the days when she was playing in St Peter Port?"

"Good gracious!" exclaimed Fiona. "What was the play?"

"*The Poor Sailor,*" replied Delancey, "and I thought it a very poor play, saved only by your acting."

"But I was playing only a small part!"

"As a girl dressed as a cabin boy."

"Oh, dear, you must think that I always dress like this!"

"The dress certainly becomes you. Where you and another girl made a mistake was to venture on the breakwater, clad as seamen and hoping to pass as such!"

"So you remember that too!"

"But do you remember me now?"

"Of course I do. You were a junior officer then—and painfully shy!"

"If you will forget my awkward manners I promise to forget your escapade on the breakwater."

"Shake hands on a bargain!" For an instant he felt her cool slim hand in his. Then he hastened to take his leave.

"I shall be here tomorrow afternoon to advise Mr Ward on some point of seamanship. I shall hope to see you then. Young lady, your servant. Mr Ward, your humble assistant!"

All this time Major Willoughby and his other guests were showing signs of impatience and Delancey presently made his apologies as they were leaving the theatre.

"No need to make excuses, my dear fellow. We all understand and I'll admit that she is a deucedly pretty girl. No one could blame you. She is as charming a girl as ever I saw!"

"In trousers, moreover, and barefoot!" added Captain Benham.

"But not a word of this, egad, to Mrs Farren!" exclaimed Colonel Willoughby. "She had best not know that you have been to the theatre at all—let alone going backstage!"

"And let alone going back there tomorrow!" added Willoughby.

Delancey had to put up with a good deal of quizzing over supper but Mather took no part in it, looking rather serious. He knew exactly what impact that girl must have had on Delancey. She had red-gold hair, dark eyes, white skin, and a perfect figure. She had a lovely voice, trained for the stage. But her beauty, startling as it might be, was less memorable than her sheer vitality. She was obviously a girl in ten thousand, one he himself would never forget for the rest of his life. As for

Delancey, he had still remembered her from a chance meeting —had it been more than that?—at the very beginning of the war. But what of his career? The war had ended. There would be no more prizes to capture, no more honours to achieve, and he was not yet a post captain. His whole future depended on a marriage which would establish his position in the service and in society. It looked now as if he might throw away his entire future for the sake of a young actress who was of no consequence even on the stage. Mather couldn't hide from himself that his own future, as Delancey's follower, was also at risk. But that, he told himself, was of little consequence. Delancey was a man who should rise high in the service if all went well but his career would come to nothing if he jilted Mrs Farren.

On the following afternoon Delancey was at the theatre and Mather, at his own suggestion, came to offer his own counsel and assistance. It was as well he did so, for Delancey, after Fiona appeared, would talk to no one else. Nor did the girl herself need any encouragement. There were young ladies in society who would make a point of being bashful in male company but Fiona's life had been spent on the stage. Observing her, Mather guessed that she would have had several lovers in her time. She was no virgin, of that he felt sure, but she retained, nevertheless, a certain quality of innocence. Forced to take over the chief role of technical adviser, Mather explained to Mr Ward that the crew's energies should be directed, first of all, towards hoisting the cutter's mainsail. He began to show how this would be done. Delancey, meanwhile, led Fiona aside and sat beside her on a bench in the wings. After a moment's hesitation he asked her about her career since they had met.

"You are not of a Guernsey family, I should suppose?"

"Why, no. I came to the island with the theatre company, being treated almost as a daughter by Mr and Mrs Bernard. Then the theatre closed down there and I tried my fortunes in London."

"I'm afraid you will have had an uphill struggle?"

"I have been luckier than many young players. I haven't often gone hungry."

"You have relatives perhaps, in London?"

"No, sir. None nearer than Scotland."

"Do please forgive my directness, Miss Sinclair, but do tell me this: Are your parents alive?"

"No, sir. I am illegitimate but have been told that my father, who never married and who died in battle, was commander of a private man-of-war. My mother was young when she came under his protection, and died when little older. I don't remember her, but I have an aunt and uncle at Dumbarton. I have been brought up on the stage and have had no other education. Now you know my whole life history! One or two men have wanted to marry me but they lost interest when they learnt that I am not legitimate. A good riddance, too! If a man cares for me no more than that, he doesn't care for me enough."

Delancey was captivated by Fiona and found himself wondering why. Her clothes had, and were meant to have a stunning effect—shirt and trousers were obviously her only garments—but she seemed almost unaware of her powerful attraction. Far from being bashful or self-conscious, she was too intent on the conversation to notice what her unbuttoned shirt was revealing.

"Tell me your name again," she demanded.

"Richard Delancey."

"I should have remembered it from our first meeting."

"When I was the Poor Sailor!"

"But no longer poor. You have been promoted, you have fought gallantly, and you have made prize money!"

"How do you know?"

"I can see it in your face. I shouldn't call you exactly handsome—"

"You are right there!"

"—But you look interesting. I can imagine men being afraid of you."

"Men, but not girls?"

"Of course not. Any girl can do what she likes with you and would know it from the beginning. Do you think me pretty?"

"You are the most beautiful creature I ever set eyes on."

"But quite penniless, almost nameless, and not a model of virtue. I am full of mischief. If we are to be friends, you must not claim afterwards that I did not warn you. I am no fine lady, no simpering miss, and no ornament to society. I am just a village girl, an orphan, and brought up on the stage."

"I have been warned and I still want you to think of me as a friend."

"In that case we are friends. You may kiss my hand."

Delancey quickly availed himself of that privilege. Then he noticed that the rehearsal had come to a pause, with Mather talking quietly with Mr Ward on one side of the stage and the players chatting among themselves, some of them glancing with amusement at Delancey. Fiona had made another conquest! They must have been familiar with the routine and might even claim to know the lines. Fiona took all this in at a glance and her face lit up with a wicked idea.

"And now you may kiss my feet!" Without a second's hesitation Delancey knelt before her and deliberately kissed each foot in turn, noticing how dirty they were, as they would be, of course, from the dust of the stage.

"And for that you deserve a reward!" She kissed him fairly on the mouth to the sound of subdued laughter. "And now I must go and rehearse with the others, after which I must change these clothes and you must go." She was gone in an instant and it seemed only a matter of minutes before Delancey found himself in the street, walking westwards with Mather.

"What an astonishing creature!" he exclaimed. "She is almost as direct as a milkmaid or shepherdess, ready to be tumbled next moment in the hay, but she has been taught as an actress to take the part of a young lady. She has no trace of a country accent. She could easily play her part as a Colonel's daughter."

"Forgive me saying this, sir, but it seems to me that you are taking a terrible risk. What if Mrs Farren comes to hear of this frolic backstage? Your whole future depends upon making a good marriage and you have the chance of a lifetime. It is not as if Mrs Farren were unattractive. I have been told that she is still a fine woman. She will bring you wealth—in India stock, too, I hear—and just the right sort of connection."

"I know that, Mather, and need no reminder."

"But it is not merely the risk of losing her. You could be accused of trifling with Mrs Farren's affections and would make enemies of the whole family."

"I realise that."

"But they might take very real offence. I should suppose, indeed, that her brother, Lord Dynevor, might call you out."

"Yes, I think he might. In his place I should do the same."

"So do please heed my advice for once. Leave things as they are and let's hope that no word of this comes to Mrs Farren's ears. Let us thank heaven that Major Willoughby and the others were not here today. It is the stage players who will gossip but they don't move in society. There is a chance of nothing more being heard about it. But please, sir, resolve never to see this girl again. Forget you ever saw her!"

"Could *you* ever forget her?"

"Well—I suppose not. But it isn't important that I should. For you, sir, it is vital."

"So you would advise me against marrying Miss Sinclair?"

"*Marrying* her? No thought of that ever crossed my mind. You must know as well as I do that she is little better than a prostitute."

"A streetwalker?"

"No. I don't mean that. But it is well-known that a young actress will gain a part in a play by offering her favours to the leading actor. I should suppose that Fiona is a woman of the world. She has done well to be playing at Drury Lane. I can only guess at the story of her rise to this prominence."

"She is no angel, I grant you that, but I should not want her to be different in any way. I could not even have wished that her feet had been clean."

When they parted, Mather headed quickly back to the theatre and arrived just as members of the cast were leaving. Fiona Sinclair was greatly surprised to see him, and perhaps disappointed, but she allowed him to escort her for the short distance to where she lodged in Hanover Place. A shy bachelor, Mather had the utmost difficulty in explaining himself. He finally made it clear that his friend Delancey was a rising officer of potential distinction and that his whole future depended upon his making a suitable marriage. He was all but engaged to a lady of high position and influence. By coming backstage at Drury Lane he had put his career at risk. By pursuing a friendship with an actress he would face ruin.

"Did he tell you to say all this?" asked Fiona bluntly.

"He has not the least idea of it," Mather hastened to assure her. "I am pleading with you for the good of the service."

"And with an eye to your own promotion?"

"I know it must seem like that. I have questioned my own motives a dozen times. But Delancey's career would be important to me even if I had not been his follower or had not been in the service at all. He will some day lead a squadron as Commodore. The whole safety of the kingdom might depend upon his resolution and skill. His name may well be remembered alongside those of Howe, Jervis, Duncan, or Nelson."

"And Nelson has done himself no good by associating too much with a prostitute called Emma?"

"I'll admit, forgive me, that the comparison had crossed my mind. Anyway, my plea is that you refuse to see him again."

"But look, Mr Mather, why don't I hear all this from him? If he is so distinguished, successful, and brave, why can't he decide for himself which girl he likes best? Why have I to decide for him?"

"Perhaps you would understand him better if you realised how his recent years have been spent. He took command of the *Merlin* at Gibraltar in 1799. He served in the Mediterranean from then until the war ended, now on convoy duty, now at Malta and eventually in the battle of Algeçiras. All that time he hardly set foot ashore. Finally, when the sloop was paid off he comes to London and falls in love with the first lady he meets and that doesn't prevent him from falling in love with you as well. Sailors come ashore starved for love—yes, like Lord Nelson himself. Believe me, we can behave very foolishly indeed. He will not listen to my advice, Miss Sinclair. Only you can save him from ruin."

"And will his marriage to this lady make him happy?"

"I don't know. I have never seen her."

"Men who marry an heiress can end in misery."

"Very true, Miss Sinclair. But it is also misery for an active officer to be left on the beach."

"But I still don't understand. As good an officer as you say he is must be needed at sea."

"Forgive me—I have failed to explain things clearly. If he jilts this lady—for his withdrawal now would amount to that—her family would see to it that he never has another command. He would be ashore for good as a half-pay Commander—supposing, of course, that he survives a duel with the lady's brother."

"I begin to understand, Mr Mather. I am an ignorant girl from the country, with no knowledge of society beyond what I learn from playing a part as Lady This or the Honourable Mrs That. I speak the lines yet I know little sometimes of what they mean. But I'll be frank with you provided that you repeat nothing of what I say to Richard Delancey, or indeed to anyone else. Have I your promise?"

"On my honour, Miss Sinclair."

"Very well, then. Your friend Delancey saw me on the stage and liked me. Years later he has seen and talked to me, to discover that he likes me more. To speak openly—as I suppose that real ladies never do—I like him too. But for men to admire me is no new experience. I need to know of a man whether he wants me enough, whether he wants me more than anything in the world. Such a man I could love but I won't accept anything less."

"Thank you for being so open with me."

"I have decided, anyway, what I must do. It so happens that I have been offered a leading role at a theatre in the provinces, far from London. I have been trying to decide whether to accept or refuse it. I have now made up my mind to go. But your plea for your friend's career has led me to a further decision. I shall go at once. I shall go without leaving an address. I shall leave my understudy to take my part. So far as Delancey is concerned, I shall have vanished. He will have his regrets but then he will remember his career and pay homage again to this lady upon whom his future depends. As for me, I too will soon forget him as a man who admired my beauty but who never really cared for me. How is that for a bargain?"

"I hope that you have not made too great a sacrifice."

"I have made no sacrifice at all. If Delancey goes back to his heiress and his chances of promotion, he is not a lover worth having. Next time he calls at the stage door there will be a note from me advising him to be faithful to his society lady. If he calls again it will be to learn that I have left London and that no one knows where I have gone. And here we are at my lodging and I must say goodbye to you. Take care of yourself, Mr Mather, don't get killed in battle, and find a nice girl to marry."

Mather walked away with an odd feeling that he had betrayed his friend. He knew that he had acted from the purest of motives. Mather could see what Delancey's temptation had been. Fiona Sinclair was a lovely girl—he had no illusions about that—and she had an honest down-to-earth quality, a directness, a lack of affectation, which appealed to him personally. Mather thought the time had come for him to leave town. His business had been done and he would do well to escape from the expenses and temptations of London. A few days later he left London by coach after wishing Delancey every success in his wooing. Delancey, he knew, had recently been seen with Mrs Farren and had not, he felt certain, been seen again at the theatre.

Chapter Three

THE PRETENDED GENTLEMAN

DELANCEY'S best friend in London was Colonel Barrington, once of the East India Company's army but now something of an invalid, living in St James's Square and seldom seen in society. It was to Barrington that Delancey finally explained his problem. This was in February 1802, some weeks after Fiona's vanishing from Drury Lane, and Delancey had since continued to pay half-hearted court to Diana. He came straight to the point and described his position.

"I have been much seen in company with the Honourable Mrs Farren, a widow of good family—"

"Yes, yes, I know who you mean. A charming woman. Her husband was killed in a hunting accident—his horse fell on top of him, poor fellow. Diana is still in good looks and owns a pretty estate in Wiltshire. When in town she stays with the Markhams. You could scarcely find a more eligible match. Your dancing attendance on her has been noticed, by the way. Someone made some comment on it only t'other day. Could it have been Tommy Onslow? Anyway, I hear that the relatives approve and that the lady is likely to say 'Yes.' I offer you my congratulations."

"The trouble is, Colonel, that I am not in love with her."

"My dear sir, marriage between persons of consequence cannot wait until they fall in love. That happens afterwards and if

it doesn't a man must make use of a chambermaid. The moment
of passion is all very well but there are more vital considera-
tions, land is one, income is another, and family connections,
as in this instance, can be more important than either. That
you are not in love does not signify. Let's see now—how old
are you?"

"I was born, sir, in 1760, almost at the same time as when
our present king came to the throne."

"So you are past forty and past the age of falling in love.
When you were twenty or twenty-five was your time for
romance. A man, sir, should not behave like a boy!"

"But consider, Colonel, how my life has been spent. At
twenty-three I was defending Gibraltar against the combined
armies of France and Spain! I was sixteen when I first went
to sea."

"I see what you mean. But why have you suddenly discovered that you don't love Mrs Farren? You have been fond of
her until now."

"I am fond of her still. I thought, indeed, that I loved her.
Then I met another girl and suddenly discovered that real love
is something different."

"Ah, there is another girl! I thought as much. But how, pray,
can you tell real love from false?"

"Quite easily, sir. When you are merely fond of a woman,
you notice her good points and regret her blemishes, weighing
up all that is for and against her. When you love her you regard
each blemish as another aspect of her beauty and would not
have it different."

"And what was this other girl's blemish?"

"Her bare feet were dirty and I did not want them otherwise."

"Zounds, man, does she sell cockles and mussels?"

"She is an actress, sir, and her part, at Drury Lane, requires her to go barefoot."

"An actress! The situation is serious indeed. To jilt Mrs Farren is enough in itself to ruin your career and damn you for ever with the present government. All that you need to do to clinch the disaster is to announce that your preference is for a whore from Drury Lane! Had she any knowledge of your position, had she any consideration for you, this girl would reject your acquaintance and leave London."

"And that is exactly what she has done!"

"S'death, then, that solves your problem. She is gone and you don't know where. You are free again!"

"But I learnt this from her, that I do *not* love Mrs Farren. Were I to propose to her I should be offering her what I don't have to give."

"But she'll know that, man, she will be in the same case and people who marry for the second time have learnt not to expect too much."

"I can't do it, sir. It is the simple fact that I can't go through with it."

"But how do you get out of it? Things have already gone too far."

"How do I get out of it? Nothing could be simpler, sir. I ask the advice of an old officer and man of the world. If anyone knows what to do, I tell myself, it will be my old friend, Colonel Barrington."

"You be damned, sir! You wish to make me your accomplice in doing something dishonourable without taking the consequences!"

The old man was white haired and red in the face but there

was a twinkle in his eye which hinted at some inner amusement. Delancey said no more but waited in patience.

"Well," said the Colonel at last, "I do recall a man who escaped from your sort of dilemma. I don't say I admire him for it, nor do I advise you to copy his misconduct. All he did was to make close acquaintance with members of the political party to which his prospective father-in-law was bitterly opposed. The match was forbidden and he left the scene with unconcealed grief. He had not jilted the lady nor had her brother any occasion to call him out. His political views were to change again at a later date but this was long after the lady was married to someone else."

"The Markhams are followers of Lord St Vincent, who supports the Prime Minister. Their hostility is directed, I suppose, at those who have chosen to support Pitt against Addington."

"Yes, but their bitterest hatred is reserved for those who promised to support Addington and then deserted him. I'll give you two names: Lord Ravenglass and the Honourable Stephen Lowther, M.P."

"I know them at least by repute. One of them owns a schooner yacht in the Lake District. She is called, I think, the *Water Nymph*."

"I never heard that and never met his lordship but I can introduce you to Lowther, his close friend and neighbour. There, I have done my best for you and wonder whether I should have done as much. Mrs Farren is a charming woman and I think you are making a great mistake. More than that, I hate to think that I may have done her a disservice."

"But what service would it be to ensure her marriage to a man who is in love with someone else? Married to a most attractive and eligible brunette I should be kind, I hope, and considerate but all my thoughts would be with a wild girl whose hair is red-gold and who counts socially for nothing at all. I don't know where she is but I am prepared to follow her to the ends of the earth."

"Pooh! You talk like a lovesick youth of eighteen! She won't go to the ends of the earth. If she is an actress she will have gone to another theatre; to Bath, for example, or Bristol. The person who will go to the ends of the earth is you, more likely, leaving her at Sadlers Wells. The present Board of Admiralty may have their revenge on you, remember. They could send you on a mission to China! They could station you in the East Indies for the next five years! Or they could send you to look for the North-West Passage—that would cool your ardour! To be frank with you, sir, I think that you are out of your mind. . . . Is she very lovely?"

"She is the most beautiful creature I ever saw."

"Ah, well. . . . You shall meet Tim Lowther in a few days' time. For the rest, I leave you to play the game your own way. Don't say that I encouraged you! I think rather that you are demented!"

Once Delancey and Lowther had met their friendship developed rapidly and a friendship with Lord Ravenglass was the natural sequel. Both were keen yachtsmen and talked a great deal about Lowther's schooner yacht *Water Nymph,* which sailed on Windermere. She had outsailed all other yachts on the lake but Lowther had now received a challenge from—of all places— the Isle of Man. The schooner *Peggy* was already famous for her speed and was on charter, for the time being, to Colonel Manning. It was at first a question whether *Water Nymph* was somehow to reach the Irish Sea or whether *Peggy* was to travel by some means to Windermere. This problem was settled by the toss of a coin and Manning was left with the problem of transporting *Peggy* on rollers. He was a man of wealth, unconcerned about the cost, but the operation was going to take time. The trials were provisionally planned for April 1802. Lowther had meant to race *Water Nymph* himself but Ravenglass had what seemed to him a better idea.

"This fellow Delancey shall sail her. He has spent his life on board ship, knows all that is to be known about every damned rope or spar. Manning will be at the helm of *Peggy* and he is a soldier, brought up in the stable yard. Manning thinks that you are to race *Water Nymph* but there is nothing about that in the terms of the wager. With Delancey we are sure to win and I, for one, will double my bet. He is a fine seaman—everyone I have talked to agrees about that. We shall stand to win a small fortune."

"Will Delancey expect to be paid?"

"No, he's a gentleman of sorts, a cousin in fact of Oliver Delancey. A bit marginal, perhaps, but I'm pretty sure that he will expect no more than hospitality. He can make his money from his own wagers."

"And that's the one thing he won't do. Oddly enough, I took him into the club the other day, assuming that he would play like the rest of us. He refused flat, and can you guess why?"

"Easily, my dear fellow. He is afraid that Diana Farren would come to hear of it! She and her family are all Methodists or little better. He, poor fellow, will have to conform to pattern. It will be worth it, mind you. She has a good holding in East India stock."

"You make a good guess, Ravenglass, but you chance to have guessed wrong. He turned to me and said, in the hearing of my friends, 'I have to warn you, Lowther, that I never gamble. My old father made me swear on the Bible that I would never play any game for money, never bet on a horse, never throw dice or place any wager of any kind.'"

"Good God! And who was his father, for heaven's sake?"

"Nobody of any consequence, I'll swear. As you said, his position in society is only marginal. He is merely the probable bridegroom for Diana Farren. His real objection to betting is probably because he has no money."

"And there could be worse reasons than that. Did he make no prize-money?"

"Not much, I should guess. His last command was only a sloop. To make money you need a frigate. He has not even been posted."

When approached on the subject of the yacht race, Delancey accepted the offer and felt reasonably sure of beating a Lieutenant-Colonel. He did not bet on the result, however certain he may have felt about it, but he seemed to have an almost morbid interest in gambling. He was often seen in the gaming rooms and sought the company of some notorious rakes. At other times he was assiduous as an escort for Mrs Farren, taking her to more than one concert of sacred music composed by Mr Handel. He could not live this double life for ever and it became apparent before long that Diana was no longer as friendly as she had been. A puzzled expression was taking the place of her welcoming smile. Things came to a head in March when Delancey found himself summoned to call on Captain Markham at the Admiralty. Markham came third in a hierarchy of which the formidable Lord St Vincent was the head. He greeted Delancey with great politeness and waved him to a chair. He had not yet achieved his flag but it was all but visibly ready to hoist. Of his competence there could be no doubt at all and it was he who spoke for the Navy in the House of Commons. He looked older than he was, a not unusual result of working under St Vincent.

"Ah, Delancey, it was good of you to call. I hope you did not conclude that I was about to offer you a command at sea. There is little I can do in that way for anyone while the country remains at peace. No, I am concerned with something more personal. As you know, my wife's sister, Mrs Farren, has been almost an inmate of my house since her husband died some years ago. She stays with us, that is to say, whenever she is in town. I have the highest regard for her and feel that she should marry again should a suitable opportunity arise. I have been aware for some time of your growing acquaintance with her and am convinced that she has a high opinion of you. I feel, myself, that you have a good war record and may well have a distinguished career. You will not take it amiss, I hope, when I have to admit, with reluctance, that you lack any family connections which would strengthen your position . . ." Markham shook his head sadly while Delancey remembered that Markham was himself the son of the late Archbishop of York. "As against that, my sister-in-law is a widow and can no longer be described as a young woman. For that and for other reasons I have looked with approval on what I hoped would prove a fortunate connection." He paused again and then resumed his speech in more solemn tones. "You will be aware, I have no doubt, that Mrs Farren is a lady of great piety. Her evangelical views are quite opposed to the frivolities of London society—plays, dances, and gambling in all its forms. She disapproves of the faction which opposes Mr Addington and could not possibly have any social relations with those who promised him their support and then went back on their undertaking." There was another pause and Captain Markham continued: "Knowing all this, I must warn you against associating with characters like Lord Ravenglass and Mr Timothy Lowther. Mrs Farren does not as yet know of your association with these men and their friends. In the event, however, of her realising that you are associated with her family's political opponents, she will have to look upon you as another member of the opposing faction. Her acquaintance with you will have to end on my advice and you must see yourself that we have no alternative. To give you these words of warning is for me a very painful duty but it was unavoidable. You will realise, I hope, that I have your best interests at heart."

"You are quite right, sir, to class me as an ignoramus in politics. I gave little consideration to Lord Ravenglass's political position and would not have known whether Tim Lowther was Whig or Tory. I have been asked, however, to sail Lowther's yacht in competition with another yacht and have accepted the task. I do not see that I can very well tell him that I have changed my mind."

"Why not? Tell him that you have had to change your plans. For that matter, you can tell him the truth."

"The difficulty is, sir, that wagers have been laid on the result and that my promising to take the helm has naturally affected the odds. I cannot, in fairness, go back on my word."

"Really, Delancey, I am disappointed in you. When so much

else is at stake—a lady's hand in marriage—a possibly distinguished career—you think that wagers in a sporting event are
more important. I cannot applaud your decision and I incline
to congratulate my sister-in-law on avoiding what could have
proved an unfortunate connection. Good day, Captain Delancey,
and do not look to this government for patronage."

Delancey bowed and withdrew. He paid a call next day at
the Markhams' house, asking for Mrs Farren, only to be told
that she was not at home. So that, he concluded, was the end
of that. His next problem was to discover the whereabouts of
Fiona Sinclair. On that subject Colonel Barrington had been
perfectly right. If she was not playing in London she would be
playing somewhere else. Acting was her trade and she had no
private means. There were theatres everywhere. Had he to visit
them all? On the day after his repulse from the Markhams' door
he walked towards Printing House Square. Would someone
connected with the press be able to advise him? No London
newspaper, he realised, would find space to comment upon a
provincial theatre. But provincial news must somehow reach
London. He decided that his best plan would be to dine that
day at the Cheshire Cheese, wherever that might be. It was the
inn, he had been told, at which hacks and scribblers were usually to be found, and he was there in time to have the "ordinary"
meal and a pint of ale. There presently sat opposite him a tall
man of pale complexion with a long nose and inky fingers,
who praised the steak pie and launched almost at once into an
attack on the government.

"You look to me, sir, like a seafaring man and I hardly need
to tell you that this peace will be of short duration. We shall
be at war again, depend upon it, within the next year or two.
Why, you ask? Because, in the first place, the terms of the peace

treaty would be impossible to carry out even if either side chose to observe them. Malta, you will recall, was to be restored to the Knights of the Order of St John, and who are they? The younger sons of the French and German nobility, each with an income from the family estate. The effect of the French revolution has been to sweep away these estates and all the revenues on which the Order used to depend. Nobody, sir, could restore the Order because the Knights would be penniless. So further war is inevitable. Now, when the last war ended it was the French plan to invade this country, using numberless small craft, flats and barges, to ferry their army across the Channel. This flotilla still exists and their invasion plan is already drawn up. Can it succeed? The admirals say that it cannot. I say that it can!"

A number of other newsmen were now listening to this speech and one of them now ventured to point out that the Royal Navy was a possible obstacle.

"Bah!" said Longnose. "The Royal Navy can be swept aside. By what force, you ask? By the use, I reply, of gunboats!"

"What is a gunboat?" asked a timid man who had just been served with a suet pudding.

"What is a gunboat, my friend? You do well to ask that question and all too few people know the answer. A gunboat is a large undecked vessel, propelled by oars and mounting a single cannon in the bows—a cannon, it may be, of large calibre. Now, I'll freely admit that gunboats must be confined to coastal waters. We must not expect to meet them in mid-Atlantic. But they pose a real threat to our Navy in the Channel and on our coast. Now you will ask what we should do—and what indeed we should have done—to counter this menace?"

Longnose looked around for a response and a young man

replied: "I suppose we should build up our own gunboats to match theirs?"

Longnose nodded approval. "Exactly, sir! We should beat them at their own game!"

The discussion became more general and Delancey found himself in conversation with some sort of editor who sat on his right. "Our talkative friend has overlooked some facts which do not suit his argument," said the older man. "He said nothing about the fate of a gunboat when hit!" Delancey agreed that this was a point which had been overlooked, adding "Nor did he comment upon a gunboat considered as a steady gun-platform." They went on to talk of other matters and Mr Elton, his neighbour, turned out to be a man of intelligence.

"Am I right, sir," asked Delancey, "in thinking that you are connected with *The Times?*"

"I have that honour," replied Mr Elton, not without a touch of pride.

"I wonder, then, whether you can set my mind at rest upon a matter which has often puzzled me. Not all events take place in London. There can be unexpected incidents in other places— a fire here, a murder there, the collapse of a building somewhere else. You cannot have a representative everywhere. Do you take copies, therefore, of every local newspaper, and see from them what deserves your notice?"

"We do indeed, sir. They come in by every coach and are studied as soon as they arrive."

"Would someone like myself be allowed to look through the files? I am trying to discover at what provincial theatre a certain player is now appearing and must assume that local newspapers would provide the answer."

"Sir, you are welcome to study these files but I fear that you may have a tedious search. Theatres these days are very numerous, plays being shown in Edinburgh and Plymouth, in Chester and Dover. You may have days of work ahead of you."

"I accept your kind offer, nevertheless. I am a man of leisure and not without my share of obstinacy."

It took Delancey a day and a half before he discovered the *Yorkshire Herald* with its announcement of a current play at the Theatre Royal, York; one in which Mr Charles Matthews played the male lead opposite Miss Fiona Sinclair. He knew now where the girl had gone and his first instinct was to go north at once. He changed his mind about that, however, and decided to begin the action at long range. He had in prospect this yachting event on Windermere for which he would have to prepare by a great deal of rehearsal. He would go there first, as Ravenglass and Lowther insisted, and on to York afterwards. So he now wrote Fiona a letter in which he apologised for seeking her friendship at a time when he was all but betrothed to a lady well known in London society. He hoped that he might be forgiven. She might now be assured that his relationship with the lady in question was quite at an end, that her family disapproved of his political associations and that he was now perfectly free to pay his respect to any other lady who was not herself already engaged. His affairs would presently take him to the north. Would she consent to see him if he were to visit York? Her reply, dated 24 March from York, showed that her departure from London had set him a test and that his finding where she was had gone some way towards gaining her friendship.

Chapter Four

"Water Nymph"

DELANCEY would never have wanted it known that his stay with Sir Roger Cartnel at Aysgarth Hall, near Bowness, was his first real experience of country life as known to the nobility and gentry. He had realised at the last moment that he would be expected to bring his own servant and finally did so, engaging an idle youth called Jenkins who at any rate looked the part. Sir Roger was far from being a leading figure in society but he was Commodore of the Windermere Yacht Club and it was in this capacity that he had offered hospitality to Ravenglass, Lowther, and Delancey. Colonel Manning and two of his friends were at the Old England Inn at Bowness, next door to the Yacht Club premises. Before leaving London Delancey had heard that the schooner *Peggy* was already on the lake but he found on arrival that this was not entirely true. She was at Haverthwaite, having been brought ashore below Penny Bridge, and her further progress was slow. She was being manhandled on rollers by shrimp fishermen from Morecambe who were available only when prevented from fishing. Manning finally paid them extra to work on Sunday, hoping that the clergy would not come to hear of it. The total distance on rollers would not be much over four miles but the process was tedious and they did not have the road entirely to themselves. Sir Roger provided horses for his guests and Delancey rode with the others to see *Peggy* for the first time on the road beyond Newby

Bridge. It was there that the two opponents, Manning and Delancey, were to meet. The Colonel was a man of indeterminate age, grey-haired, sallow-faced, with a permanently sad expression. He was friendly enough, as were his two companions, Major Forest and the Honourable Mr Stephen Fitch. *Peggy* was mounted on a cradle which rested in turn on six wooden rollers, four supporting the schooner at any given time, the other two rolled ahead and placed in position. There were 25 men in all, supervised by Mr Waller, Sir Roger's Water Bailiff, who had once been a sergeant in the Marines.

"He served in America during the previous war and saw how things were done around Lake Champlain," explained Sir Roger, and Waller certainly seemed to know what he was doing. Delancey watched the team's progress with interest but was still more intent on *Peggy* herself. She was a fine boat, there could be no doubt of that, undecked but in beautiful order, covered for the time being by a tarpaulin. Her mast, sails, and cordage had gone ahead by wagon to a point near Staveley where the vessel was to be launched again.

"I lost the toss," said Manning, "and have to race in Lowther territory against people who know the lake."

"We shall need some advantage," replied Delancey, "if we are to keep level with *Peggy*. And you will have two local men in your crew."

"I know that I am allowed two local men but I shan't have them. My crew have worked together for four years and I should be loath to leave any of them ashore. They are at Bowness now, using a borrowed craft so as to get the feel of the lake."

After dinner that afternoon Sir Roger spread a map on the dining table and explained how the race would be sailed.

"The lake divides almost equally into north and south, Belle Island forming the narrows here opposite Bowness. The probable course is from a start line just south of Belle Island to a flag buoy which you must round opposite Town Head, up the whole length of the lake to the Waterhead flag buoy below Ambleside, and so back again to the Ben Holm flag boat which is just north of here and marks the finish."

"What is the total distance?" asked Delancey.

"Eighteen miles," replied Sir Roger. "We can do it in about two to three hours, given a fair wind. I believe the record stands at one hour and twenty-two minutes but that was under ideal conditions. We seldom race as early in the year as this, the club matches being sailed in June or July, often with a large crowd to watch the finish from the shore just north of Bowness. To race in April is to gamble on the weather but I know that you have a taste, Lord Ravenglass, for games of chance."

Ravenglass was a fair-haired man endowed with good looks and a large fortune, extremely well-dressed but with an inadequate supply of brains. He had been coached as a yachtsman by the Honourable Stephen Lowther (always called Tim), who was a young relative of the Earl of Lonsdale and had known Windermere since childhood. They were boon companions, these two, gamblers both and destined later to become friends of the Regent. As the older of the two, Tim took the lead and more especially on this occasion in that *Water Nymph* was his own dearest possession and the fastest yacht on the Lake. He had not been nearly as successful with racehorses, which made him all the keener on yachting.

"You were saying, Sir Roger," said Ravenglass, "that you have crowds here in summer. These are mostly visitors, I should suppose?"

"Well, you know what the effect of the recent war has been. Folk who would previously have gone on tour to the Rhineland and Italy were unable to land on the Continent with any safety. They made Westmoreland a substitute for the Alps. Then this fellow Wordsworth came to live at Grasmere about three years ago—"

"But he was born here, surely?" Lowther interrupted.

"He was born at Cockermouth in Cumberland. Then comes this other fellow Coleridge—heaven knows where he comes from—and the Lakes are made fashionable. Now I say nothing against these poets. They are not my sort but it takes all kinds of folk to make the world we know and I am as broadminded as the next man—"

"Nobody more so," said Lowther.

"But I could wish that these scribblers would leave us alone and write about Ireland or the Hebrides. Perhaps, however, the peace will encourage them to live in France or Holland and lead other people to go there as well. I can't say that the peace had made much difference as yet. Keswick is a place I hardly recognise these days!"

"I should imagine," said Delancey, "that Windermere is subject to sudden squalls, to gusts of wind between the hills."

"That is so," replied his host, "and more especially in the spring. A storm can blow up in a matter of minutes and end as suddenly within the hour. But Tim here knows all about it and will be able to warn you."

"I know as much about it as anyone," said Lowther, "but will be just as surprised as a stranger when the yacht is suddenly on her beam ends. One needs to be alert, by God!"

"It looks to me," said Delancey, "as if you will seldom have occasion to beat to windward."

"Very true," replied Lowther. "Winds are usually from the west or east, only rarely from the north or south. With a strong northerly wind you could not pass the narrows at all, not in a yacht of any size."

"And certainly not in *Water Nymph*," Delancey agreed. "I look forward to trying her paces but *Peggy* looks to me a formidable opponent. She has beautiful lines and must be a pleasure to handle."

"*Water Nymph* will be in the water tomorrow," rejoined Tim Lowther, "and she is the fastest yacht in this county. We have to win, moreover, because I can't afford to lose. Manning is a man of wealth who dares to wager as he is said to have done. Should my yacht be beaten I shall have to borrow money at a high rate of interest. I shall be going, cap in hand, to the Jews."

Delancey was present when *Water Nymph* was launched from the slipway at Bowness and was duly impressed by her lines and by her excellent state of repair. Nor was he disappointed when he saw her with masts stepped, rigging set up, and sails bent. She was a beautiful craft and as easy to handle—and quite as fast—as he had supposed her to be. He spent a long day cruising in the upper lake with a fine breeze and returned to Bowness with a good opinion of the yacht and an enhanced opinion of his crew. Ravenglass might be amateur but Tim was skilful and the two hired men from Morecambe were very good seamen indeed. When they dropped anchor it was early evening but there was light enough to glimpse a distant sail to the south-east. Delancey raised his telescope and confirmed his first guess. Yes, it was *Peggy* all right and Manning was already exercising his crew near Storrs Hall. Delancey had the strong impression that the Colonel was a very good helmsman and one with considerable experience. They would see more of each other before the race took place. It was evident, moreover, that they would have the lake to themselves. As judge, Sir Roger would be afloat but in a much smaller craft, just large enough to mount a small brass swivel gun, the weapon which would start and finish the race. Delancey knew already that lakeland craft all mounted small guns. He could not imagine why but learnt presently that the object was to make an echo which would resound from the fells on either side of the lake. Even rowing boats carried a shotgun with blank cartridges and, as for *Water Nymph,* she normally bristled with artillery. She mounted none when racing, however, and *Peggy's* armament had also, he heard, been left ashore. Watchers along the lakeside had been timing both yachts over a measured mile and the local odds were now about even. After three days of exercising in different states of wind and weather, Delancey came to the conclusion that *Peggy* was probably faster than *Water Nymph.* The odds now being offered were proof that other folk were coming to the same conclusions. There were to be three races on successive days beginning on 16 April, the winner the yacht which had the best result of three.

The 16th began as a fine day with a south-westerly wind, the lake looking its best with a gleam of sunshine. The two yachts were level and coming up to the line when Sir Roger fired his gun. *Water Nymph,* to windward, had a slight advantage over the southward run, holding nicely to the wind, but lost ground again after rounding the buoy. The two yachts were almost level off Bowness, *Peggy* slightly ahead at Ecclerig and still further ahead in rounding the Waterhead Buoy. It was about then that the sky darkened and the day seemed suddenly colder. Tim Lowther looked fixedly at the sky and gave it as his opinion that the wind would presently veer to the north-east. For the next half-hour the breeze was fitful, gusting from different directions and sometimes dying away to nothing. In these conditions Delancey contrived to gain ground and had even, at one time, a very slight advantage. Then the breeze steadied in the north-west and *Peggy* showed her speed with the wind abaft. By Elleray it was evident that the race was lost and Delancey, for one, was willing to admit that *Peggy* was the faster yacht. In the actual approach to the finishing line, however, the wind blew suddenly from the north-east, just as Tim had predicted. Seeing the darkening line on the water and warned by a shout from Tim Lowther, Delancey put the helm over and presented the yacht's stern to the coming gust of wind. *Water Nymph* then came round again on course but Ravenglass pointed excitedly toward *Peggy*. Her jib had carried away as she heeled before the wind. To bend the jib again was a matter of minutes for *Peggy*'s experienced crew but the mishap could not have happened at a worse time. There was frantic activity as *Water Nymph* drew ahead and then, after about three minutes, *Peggy* was back in the race and overhauling her opponent. It was all too late, however, for *Water Nymph* was nearly at the finishing line. A gun boomed and the race was over, with *Water Nymph* the winner by a very narrow margin.

At dinner that day Delancey had to confess that the final result was not in doubt.

"There can be no question about it," he concluded. "The Manx yacht is the faster of the two. We won today by sheer luck and through Lowther's warning me about the coming change of wind direction. It is too much to expect that to happen again."

"If we were lucky today," said Ravenglass, the gambler, "we

may well be lucky again tomorrow. It is all, in the end, a matter of luck."

"And local knowledge," said Lowther.

"We are to windward of the Manxmen there," replied Delancey. "Manning might have done better to have local men aboard."

"But these fishermen from Morecambe are not really local," objected Lowther. "They may know the ropes but they don't know the lake."

"And that's true," said Sir Roger. "Anyway, we have given the people round here something to talk about. I hear, however, that the odds are still in favour of *Peggy*. Manning's seamanship today was good, or so it seemed to me."

"He did very well indeed," Delancey concluded. "His only error was in looking towards the finish instead of looking over his shoulder to see the danger that threatened him. He'll not make that mistake again."

The next day's race was a tame affair in which *Peggy* secured an early lead and never lost it, crossing the finishing line two cables ahead. It was a beautiful day with moderate westerly wind and Delancey enjoyed the sail and loved the scenery. He felt pity, however, for Tim Lowther, who looked more and more distressed as the race came near to its inevitable end. The trouble was that *Water Nymph* had won all the local races for the last six years so that defeat had seemed to him all but impossible. He had placed his bets accordingly and not on the scale appropriate to a younger son. Who would expect to be outsailed by a soldier in a craft brought from the Isle of Man? The third race would decide the match and Tim's finances would be crippled for years to come. The example was not wasted on

Delancey to whom gambling had never been a temptation but who resolved now against ever betting on anything. He had to take chances in battle, venturing other men's lives as well as his own, and this was a fact of his trade. Mere gambling was a pastime for people who had nothing else to do, but passing the time had never been his problem. He came near to it in this sailing match but the whole exercise had a different purpose. It was *Water Nymph* which saved him from making a foolish marriage and gave him the chance of marrying Fiona. She had not accepted him as yet, to be sure, but he hoped and believed that she would.

The third and final race began in what was nearly a dead calm, the lake grey and still, the clouds low and with very occasional gleams of sunshine. The two yachts drifted down the lake with fitful westerly puffs of wind, neither having any considerable advantage but Delancey proving a little quicker in using what wind there was. At a snail's pace they rounded the Town Head buoy with *Water Nymph* just ahead but the wind stiffened on the run north and *Peggy's* superior speed soon became obvious. When they passed the narrows near Bowness, *Peggy* had a steadily increasing lead. Overhead dark rain clouds were gathering by now with ragged edges blotting out the mountains. The water darkened and waves began to dash against the yacht's port beam, the spray passing overhead and the craft gathering speed. The wind rose to a shriek and the yachtsmen could no longer see the shores. The mountains had vanished and so had the rival yacht, there being nothing to be seen but a wild waste of surging waves and drifting mist, nothing to be felt but blinding rain and stinging hail. Suddenly there came a screaming gust of unexpected fury, *Water Nymph* was knocked on her beam ends with masts and sails in the water, her crew clinging to her rigging as water poured over the starboard gunwale. With the yacht no longer answering to the helm, Delancey could do little except tell the others to bale and prepare to cut away the masts. They were saved the trouble, however, for both masts broke at this point and the yacht slowly righted herself, leaving booms, gaffs, and canvas in the water. Frantic baling followed amidst a further hailstorm and then the storm passed, the wind became a mere breeze, the waves disappeared, and the mist vanished north-west towards the head of the lake. As when the curtain rises at the theatre, the clouds, dispersing, revealed the fells on either side. The scene momentarily sunlit was one of breath-taking beauty but Delancey was not looking at the landscape. His attention was fixed on *Peggy* and he was relieved to see that she also was dismasted but afloat. Both yachts were at a standstill, with much of the course still to sail. Delancey began at once to make a plan. If he could rig some sort of jury mast and set even the jib alone, *Water Nymph* might still reach Waterhead and return to the finishing line. It would take hours to be sure, but it was still possible for him to win the race. He was still thinking furiously along these lines when there came the boom of a gun from the judge's boat, accompanied by a signal which Tim Lowther was able to interpret. "The race is over," he announced with obvious relief, "and the result is a draw." Sir Roger's decision was a sensible one for the race, if continued under jury-rig, might not have ended until after dark. It was obvious, at the same time, that Manning had been cheated by ill-luck of a victory which he certainly deserved. As for Ravenglass and Lowther, they had been saved by the Goddess of Gambling to whom their prayers had been directed.

It would have been physically possible to re-rig the two

yachts and stage another race in June but Lowther pleaded technical difficulties and Delancey made it clear that the race, if it took place, would happen without him. He spoke of another engagement and hoped inwardly that it would prove to be more than an excuse. The whole affair ended in friendly fashion, it being generally agreed that *Peggy* was the faster yacht and that Manning was as good a helmsman as his opponent. Delancey himself would have allowed that Manning was the better of the two, having had far more experience with that type of craft. For him, however, the whole affair was over and his only ambition was to reach York without further delay.

Chapter Five

THE "CHARLOTTE DUNDAS"

THE COACH was approaching the City of York, where the lights were already lit. The rumbling of the coach wheels became louder as the vehicle passed through the city gates and now the coachman was flicking his horses into a final burst of energy so that he could arrive with a flourish. With stables almost in sight, the horses broke into a canter. The guard sounded his horn, some children waved and cried out, and then the coach swung into an inn yard, the horses plunging as the ostlers ran forward to hold them. The journey was over and Delancey told himself that Fiona could not possibly be there to meet the coach. The letter in which he had given the hour of his arrival would not have come in time. In any case, she would be on stage all the evening. He might expect to see her next day, at the earliest. After all, an actress, a leading lady has her work to do, her parts to learn, her rehearsals to attend. . . . Then, somehow, she was in his arms! Kissing him on the mouth, she cried, "You *shall* marry me!" Kissing her back he asked, "When?" To this she replied, "Soon!" In the inn yard while the coach was emptied of its luggage, while the horses were led away, while other passengers were greeted by their friends, they hugged each other and Fiona shed a few tears even while laughing.

"It seemed so long!" she explained.

"It was an eternity!" he agreed, adding, "You are more beautiful than I remembered."

"And you look younger," she replied, "perhaps because you are on holiday."

"Or perhaps because I am in love."

"Like you were with Mrs Farren?"

"Like I never was with anyone."

"Where are you to stay?"

"Here, at the—"

"Shall we have supper here?"

"Of course, but what about the theatre?"

"I took the evening off so as to give my understudy her chance to play the part. She will be one bridesmaid and the theatre, I find, is in the parish of Michael-le-Belfry. How would that do? It was where Guy Fawkes was baptised."

"And do you think Scarborough might be the place for the honeymoon? I was never there but it seems to be fashionable."

There was much to discuss and Delancey took Fiona back to her lodging after supper. Saying goodnight to her on the doorstep, which took a surprisingly long time, Delancey confessed he had gone through agonies on the journey, especially over the last few miles. "I half expected to find you betrothed to someone else—to Mr Matthews, for example."

"He is married, love. But I thought maybe you would worry and decided to accept you at once. I'll confess now that I never had the least idea of marrying anyone else. Well, it would be absurd, wouldn't it? Mr Matthews has promised to give me away and he has a niece who will be the other bridesmaid. I have asked about Scarborough and we can't easily reach there in one day—not, I mean, allowing time for the wedding. We shall have to break the journey in Malton, staying perhaps at the Green Man in the Market Place. There is a good inn at Scarborough called the Royal but it is more the fashion to take lodgings there in the Crescent."

"Are the lodgings engaged, my love?"

"No, but I have the address. Why are you laughing, dear?"

"I was laughing at the fears I felt that you would refuse me. While I was worrying about that you were deciding what to wear at the wedding!"

"The dress is not bespoke but I have chosen the cloth. . . . No, love. I had not the least idea of refusing you! I liked you from the day we met. Who did you think of asking to appear as best man?"

"I hadn't thought about it at all! You are miles ahead of me. But my former First Lieutenant lives in Westmorland, not all that distant, and might make the journey that I have just made. He would come to the aid of an old shipmate, I daresay."

On his way back to his inn Delancey reflected that an actress needs as much practical ability as a naval officer. She must be as ready for the curtain's rise as any lieutenant must be ready for the morning watch, nor must she fail to cover up when someone else has missed his cue. There could be no doubt about the organisation of the wedding, due not to the bride's parents but to the resourceful bride herself. All went as well as he expected and the eventful day ended, as planned, in the best inn at Malton where Fiona and Richard entered into a relationship which was to be passionate, loving, complete, and permanent.

On the second day, going to bed at an earlier hour than some fellow guests thought was decent, Fiona and Richard had time to talk.

"By rights I should have hired a lady's maid for you."

"I've no need for one. You found how to undress me quickly enough."

"But what about dressing?"

"That is not as important. You married a slut."

"I married an angel!"

"You came nearer to marrying a whore. You are the seventh man to have taken me."

"As if I cared! Was I the best, though?"

"Far the best, darling. For one thing, you—oh, well, never mind—what really matters is the way you treat me like a goddess."

"You are a goddess!"

"I'm not even a lady!"

"You are, my dear. I have made you one."

"How?"

"I am an Esquire by virtue of holding the King's commission. The King's servants address me as Esquire when they write to me. The wife of an Esquire is a gentlewoman."

"But my position is not quite the same. You have made me a lady, nevertheless—I see that—and I have a part to play from now on. I am Mrs Delancey and you shall see me play it to perfection."

"Don't overplay it, love. You could be *too* ladylike!"

"Warn me if I overdo it. While I quit the stage, I shall not cease to play a part. It will become habitual but all the time you will know that there is another Fiona. If ladies reluctantly submit to love making, as I am told they do, you will know that I demand it!"

"You may have more than you bargained for. What then? You cannot reject me and go back to your family!"

"No, I can't do that. I weep to think that I am at your mercy.
I do believe, however, that we should visit my aunt and uncle
at Dumbarton. They are my only relatives and I want to tell
them how badly you are treating me."

"We'll do that. When we come south again you shall then
visit my sister at Bristol. I want to tell her how deceived I have
been by a girl with all the airs of a great lady who is really no
better than she should be."

So the journey to Scotland was agreed upon following their
stay in Scarborough. They went by coach to Newcastle, sailed
from there to Leith by a coasting vessel, and so went by coach
again to Dumbarton which is some fourteen miles from Glas-
gow. It was a place of no great commercial importance, once
the site of a castle built at the confluence of the Clyde and the
Leven. It was not then, nor is it now, a scene of great events
but it is placed within easy reach of places which were to be
the very heart of Scottish industry. Mr and Mrs Sinclair turned
out to be an elderly couple living in a cottage to which the
Delanceys were made very welcome. Mr Sinclair, like Robert
Burns in at least this one respect, had spent most of his active
life as an exciseman. It was not a career which was consistent
with great popularity and he had been glad to move from Perth
on retirement to this cottage which his wife had inherited. Taking Richard to look at his garden, he explained that he had not
seen Fiona for some years. "My younger brother Hamish," he
explained, "was a wild young man, would not settle down to
any steady occupation, but was clerk for a time to a merchant
who did good business at Leith. He never married but he lived
for some years with a bonny Highland lass called Katrine. There
was the one child, Fiona, and then Katrine died in childbirth
of her second, a boy, who never lived. Fiona was brought up

by poor Katrine's sister, another wild creature—that is, after Hamish died—and I scarcely wonder at her living the life she did at one time. I cannot tell you what pleasure it gives me to see Fiona married to a good man who will know how to keep her in order. She is bonnier than her poor mother was—and *she* was among the prettiest lassies you ever saw—but she seems to be steadier these days and something of a lady and an officer's wife. She'll settle down even better after she has had a child or two."

Mrs Sinclair also took Richard aside and expressed her own relief that Fiona was so well married. "She had no sort of chance in early life with her mother dying so young and her aunt drinking too much and scarcely ever seen in the kirk. She was a handful as a child, or so I've been told, but never did real harm. She was always affectionate, you know—too much so with some of the boys—but kind to younger children. She is a good girl at heart."

When family matters had thus been settled, Mr Sinclair took Delancey to his workshop and revealed what was clearly his main interest in life, the building of ship models. The point of his models, however, was that they were propelled by steam. He was no inventor but had closely followed the work of Mr William Symington whose first steamship had been launched on the river Carron in 1789. It was this vessel that Mr Sinclair had carefully imitated, his working model having two paddle-wheels on the same side. She had belonged to Mr Patrick Miller of Dalswinton and had been tested on Loch Dalswinton, reaching a speed of no less than five miles an hour.

"But all this," said Mr Sinclair, "is only by way of experiment, you'll understand. Mr Symington has now completed another steamboat. This has been built for Lord Dundas and is for use on the Forth and Clyde Canal. My model here is an exact replica, from which you will see that she is driven by a single stern-wheel. On a trial trip in March, only a few weeks ago, she covered a distance of nearly twenty miles at over three miles an hour."

"So she was not as fast as Symington's first ship?"

"Aye, but she had two barges in tow and was steaming into the teeth of a gale."

"So the trial was judged a success?"

"Weel, it was and it wasna. The engine did fine but some gentlemen of the Canal Company were worried about the effect on the canal banks."

"I can understand that."

"Weel, I'll confess that my interest is merely in the engine itself. The point about it is that the steam acts on each side of the piston—Watt's idea, as you know."

"Just so."

"The piston then works a connecting rod and crank—as you see in the model—*here*."

"Quite, I see that."

"Then the crank is joined with the axis of the paddle-wheel, as you can see for yourself."

"Very clever indeed."

"Yes, but copied from Pickard's invention of 1780—the idea for the reciprocating action on the connecting rod."

"So Pickard should have some of the credit?"

"Yes, but the paddle-wheel we owe to Miller."

"Well, I am amazed—and not least so by the skill with which you have built your model. What is this latest steam-boat called?"

"The *Charlotte Dundas,* named after his lordship's daughter."

"Would it be possible for me to see her in motion on the canal?"

"It shall be arranged. I know all the gentlemen concerned. It so happens, moreover, that we are expecting a visit from an American gentleman, a Mr Fulton, who has made just the same request. You and he can visit the *Charlotte Dundas* on the same day and perhaps take a short trip in her. I hear that the Duke of Bridgwater is interested. We may expect a visit from him some day. Steamboats are very much the thing of the future."

In bed that night, Delancey told Fiona about the local interest in steamboats.

"Your uncle told me about cranks and connecting rods, about ratchet wheels and cylinders, and I haven't the least idea what he was talking about."

"You poor dear. It is the Sinclairs who have the brains."

"But I'd like to see this steamboat, wouldn't you?"

"Yes, I should. But why the fuss about it? When you have your frigate, the wind will blow it along and the wind will cost you nothing. But a steamboat has to be driven by a furnace which is so greedy of coal that the vessel can carry nothing else, neither guns nor cargo. It makes no sense at all!"

"It might make sense if there is no wind or again if the wind blows from the wrong direction."

"And then the smoke will blow into your eyes and dirty your linen. I'll look at this steamship but I shall say nothing in its favour. I prefer ships with sails."

"So do I, darling. We mustn't stay too long with your aunt and uncle. They don't have too much money."

"I know, dearest. So I have been giving money to my aunt without my uncle's knowledge. We'll go soon after we have seen the *Charlotte Dundas* and make our way to Bristol. Do you think we shall be at war again soon?"

"By next year, I should think."

"Then we shall be in London again by the end of this year. . . . Do you still love me?"

"But of course, darling!"

"Why don't you prove it?"

They talked no more that night about marine engineering.

Delancey first saw the *Charlotte Dundas* on a date in early July. She was at Lock 20 on the Forth and Clyde Canal and Mr Symington was already there, the furnaces stoked and a thin column of smoke ascending from a tall funnel into the windless air. There were several artisans at work on the engine, one with an oiling can, and two boatmen forward, keeping well away from the noise and dirt. On the road opposite the lock there were half a dozen carriages drawn up with grooms holding the horses' heads. Some of the gentlemen to be seen were casual visitors but two, standing by the gangplank, were evidently there by invitation. Symington presently came ashore to greet them and then extended his greetings to Mr Sinclair and Captain Delancey. Introductions followed and it appeared that Symington's other guests were Mr Fulton and Mr Williams. Fulton's accent was plainly American. Mr Williams was obviously from the less fashionable part of London. Both were engineers and both were fascinated by the *Charlotte Dundas*. Fulton was tall and handsome, aged 37 and a man of culture, accustomed to good society and known (Sinclair had whispered) to the Duke of Bridgwater himself. Williams was an older man, aged perhaps 45, and probably unknown to anyone of consequence. Unlike Fulton, he looked like a man who could work with a spanner or even with a shovel. Symington, a little older than

Fulton, was an eager-looking inventive person, keen to talk about steam navigation to anyone who would listen. The group collected round him and stared down at the queer-looking vessel in which the engine had begun to vibrate. She was of no great size, the machinery occupying the stern half of the vessel and leaving little room for anything else.

"Pray step aboard, Mrs Delancey," said Symington. "Come gentlemen. If you go forward in the bows you will find that the smoke all goes astern."

They went aboard and forward as advised and felt the vessel shaking under them as the engines worked up to a higher speed. Disturbed by this sensation Fiona held Delancey's hand tightly. Then the engines stopped abruptly and the vibration ceased. Joining them, Mr Symington explained that there was a minor adjustment to be made. It would take no more than a few minutes. He pointed out, in the meanwhile, that there was an east wind, blowing almost directly down the canal. He would take the *Charlotte Dundas* into the teeth of the wind. "We have sails," he went on, "and we use them if the wind is favourable, as it will be on our return. With a headwind like this, we shall hoist no sail but rely solely on the engine." Within a minute or two the engine restarted noisily and the vibration intensified. "I'm frightened," whispered Fiona, and Delancey's arm tightened round her waist. "There's no danger," he assured her as the mooring ropes were cast off their bollards.

The boatmen pushed the craft away from the wharf and she began to sidle into the middle of the canal. The stern-wheel started to revolve and the canal banks slowly slipped past. The vibration increased and the sound could be heard of more coal being shovelled into the furnace. The smoke all went astern as Symington had predicted and the passengers went further aft to see the engine at work. It was an impressive sight and the paddle-wheel's action, beating the water into froth, was as novel and exciting. An engineer pulled a lanyard and there came a hooting noise from near the funnel, which alarmed Fiona still more. Now far astern, the grooms could be seen trying to calm the frightened horses on the quayside. A great adventure had begun but the novelty had worn off in half an hour. The speed, which Symington estimated at four miles an hour, was impressive only in being against the wind, and when the craft went about, hoisted sail, and began the speedier return voyage, the smoke drifted more forward than aft. Passengers tended to choke and cough, Fiona brushing the soot off her dress and everyone being rather relieved when they were back at Lock 20, dirty but impressed. When the engine had been stopped, Mr Symington made a little speech:

"You have seen, madam and gentlemen, what the *Charlotte Dundas* can do. What you must understand, however, is that we are in the very early days of steam navigation. There are many problems still to solve but I myself have no doubt that steam is the thing of the future. The first use of the steam vessel will be to tow sailing ships in and out of harbour when the wind is contrary. Think of the time wasted and the mounting expense when an outward-bound merchantman is windbound, perhaps for weeks at a time. Later, and perhaps within our lifetime, there will be the man-of-war fitted with an engine, able to progress in a flat calm or against a contrary wind. Then will come the merchantman under steam herself. What you have seen today is just the beginning of a revolution in nautical history!"

He was applauded, congratulated, and thanked, his passengers then making their way, in conversation, towards where their carriages were waiting. After saying goodbye to them, Symington made his way back to the engine. Delancey, making a quick decision, asked Fulton and Williams to have dinner with him and Fiona at the Burnside Inn, which would be on their way back to Dumbarton. The two gentlemen accepted and the party foregathered for a simple meal, in which haggis was the main feature apart from boiled mutton. All the talk, inevitably, was about steam navigation, Fulton taking the lead:

"It is in America," he maintained, "that we shall see the most rapid progress. We have great distances to cover, with rivers and lakes affording our only means of transport. Here in Britain the distances are small and you already have a good system of roads."

"Very true," said Delancey, "but our immediate problem is how to thwart the designs of Bonaparte. Shall we apply the steam-engine to the purposes of war? It seems to me, I might add, that the basic idea in this invention is simple enough. You take the steam-engine, familiar to Cornish miners, and apply it to the waterwheel, the ordinary mill device with the process reversed. It takes no genius, surely, to think of that. The real problem is to design and construct the actual machinery, making each part with sufficient accuracy and fitting the piston to the tube. But suppose the engineering problem solved, how do we apply the machine to the war at sea?"

"First of all," replied Fulton, "its use must be confined to small craft in coastal waters. At the end of the last war, Napoleon had collected a vast number of vessels in which to ferry his army from France to England; a distance from Boulogne of, shall we say, thirty miles? These craft still exist. Should the war be resumed, his first idea will be to think again of invasion. He is a soldier and that is how his mind works. Now, were you,

Captain Delancey, to have a steam-vessel, perhaps of twice the tonnage of the *Charlotte Dundas* you could attack these invasion craft during a dead calm when they would least expect it. The effect on their morale would be out of all proportion to the actual damage done. Suppose, however, that you had a dozen steam-vessels, the French would have to abandon their whole idea as something too hazardous to contemplate. I see no reason why a dozen such vessels should not be built."

"Is it as easy as that?" Delancey asked. "How many men do we have who can build an engine? How many engineers are there in this country?"

"Very few, I grant you, but they can be trained, and it would all take about a year."

"I agree with that, Mr Fulton," said Williams. "You've hit the nail on the head. Our difficulty must be to convince their lordships of the Admiralty, and we shan't have done that until the war is over. Now my plan is to build a steamship of my own and show the Royal Navy what it can do—at sea, mind you, not on a canal. I have a shipbuilder friend at Woolwich who can do the construction of the vessel and there are engineers in London who can build the engine. I don't mind revealing to you gentlemen that I am in touch with one of the greatest inventors of all time, Joseph Bramah himself, a genius of our age. With the help of these gentlemen known to me, I can give Britain a naval superiority over every other country in the world."

"But that we already have, Mr Williams," said Delancey sharply. "What more superiority do we want?"

"Why, Captain, we can have superiority, in addition, over wind and tide!"

"Well, gentlemen," said Fulton, "I have plans, too, but have had little encouragement from your Navy Board. I shall have to offer my inventions to Bonaparte."

"Would you not rather assist us against this tyrant?" asked Delancey. "Do you want to see him rule the world?"

"I am a citizen of a country which is neutral, sir, but remember that we owe our independence to France. Our traditional alliance is with the French and our traditional opponent is King George. We did not grow to national manhood with any prejudice in your favour. No, sir. But I have treated you more than fairly. I have offered my help and it has been rejected. You may think that the steamship is a simple device and so it is, but what would you say to a craft which can travel below the surface of the sea?"

"I should say fiddlesticks!" replied Delancey. "The thing is impossible."

"No sir, it is not impossible, and I am prepared to prove it. I have built just such a vessel and called her the *Nautilus*."

Chapter Six

THE "STARLING"

THE DELANCEYS' visit to Bristol was a great success. Rachel, his sister, was still the respected wife of Alderman John Sedley, the West India merchant, and still lived at her old address in Queen's Square. Her children, however, had all left home by now and even the youngest daughter had married. There were nine grandchildren all told, and peacetime had brought greater prosperity to the whole family. Rachel and Fiona became great friends at once while Richard was introduced to several of John's associates, all merchants of note, some of whom he had met during his previous visit in 1798. The Delanceys were pressed to stay for a long visit but Richard explained that Fiona had still to see her new home in Guernsey. "I have a small estate there," he explained, "a place called Anneville Manor. I have been making it habitable over the years, making improvements as I could find the money, and the time has come for my wife to see where she is to live and meet our neighbours. I had thought of travelling to Southampton and sailing from there." This was a reasonable plan but fate decreed otherwise. At a dinner party, the Delanceys met a young naval officer called Le Page, who commanded a cutter called the *Starling*. He was under orders to sail for Portsmouth but he was a Guernseyman and had a premonition that he would be compelled by weather conditions to seek shelter in St Peter Port—the home, as it happened, of the girl he hoped to marry.

In a convivial mood, he offered the Delanceys a passage, an offer which he confirmed on the following day, and the opportunity seemed too good to miss. All was arranged and Le Page was paid something for the use of his cabin. The *Starling* had been sent on some errand to Ireland and was making a leisurely return to her home port. Lieutenant Le Page was a breezily confident youngster who evidently did not expect to be questioned too closely about where he had been and why. The cutter herself was an almost new craft and in very good order. Fiona, for one, looked forward to the voyage and to seeing Anneville. Delancey himself saw that favourable winds could well make this the quickest way of reaching Guernsey. As against that, contrary winds were to be expected in a voyage during which the original course would be south-west and the subsequent course nearly due east. It was to be hoped that the cutter could keep close to the wind, as might be expected of a vessel with her rig. As for distance, he would guess that the nearest route to Guernsey would be about three hundred miles as a seagoing steamship would steer (supposing that such a craft existed). With reasonable luck, the voyage could be done in three to five days. The cutter, incidentally, had not come up the Avon to Bristol but was at anchor in the King Road, a sensible precaution against being windbound.

Sailing before daybreak on a September morning meant a long pull in the ship's boat on the previous evening but Delancey saw to it that Fiona was warmly wrapped in a boat cloak over all. Le Page's quarters, which he had lent them, were necessarily cramped but a coasting voyage had at least the merit of involving fresh food on the table, with milk even on the first two days. Although Delancey was on deck to watch the cutter sail, Fiona was wisely asleep and woke only off Ilfracombe to have, presently, a distant view of Lundy on the starboard bow. The wind was fair for Land's End and seemed to have settled in that quarter, foreshadowing a tedious beat up Channel.

Delancey came to the conclusion, meanwhile, that *Starling* was navigated by a young man of rather less than ordinary intelligence. He should at least be familiar with the approach to Guernsey, which was a consoling thought, and he had a reasonably good crew, weakened however by the sickness of the boatswain who had been left ashore, but his own experience was limited, and the *Starling* was his first independent command. Off Land's End there was enough of a sea to make the cutter pitch and roll. The wind dropped later and Delancey decided to go on deck, where he found that the cutter was on the starboard tack with no land in sight. There was so dense a mist that no observation was possible. Le Page now had the ship's bell rung at intervals but there was no answering sound from any other vessel. Although heading up Channel in one of the busiest highways the *Starling* seemed to be alone in the world. She sailed on slowly as night fell. By the morning what had been mist had turned to fog.

Le Page had so far been very much in command but he was now worried enough to call Delancey into consultation. In the cabin he unrolled the chart and showed Delancey his pencilled calculations. "But where are we?" asked Delancey, and was shown a hesitant pencil mark in mid-Channel due south of the Lizard. "What was your last observation?" "When I sighted Land's End." Le Page pointed to a firm pencil mark with the bearing shown. "All since is by dead reckoning . . ." Delancey realised that the cutter's estimated position could be five or six leagues out in any direction, and that she was certainly not in soundings. "If I were you," he said at last, "I shouldn't lay a course for Guernsey. I should make for Start Point and hope to sight it in the morning. Then you could approach the Channel Isles on a known bearing, and maybe meet with some fisherman on the way who might know where he is." After some hesitation, Le Page agreed to this plan and Delancey stiffened his resolution with a glass of brandy. They both knew that Guernsey was the last place in the world to approach in a fog with one's last position in doubt. There were rocks everywhere and a strong tidal current, some areas to the south-west and north-east being mere graveyards for incautious mariners. During the night the bell was sounded at intervals, no other bell was heard, and daylight revealed a fog which was thicker than ever. "If my calculations are right," said Le Page bravely, "Start Point should be somewhere on the starboard bow." Delancey studied the chart afresh and then summed up the position with finality. "We are lost," he concluded briefly. "We have no idea of our true position."

More by luck than science, the *Starling* struck soundings that afternoon in 23 fathoms, which proved that they were somewhere on the English coast. Better still, the fog lifted for a few minutes and gave them a distant glimpse of Portland Bill to the eastward.

"Now we know where we are," said Le Page. "A course almost due south will bring us to Guernsey. If this wind holds we shall be there by noon tomorrow."

"But what about the fog?" asked Delancey.

"It will probably disperse during the night."

Delancey could not accept this conclusion. Had he been in command he would have dropped anchor somewhere off Bridport and waited for the fog to clear. But was he being over-cautious because Fiona was on board? As against that, Le Page was ready to take risks in order to reach his girl in St Peter Port. Lord St Vincent hated his officers to marry—as if their being single would make them sexless!—but sex was the force that could distort judgement and he could not swear that his own judgement was unaffected.

The fog thickened again as the cutter headed south and Le Page plunged into calculations about the tidal current.

"I shall keep well to the westwards," explained Le Page. "It doesn't matter if we pass Guernsey on that side. If we go too far to the eastwards we could hit the Casquets before we are in soundings."

This was profoundly true and Delancey agreed that it was better to err in that direction. He went below and did his best to entertain Fiona, reading to her until it was time for sleep. He was on deck at first light, only to find that he could see for no more than a cable's length. The fog, although patchy, was persistent and the cutter was sailing on a course of south by west, sounding her bell at intervals and checking her speed by the log. As the day wore on, Le Page was increasingly worried. Turning at last to Delancey he said that his calculation of the distance run put the *Starling* actually beyond Guernsey on the chart and heading, therefore, for the French coast. Supposing, however, that Guernsey had been passed, he did not know on which side. Delancey took the chart below and studied it on the cabin table. "Yes," he concluded, "if we were south of Guernsey we should be in well over twenty fathoms. I can't believe that we have passed north of the Casquets—we should be aware by now of the Race of Alderney. If your calculation of distance is right we are about here, north of Sark."

Knowing these waters but ignorant of their own position, he remembered all the rocks which cluster around Sark and Herm.

"Your best plan," he said finally to Le Page, "is to go about, set a new course to the north-west or as near as the wind will let you, keep under easy sail, and listen hard for the sound of breakers."

The fog seemed to be clearing, affording a view of perhaps two cables ahead, but there was nothing to be seen or heard. An hour passed and Le Page made preparation for lowering the two boats should the emergency arise. For his part, Delancey joined the lookout in the bows, watching and listening intently. More time passed and then, suddenly, he heard the surf and saw a white line across the cutter's bows. Turning aft, he shouted "Hard a-starboard! Quickly!" The helmsman obeyed and Le Page hurried forward to join him, as the cutter swung broadside to the shore.

"Look!" said Delancey. "At least we know where we are!"

"What d'you mean, sir?" asked Le Page.

"Can't you see the whiteness beyond the breakers? That is the shell beach on Herm—couldn't be anywhere else for a hundred miles around. We were heading straight for it and would have been wrecked in another two minutes. We should have been as certainly wrecked had we turned the other way. Now tack, head north-east for half an hour—we must clear the Bonne Grune—then head due west and we shall be in the Little Russel and so on course for St Peter Port."

Now that their position was clear the fog began to lift, affording glimpses of Herm and, soon afterwards, of Guernsey itself. There, presently, was the Brion Tower and Vale Castle. The cutter made more sail as Fiona came on deck and there was even a passing gleam of sunshine to prove that all was well. Forward, a group of seamen had gathered round a four-pounder which presently saluted Castle Cornet, from which the saluting battery replied, amid a chorus of protest from the seagulls. Delancey had the sense of homecoming which he always had when entering St Peter Port. The red roofs climbing the hillside, the tower of the town church, the ramparts of Castle Cornet on its island, the masts of the shipping, the distant glimpse of Fort George—all these had formed the background to his boyhood. It was good to be home, better to think that he actually owned what was no longer a ruin, best of all to remember that his bride was with him. Sail was reduced until, finally, the cutter glided into the anchorage under her jib alone. The cable slid through the hawse-hole, the anchor struck bottom, and the voyage was over. The boat was now manned which would take them ashore. "Thank God for that!" said Le Page, and Delancey replied "Amen."

Chapter Seven

"VENGEANCE"

THEY STAYED on arrival at the Golden Lion and dined there on the following day. As they sat down to dinner a number of men recognised Delancey and came over to greet him in French. He replied in the same language, presenting them to Fiona as Nicolle, Henri, Michel, and Jean-Pierre.

"Michel," he told Fiona afterwards, "is a smuggler in quite a big way of business. During the war the others there were privateersmen, Jean-Pierre being the most successful of them. Now we are at peace they must be doing something else. Or perhaps they are merely hoping for a renewal of the war. The younger privateersmen will never have had another trade. I myself commanded a privateer at one time. That was back in 1795."

"After the time we first met?"

"Yes, a year or so later. I was given the command of a privateer called the *Nemesis*. I was lucky enough to capture a French merchantman called the *Bonne Citoyenne*. It was that prize which enabled me to purchase Anneville."

"And what happened to the *Nemesis*?"

"She was caught by a French corvette and driven ashore by gunfire. I was lucky to escape from Spain, where I was prisoner, and owed my life to a smuggler called Sam Carter, who is master of a lugger called the *Dove*. You will meet him some day for we have remained friends ever since. We have often

90

supped together here at the Golden Lion. This is where the privateersmen used to meet and exchange information, making plans and agreeing sometimes to work together. If they meet here still, and it looks as if they do, it will be to talk about old times. They have made a fortune, some of them, and you can see their fine houses along the Grange or in Clifton. I was not a privateer captain for long. I went back to the Navy and was here again as a lieutenant, supping here when off duty and whenever I could afford it."

It was thus on a fine day in early October 1803 when Fiona had her first sight of Anneville Manor. She saw a granite building, hidden from the road, slate roofed, with deep window embrasures, showing a hint of battlements and the roof, beyond, of what had been the chapel. There had been little attempt at gardening, the immediate surroundings looking wild and unkempt. Across the field a glint of sunshine revealed a silver inlet of the sea.

"It is really a coastal fortification," explained Delancey, "but the present Governor has a plan for reclaiming all the land to the north of us. The Vale is now an island, connected with Guernsey proper by the bridge at St Sampson's. Sir John means to change all that, much to the annoyance of the fishermen."

"But what is his object?"

"He has to defend the island and he has no means at present of rushing his artillery to the north-west corner of it. He wants firm ground and he wants a good road and I can't blame him. We shall be the losers to this extent, that we shall be further from the sea. We shall gain in being able to keep a carriage. We shall also gain in having easier access to St Sampson's for shopping."

"Let's look at the house from the direction in which it faces," said Fiona, and then presently clapped her hands and exclaimed, "It is like a miniature castle in some romantic novel. No, it is more like a castle on the stage. It is far prettier than I thought it would be!"

"The coach house is detached on the left, then there is the gateway and courtyard and the main building, then the kitchen under the battlements, and, last of all, the Chapel of St Thomas. It is said to have been built in about 1300 but there may have been earlier buildings before that. I have tried to make the place habitable. It has a roof on, for instance! But there will be a hundred things you will want to put right. I have directed operations from a distance and the builder has not always done what I wanted. There is only the one servant at present, the woman who acts as caretaker, and the garden is little better than a wilderness. We shall have years of work to do!"

"And you'll run away to sea and leave me to do it! Well, never mind. That means I shall have my own way about everything. And one thing I've decided already. It is no good aiming at formality here. The style must be rustic and gothic, a planned disorder—don't you agree?"

"That is my own plan in so far as I have had one."

"Good! Now let's go inside."

Old Mrs Mahy met them at the main entrance with greetings in the local dialect, which Delancey was able to return, and they looked at the hall, the kitchen, and the dining room with its great fireplace and furze oven.

"At last," cried Fiona, "I have a home of my own."

Delancey's next care was to call on Sir John Doyle, the Governor, and make his presence known to Sir James Saumarez, to Captain Savage, and to many old friends, not forgetting Sam

Carter. Convinced as he was that a renewal of war was certain, he ensured that Fiona should have plenty of good neighbours, people who would care for her while he might be at sea. Three months of activity followed, and the Delanceys finally spent Christmas in their own home. It was a happy time for both of them and Delancey had intense pleasure in watching the perfection of Fiona's manners and the good impression she made on all her acquaintances. It was, as he had guessed, her training as an actress that had prepared her to play any part, and now she played to a nicety the part of a senior officer's wife. She could have been a great lady with equal ease but she knew, by instinct, that she could give offence by being too grand. She knew her position to within an inch, being always kind as well as polite, simply but correctly dressed for every occasion, remembering everyone by name and being properly deferential to all who might regard themselves as senior to Delancey. She regarded it all as a game and one of which she must know the rules before she dared laugh at them. To watch Fiona's artistry on every social occasion, whether she were hostess or guest, gave Richard an intense pleasure which was destined to be his for as long as they were together. He never saw her make a mistake.

As the rumours of war were heard more often, Delancey learnt, through Sir James Saumarez, that he was no longer in such disfavour at the Admiralty. It was the same administration, to be sure, but his treatment of Mrs Farren had been almost forgotten. The fact was that she had since made a very good match with the wealthy Sir Jocelyn Baxter, Bt.—a match compared with which her marriage to a mere naval officer (and one without post rank) would have been a disaster. Their lordships may have felt no great warmth towards Delancey but they had to admit that he had served with credit. He was, after all, the man who had destroyed that French 74, the *Hercule,* on the west coast of Ireland. It was more than everyone could boast! When they received his application in writing, with war now imminent, they appointed him, after some hesitation, to command the small frigate *Vengeance* (28) destined for service under Saumarez in the Channel. He clearly owed this appointment to Sir James's recommendation and it brought him the post rank which put him, at last, on the road which might lead to high command. He would now be a full captain, no longer Master and Commander, the equal of an army Colonel. That main point gained, the fact had still to be faced that the *Vengeance* was not the crack frigate about which he might have dreamt. She belonged rather to a semi-obsolete class, the 28-gun Sixth-Rate ships, mostly built during the previous war, the latest in 1787 and the earliest—heaven help us!—in 1737. The typical ship in this class was the *Enterprize* built at Deptford in 1774, the ship from which many of the others were copied. The *Vengeance* was one of these and came immediately above the *Vindictive* in the Admiralty list—the *Vindictive* being (oddly enough) the Admiral's house at Sheerness. Like the *Enterprize,* then, but built at Deptford in 1779, *Vengeance* measured 394 tons and 120 feet 6 inches on the gun deck, mounted twenty-four 9-pounders and four 6-pounders, and was established for a crew of 195. She was a good ship, over twenty years old, but was not to be compared with the newer frigates in the superior classes mounting 32, 36 or even 38 guns. Delancey had never seen her but he knew other ships of her class and had no illusions about his new command. He had been given what was left over after the more important posts had been filled. And what else could he expect, the most junior post-captain on the list? To Fiona he said, "*Vengeance* is mine, saith the Lord. I must leave at once for Chatham." Quickly changing his mind, he added, "No, I must go to London first and try to secure Mather as my First Lieutenant." Changing his mind again, he went on, "I mean to say that *we* should go to London together—it will give us the chance to revisit Drury Lane."

"Very well, Captain sir,—no, I mean 'Aye, Aye!'—but I am coming to Chatham as well. I shall see to it that your cabin is properly furnished. Now you are a great man, you must have carpet on the deck, a proper table, decent curtains, and a tablecloth to look the part. You must be prepared, sir, to welcome me aboard!"

Leaving Mrs Mahy to look after Anneville Manor, the Delanceys presently set off for Southampton, for London, and so to Delancey's old lodging in Albemarle Street. At the Admiralty it was obvious enough that war was now expected. Ships were being commissioned and manned, appointments were being made, and plans drawn up. Defence against invasion had been given an early priority, hence the bringing forward of ships destined to serve in the Channel. In one thing Delancey was disappointed. Mather and certain other followers of his were not immediately available, having been sent to recruit seamen at Whitehaven. It was agreed that Mather should join him later and he was consoled in the meanwhile by the appointment, on a temporary basis, of a one-legged officer called Atkinson, a useful man in the fitting-out process. The frigate *Vengeance,* when he first saw her, was still in dry dock under repair. She would be seaworthy, he was assured, but had never been famous for her speed. Faced by a French 36-gun frigate, she could neither win nor escape but she was in other respects a useful man-of-war. While Delancey talked with the dockyard officials, Fiona measured the captain's cabin for carpets and curtains, demanding extra cupboard space with storm-proof racks for china and glassware. Back in London after their first visit to *Vengeance* they paid a call on Colonel Barrington, who looked at Fiona with more than ordinary interest.

"So this is the young lady for whom you sacrificed the Admiralty's favour! But for you, Mrs Delancey, the Captain here could have selected his frigate and chosen his station. Lord St Vincent would have been civil to him. Troubridge would have looked on him with favour. Markham would have sent him to a cruising ground where Spanish treasure ships are seen every day. He would have had a country estate and a town house, a seat in Parliament, and a host of influential friends. All this he sacrificed, ma'am, in order to marry the prettiest girl he had ever seen; a lass he glimpsed on the stage at Drury Lane and with whom he instantly fell in love. Yes, ma'am, it was a heavy price to pay. . . . But now I have seen you, I conclude that he was right and that I should have done the same had I ever had the chance! Ma'am, I freely admit that you are worth more than all the favours that could be offered by King or Parliament, by the Prime Minister or Lord St Vincent, by the Markham family or the Clapham sect. More than that, I give it as my opinion that a single kiss from you would be worth more than the Order of the Bath!"

Fiona could take a hint and the Colonel had his kiss. He then proposed that the Delanceys should stay with him in St James's Square, leaving their cramped lodging in Albemarle Street.

"Had you been writing your memoirs, Delancey, or had you been a poet like, say, Wordsworth, there would have been some point in living near your publisher, but you, as a post captain, deserve a better address. Besides, you will be more comfortable here and this house is too big for a widower like me. You can use my carriage, too, for I seldom go out these days and the horses need exercise. Come, sir, I'll take no denial! Come, ma'am, give pleasure to an old man by giving him a glimpse of youth and beauty. Let's agree that you move here tomorrow!"

Move they did and they were often to be the Colonel's guests in the years to come. It was a good arrangement from every point of view and it gave the Delanceys some limited access to London society. They could not pretend to be folk of any consequence—wartime Captains in the Navy were thick on the ground—but they no longer arrived anywhere in a hackney carriage.

Once thus established in London, Delancey decided to visit Mr Williams at Woolwich and see what progress he had made with his steamship. He knew only vaguely where she was being built but an inquiry on the spot produced a prompt direction "Oh, that lunatic craft! The *Invention* she is to be called, seemingly. She is on the slipway at Mr Earnshaw's place —down the road and the third yard on the right." There she was, sure enough, and no one objected to his looking around, even with Mr Williams absent. He could not help being rather impressed. The vessel was far bigger than the *Charlotte Dundas* and could measure perhaps a hundred or a hundred and twenty tons. Instead of a stern-wheel she was to have a paddle-wheel on either beam. The wheels were not yet installed but there was a housing for each which showed where they were to go. The engine had not arrived but it was plainly to occupy the

midship section, with all the space aft given to coal. The masts
had not been stepped but she looked rather like a bomb ketch
with space forward for a heavy cannon on either bow and, a
little further aft, a possible emplacement for a heavy-calibre
mortar. All living accommodation was forward and the steering wheel was to be just forward of the funnel. Disliking the
whole concept, Delancey was impressed in spite of himself.
Given a French flotilla in a dead calm, a vessel like this could
play havoc from a chosen range, steaming in circles round her
wretched opponents. Twenty of them could bring Bonaparte's
plans to nothing. Williams was no fool and he was right to
reject the stern-wheel, whatever the resulting strain on the
engine. The *Invention* was a formidable weapon of war, and
might be used in a dozen different ways. On a windless day
she could tow a man-of-war into action and tow her out again.
She could rescue a ship crippled in battle or assist in a fireship
attack. Thinking of all these possibilities, he found himself
becoming almost enthusiastic over the project. Then he went
back to his earlier thoughts on the subject. What might be useful to Britain would be doubly useful to France. Nor did the
Invention represent the limit of man's ingenuity. If she were three
times the size of the *Charlotte Dundas,* another steam-vessel
could be twice the size again with engines proportionately more
powerful and guns more numerous.

He was still thinking on these lines when Mr Williams
appeared in person, recognised him at once, and plunged into
technicalities about the engines and steering gear. He also
confirmed what Delancey had suspected, that the *Invention* was
to be ketch rigged and was to mount a large mortar and
two 32-pounder guns. The crew would number thirty and the

engineers would number four. "Here," he concluded in triumph, "is the man-of-war of the future." Delancey had to agree, mentally consigning that future to some period after his own retirement.

"I commend your patriotism, Mr Williams," he said aloud. "You are spending a small fortune on a ship of no commercial value, with no chance of any return unless the Navy Board should purchase her."

"Well, sir, I am a patriot and would do all in my power to bring about Bonaparte's downfall but I do not depend entirely upon that spirit of enterprise for which the Navy Board has never been famous. I shall apply, sir, for Letters of Marque. This vessel will sail as a privateer."

Delancey took his leave, after further compliments, and made his way back to London. At dinner that day he told Fiona and Colonel Barrington about his trip to Woolwich. He expressed reluctant admiration for the *Invention,* adding his devout hopes that she would prove a failure. The Colonel was more tolerant and could see such a vessel playing havoc among the French invasion craft. "But then," he added, "a privateer would go after a different kind of game."

"Frankly, sir," said Delancey, "I can't take the *Invention* seriously as a privateer. Letters of Marque will give Mr Williams a good excuse for putting to sea without convoy but this vessel would be useless as a private man-of-war. She has heavy guns and a small crew. If she intercepted a French merchantman, her prey would be smashed and crippled and Williams would lack the men to bring her into port. A privateer is something entirely different, needing small-calibre guns and a swarm of men."

Delancey was henceforth to divide his time between London

and Chatham, now watching the repair of the *Vengeance* and now attending the theatre with Fiona. All the talk was of war and the Delanceys were actually present when the King himself announced the outbreak from his box at Drury Lane. It was the Command Performance and all present rose to applaud Addington's decision to make war on France. Poor Fiona wept as the carriage rolled back to St James's Square. "You'll go to sea, darling, and I shall be left in Guernsey to wonder whether you'll be wounded or drowned."

"Not in the first instance," Delancey replied. "When the *Vengeance* sails for Guernsey—and that, I hear, is to be her immediate destination—you shall come with me. If we are to sink on the way we shall thus go down together!"

"Stop teasing me! I'll sail with you but will be sick all the way, I expect."

"You'll have more room for it than you had in the *Starling,* and anyway, I can tell you a sure remedy. All you need do is to go and sit under a tree. Nor will you run any risk again of being wrecked on the shell beach. It will take young Le Page many years to live that down! As for the *Vengeance,* you must admit that she looks better since she came out of dry dock. Confess now, you were shocked when you saw her in the hands of the shipwright, presenting a scene of chaos. But since she was painted and now she is rigged she begins to look the part. Buff and white and a touch of gold, with a frowning figurehead and red gunports, you must admit that we are entitled to feel proud of her. There are better frigates, I'll allow, but this is the one I've been given and I must do the best with what I have. Cheer up, dearest, you married a man whose trade is war. You made the right decision—it would be absurd, as you must admit, for you to have married anyone else—but there are certain drawbacks, as I have to admit. If I stay ashore, I am penniless and everyone thinks me a coward. If I go to sea I am separated from the most wonderful girl in the world. There is my dilemma but I don't really have a choice. I must go to war as soon as *Vengeance* is manned and ready for sea."

Chapter Eight

THE "INVENTION"

WHEN THE frigate *Vengeance* finally left Chatham, mooring at the Nore, Delancey was faced with the problem of manning her. All he had at this stage were his officers, some of them temporary, his warrant-officers, his midshipmen, his boys or second-class volunteers, and his detachment of marines. There were over a hundred more men to recruit and all the other men-of-war were equally seeking what they might devour. With the actual outbreak of war, however, press warrants were issued and the press gangs became active. The best seamen were removed from the merchantmen entering the river, some without information that the war had begun. The worst were those sent down the river by the London magistrates, having been given the choice between prison or the Navy. Although the manning problem was difficult enough it would certainly become worse as the war went on. Delancey's two lieutenants (apart from old Harrison) were constantly out with the boats or ashore in Sheerness but the process of manning went slowly and the men press-ganged were, many of them, without sea experience. After weeks of effort Delancey at last had a crew of sorts and was able to sail. It was at this point that Fiona came down from London by coach and joined her husband's ship for what would be her first voyage in a man-of-war.

It was a fine morning when *Vengeance* finally sailed and Fiona was found a corner of the quarterdeck where she would be out of everyone's way. Harrison had charge of the deck and it was he who gave the order "All hands make sail!" There was hectic activity as the seamen ran to take up their positions. "Away aloft!" sent many of them up the shrouds. After which came the order "Man the topsail sheets!" and "Let fall!" To Fiona the scene was one of furious confusion but she wondered at the rapidity with which the sails were set and sheeted home. But no speed in action could satisfy the boatswain or his mates, who called the men lazy lubbers; using different terms, however, when they thought that she was out of earshot. Harrison presently apologised to her for all the shouting. "We have too many landsmen aboard," he explained, "and what we do is under the eyes of the other ships. We don't want to earn a reputation for slackness."

The frigate was presently out in the Thames estuary, heeling gently before a sou'-westerly breeze. Soon afterwards came the order to exercise the great guns and Fiona watched while the cannon were loaded and the matches, crowbars, handspikes, and spunge staves were laid beside each gun. Then followed the order for silence and further orders in the sequence:

"Cast off tackles and breechings."

"Take out the tompion."

"Take off the apron."

"Unstop the touch-hole."

"Handle the priming wire."

"Prick the cartridge."

"Prime."

"Cover the vent."

"Aim."

Instead of firing the guns the seamen then repeated the whole exercise while Mr Harrison timed it with his stopwatch.

"Dreadful!" he moaned. "Shocking!" said the boatswain, and the exercise continued.

On that day Delancey dined alone with Fiona and she expressed her surprise at the examples she had seen of naval routine.

"What I can't understand, dearest, is the way each action, however trivial, has to be at the word of command. We have to do some of the same things on the stage and we even use some of the same words, as when we strike some property in the wings or lower the curtain. But everyone knows what has to be done. We don't have to shout all the time!"

"It may seem silly, love, but there are some facts you need to know. It is not true that everyone knows what has to be done. Many of the men you see were working ashore a week ago, one as a workman in a brewery, another as an errand boy. You then have to realise that these commands as affecting the cannon will not be used in battle, nor would they be heard if we shouted them. Our aim is to make people learn a certain sequence in what they do, learn it until the actions become automatic. They have to be done, remember, under the enemy's fire. As for actions being trivial, they are anything but that. Take, for example, the order, 'Take out the tompion'—"

"That bit I understood. The tompion is a sort of cork thrust into the cannon's muzzle. You take it out as you might uncork a bottle."

"Quite right. But what is it for?"

"To keep the gun clean?"

"Well, to keep it dry, mostly. Now, suppose you left it in and fired the gun, what would happen?"

"You would lose the tompion."

"You would more likely burst the gun and kill most of the

gun's crew. Then take the order 'Cover the vent.' What would happen if the vent were left uncovered?"

"The powder might get damp?"

"So the gun wouldn't fire. Or else it would fire by accident before men were ready. We have to depend upon a lot of men who are new to the sea, many of them fairly stupid. Then we have so to drill them that they will carry out the correct sequence even when the orders are inaudible, the gun deck full of smoke, and the noise deafening. Nor is it enough for the majority of them to do what they have been taught. They work as a team and rely upon each other, so that every single one of them must do his part correctly—one to remove the tompion and another to cover the vent. Their lives—and all our lives—depend on doing it correctly."

"And it's the same, I suppose, with the sails?"

"Just the same. You may think that we are all mad to repeat the drill, stop-watch in hand. But the day may come when we are heading for the rocks and our lives depend on the speed with which we can put the ship about!"

"Like that time when Le Page nearly put the *Starling* on the shell beach?"

"Exactly! I am forgetting that you have been at sea before— that you were a cabin boy when first I saw you and still a cabin boy years afterwards!"

"You would have thought that I should be more than my master's mate by now."

"But you are. You are a goddess, remember?"

"You think I might serve as a figurehead? I hate the one we have."

"So do I, love, but we can do nothing about it. All the seamen believe that altering or replacing a figurehead will bring bad luck. They may be right for all I know. I had to pay for the gold leaf myself and hoped that it would improve her. It has made her, if anything, worse. We see little of her, luckily, so long as we remain on board."

The voyage continued and Delancey had his officers and midshipmen to dine with him on the following day, noting the looks of dumb admiration they directed at Fiona. He realised at the same time that he could not have his wife on board except on such a short voyage as this. It was wonderful to have her near him, wonderful to think that she would be there when he finally turned in, but her presence was bad for him and worse, he thought, for everyone else. He could order no flogging, for example, while she was on board, and the men knew it. In the ordinary way he always hoped to avoid punishing men except by reproof or loss of privilege. That was his rule with a disciplined crew but it could not be his practice during the first month of the commission. The men must come to realise that orders are to be obeyed and that covert insolence— even to the youngest of the young gentlemen—will never be overlooked. He knew by now who the troublemakers were and all five of them, but for Fiona, would have been brought to the gangway by now. Nor was he certain that her presence was good for his own sense of duty. He hated to disturb her sleep but how could he avoid it? On two occasions he had stayed below when he would, as a single man, have been on deck in a flash. It had not mattered but the day might come when it could matter a great deal. He loved Fiona more than anyone in the world but the time was coming when they must part. It was almost her cue to go ashore.

Anchoring at St Peter Port on 9 August 1803, Delancey expected to pay his respects to Sir James Saumarez, under whose flag he was to serve, but was unable to do so. For one thing, Saumarez was not there. For another, the Guernsey division of his squadron had been placed under the command of Commodore Clinton, whose business it was to keep the French coast under close observation. He was a handsome and well-bred officer with a gallant record but only moderate intelligence. He had a temporary headquarters ashore and explained that his ships were deployed between Cherbourg and Granville.

"We shall probably raid the French coast this autumn so as to gain intelligence but we hardly expect them to attempt anything much this year. If the French try to invade England it will be in the summer of 1804. Until then our work will be routine but we have had one item of intelligence that remains something of a puzzle. We captured a French brig last month. The master was a stubborn sort of character but as she was out of Granville we tried to make him talk. In the end my interrogator got him drunk and he was eventually forthcoming on the subject of a mystery vessel called the *Nautilus*. She is nearing completion at Granville and would seem to be some sort of explosion vessel. She is being built under cover, though, and we don't think our man had actually seen her. Their security precautions have been elaborate and we don't think he was doing more than repeating the local rumours. To judge from his drunken mutterings the *Nautilus* is Bonaparte's trump card, the ace in the pack. But this fellow's French was difficult to follow even when he was sober—and by then he would tell us nothing more. We had a local man to help us, for it is a Norman French that people speak here, but we are very uncertain whether we understood him aright. It may all amount to nothing but I should like to tell the Admiral what the French idea is."

"It happens, sir, that I can tell you something about it. I was recently in Scotland watching an experimental steam-vessel on the Forth and Clyde Canal, the *Charlotte Dundas*. Another visitor on the same day was an American, Mr Fulton, who has also built a steam-vessel and who is the designer of the *Nautilus*."

"Is he, by God? I heard something about the *Charlotte Dundas* but that scheme really depended on the Duke of Bridgwater, who has since died. So the *Nautilus* is another steam-vessel?"

"No, sir. She is a craft designed to travel under the surface of the water."

"Your Mr Fulton must be a lunatic!"

"He appeared to be sane, sir, and I understand that the *Nautilus* has been on trials without disaster."

"Propelled by what, for heaven's sake? By a steam-engine?"

"No, sir, by a hand-propelled screw."

"And what is that?"

"Well sir. Imagine a small windmill, with sails about a foot long. It will revolve in the wind. Well, if you reverse the process in a dead calm, revolving the sails with a crank handle, you will produce an artificial breeze, a type of fan. Do the same thing under water and you can propel a vessel very much as with a pair of oars, with speed and range limited by the human strength that can be applied. I suppose the crew to number perhaps two or three. I should judge it to be quite feasible."

"But what purpose is served? Supposing I approach your frigate under water and unobserved, what do I do next?"

"I understand, sir, that you would attach an explosive below the waterline of the target ship, set the fuse for, say, half an hour, and beat a speedy retreat."

"But how, for God's sake? How could you even see what you were doing?"

"I have no idea, sir. These are problems which Mr Fulton claims to have solved."

"He must be out of his mind. Anyway, I am grateful for the information. I can't see the *Nautilus* as a threat to our naval supremacy."

"Nor can I, sir. I incline to take the steamship more seriously. It could be of material use in enabling the French flotilla to leave harbour under conditions of a flat calm."

"I see what you mean. But this invasion, if and when they attempt it, will never happen in this vicinity. The short sea passage is opposite Calais and Boulogne. It has to be in the narrows, allowing the craft a quick turnabout and so back for another load."

"So there are no invasion craft at Granville?"

"Not as far as we know. There are gunboats but they will probably go to Boulogne before the invasion attempt is made. I can't see, for that matter, what the *Nautilus* is doing at Granville. It is not a port of any importance. Perhaps the idea is to base this crazy vessel in a place we are unlikely to attack. It remains to see what Sir James thinks about it. He may decide to raid Granville and see what the French are doing there. It may be better to do that than do nothing."

When Sir James Saumarez appeared his flag was flown in the frigate *Cerberus* (32) and he had left the remainder of his squadron at St Helier, Jersey. The purpose of his visit, as Delancey learnt from Clinton, was to hold a conference with Sir John Doyle, the Lieutenant-Governor. Rather to his surprise, Delancey was one of those summoned to Government House, along with Clinton, Captain Selby (flag captain), and Doyle's chief of staff. The Lieutenant-Governor lived in a house on the landward side of the town but so placed as to overlook the harbour, affording a view beyond towards the islands of Herm and Sark. On this day it was also possible to glimpse the coast of France in the far distance. All this sunlit scene could be viewed from the bay windows of the room into which the visitors were shown. Sir John's writing desk was so placed as to afford him a view of this potential battlefield. He could see each ship in the anchorage and see whatever craft might be approaching.

When all were seated round the table Sir James explained that the French were developing a secret weapon at Granville. Captain Delancey had reported that it was a vessel capable of travelling below the surface and delivering an explosive device at some point below the waterline. It was the invention of an American, a Mr Fulton, who appeared to be working for the French Ministry of Marine. The question they had to consider was whether a raid on Granville would be justified, and what form such a raid should take.

"Why didn't Fulton offer his invention to us?" asked Selby.

"He did," replied Delancey. "The Navy Board rejected it."

"Which suggests," said Sir John Doyle, "that Fulton's invention is of no great value."

"That is a possible conclusion," said the Admiral, "but Fulton may have improved upon his original design. The French, at least, appear to be interested. The ideal plan would be to inspect the vessel and then destroy her, and this would mean a conjunct expedition. Could you, Sir John, provide us with the troops—say, in battalion strength?"

"No, Admiral, I could not. My orders are to hold Guernsey, for which the present garrison is only barely sufficient. Now if I lose men in a raid on Granville, I may be thought to have endangered the place I have been ordered to defend."

"I feared you would say that! In that case we can do no more than bombard the place. Two bomb vessels have been ordered to join me and we may be able to achieve something on our own."

Soon afterwards the other officers were told to withdraw, leaving Sir John and Sir James together. "I know what's happening," said Selby. "The Admiral is trying to make the Governor change his mind. I'd bet ten guineas that he won't succeed. What do you think of the bombardment plan, Delancey?"

"The target is insufficiently defined. For all we know, the *Nautilus* may be a mile inland. We have no recent intelligence about Granville, or none that I have seen. It would seem from the chart that we shall be firing at extreme range and aiming at nothing in particular."

"What would you do then?" asked Clinton.

"I should spend a few evenings at various quayside taverns and talk to any smuggler who has recently been in Granville."

"Good God!" exclaimed Selby. "Do you mean to tell me that there are men in St Peter Port who trade with the enemy?"

"I should be surprised if there aren't. How else are smugglers to live? They have to trade with somebody. But Sir James knows this as well as I do. My fear is that he is under orders from someone who knows a great deal less."

Delancey was now able to establish Fiona ashore at Anneville Manor with a domestic staff presided over by an old manservant called Le Breton. She would be visited by many kind neighbours, Captain Savage being particularly attentive, and she was rapidly making Anneville a very comfortable home.

The heartbreaking moment came when the *Vengeance* had to sail, Fiona going down to the harbour to say goodbye.

"We are sailing no further than Jersey," he comforted her. "We shan't be far away and will be back, I daresay, in a matter of days."

Fiona was not deceived. "I know where you are going. All St Peter Port knows. But you won't be very near the target—Captain Savage says that the depth of water is insufficient."

"The Admiral might just as well have called you into conference!"

"I should have told him, if he had, that the whole thing is foolishness—everyone says so."

"Could you have told him where the *Nautilus* is?"

"No, but she's not at Granville. That information was false—that old seaman was not as drunk as he pretended to be."

"Why do we bother about secret agents when our wives can tell us all we need to know? Goodbye, love, and take great care of yourself. You'll never know how much I love you because I've never been able to explain, and don't suppose that I shall ever find the words."

"It's not a matter of words. I understand you well enough. Goodbye, my love, and run no foolish risks."

He was presently in his gig and on his way out to *Vengeance*. He gave orders at once to up anchor and make sail. Fiona was still waving as he looked back. He waved in turn and then concentrated again on his work.

A few days later Sir James Saumarez collected his whole squadron off St Helier: the frigates *Cerberus* and *Vengeance*, the sloops *Charwell* and *Kite*, the bomb vessels *Sulphur* and *Terror*, the schooner *Ealing* and the cutter *Carteret*. To the assembled captains his orders were brief. "We have been instructed to bombard the town and port of Granville. It is said that this is the scene for the development of a new and secret type of vessel called the *Nautilus*. Should this be so, we still lack any information as to where she is. Our only known targets are the gunboats in the harbour, perhaps twenty of them. Our chief danger arises from the tidal range, which is dramatic on that part of the French coast. If we put any vessel on a sandbank we had best do it on a rising tide. The operation will begin on 13 September, the frigates and sloops to lead the attack, the two bomb vessels to be covered by them, the *Ealing* and *Carteret* to remain under sail and go to the aid of anyone in trouble." That was that and the captains remained for dinner on board the flagship. This gave Delancey the opportunity to have a private word with the Admiral.

"It is my belief, sir, that the *Nautilus* is not at Granville. I think we have been deceived about that."

"What has led you, Delancey, to that conclusion?"

"The master of that brig knew about the *Nautilus* but he did not himself come from Granville. That brig sailed from Le Havre, and that, I suspect, sir, is where the *Nautilus* might be found."

"But that is no more than a wild surmise."

"Perhaps I flatter myself, sir, in preferring to think it an intelligent guess. The *Nautilus* was built in Paris, so much I know from Mr Fulton. If she were to undergo sea trials, the obvious place would be Le Havre. She could be taken down the river without difficulty and would have her mooring well up the estuary and beyond our reach."

"Why did you say nothing about this when we met together in Guernsey?"

"I did not know then that the brig came from Le Havre."

"If we accept your theory, one wonders why that Frenchman told his lie about Granville."

"I expect he had a grudge against the harbour master. Perhaps his mother-in-law lives there near the quayside. Someone at Granville cheated him once over a barrel of fish."

"Well, whatever the truth may be, we are committed to this attack. I can't cancel it now."

"That I fully understand, sir."

"And don't think that this bombardment or any other is a waste of effort. All round the coast of France, all round the coasts occupied by the French, there are garrisons, batteries, patrols, and sentries, a whole army of men with thousands of guns which Bonaparte could otherwise employ elsewhere. If we never did anything these garrisons would be weakened and his armies in the field would be correspondingly strengthened. I don't suppose we shall achieve anything at Granville. A few gunboats will be damaged, a few guns dismounted, a dozen men killed or wounded. But some general will report that his coastal defences are too weak. He doesn't know what place will be attacked next. How *can* he know? *We* don't know. We haven't decided. So more effort is made and more men wasted. Our allies sometimes complain that our military effort is too feeble. Whether that is true or not, our men-of-war are engaging the equivalent of an entire French army. I repeat, Delancey, that this attack will not be a waste of time."

Delancey's letter to Fiona left for Guernsey in the packet *Swallow*, the master of which had the shock of his life while his men were making sail. An odd-looking vessel was attempting to enter the anchorage—against both wind and tide; a feat which any schoolboy knew to be impossible. Apart from that she seemed to be on fire. Clouds of black smoke were billowing out from somewhere amidships and it seemed only a question of time before the vessel blew up and sank. It was then apparent, to him and others, that this extraordinary craft had sails but all of them furled. She was approaching for all that and had a bow wave to prove it.

"Cor, damme!" exclaimed the old seaman. "What in God's name is that supposed to be?"

The same question was being asked by everyone in sight and Delancey, among other captains, had an urgent message from Stirling, who was officer of the watch—would he come on deck immediately? He did this in a flash, telescope in hand, and focused at once on the on-coming vessel. It was the *Invention,* sure enough, the vessel he had last seen at Woolwich. He even had a glimpse of Mr Williams, dressed now as a privateer captain. There was probably no other man in the harbour or anchorage who had seen a steamship before and it would be evening before everybody knew that this astounding vessel was not, and had never been, on fire. The *Invention* dropped anchor and lowered a boat which headed for the *Cerberus.* Williams evidently meant to pay his respects to the Admiral and probably offer his services. That there was to be a raid next day on Granville was now a matter of common knowledge. It was obvious to him, if not to anyone else, that a steamship might, on this occasion, play an extremely useful role.

Later that day, after the *Invention's* funnel had ceased to smoke, the flagship signalled Delancey to come aboard. He found the Rear-Admiral at once puzzled and impressed.

"Ah, Delancey, I want to talk to you about this steam-vessel. I understand that you have seen her before and that Mr Williams is known to you. He has offered me his help in the bombardment of Granville—heaven knows how he came to know about it, the plan being secret, and I am a little disturbed to think that his two 32-pounders are heavier in fact than any other guns we have. However, I must accept the fact that he has made me a generous offer of assistance. He stands to gain nothing and I don't suppose that any underwriter would have insured his vessel. I have still to decide whether I want his help. As you know more about steam-vessels than I do—and you could not possibly know less—it seemed proper that I should seek your advice. Shall I accept his help?"

"I suggest, sir, that you should."

"But what puzzles me is how the fellow has any coal left after his passage from London River."

"He will have made his passage under sail, sir, using his engine merely to enter the harbour and make a suitable impression on you."

"And what good will that do him?"

"Why, sir, it is not unlikely that some of us may run aground off Granville. The *Invention* could tow us off. You would report this and the Navy Board might give Mr Williams a contract to build twenty more steam-vessels, likely to prove invaluable on similar occasions. I think, sir, that he is a businessman as well as a patriot. For that matter I rather doubt the effectiveness of his guns. He lacks the experience and he's hardly had time to train his men."

"But you would still make use of him?"

"I think we might be blamed if we did not."

"If I accept his help I shall keep him far astern, to begin with, and later to leeward. There is the risk of fire, the result of sparks from his funnel."

"I quite agree, sir. I certainly don't want to have this contrivance alongside my own ship."

"But what control shall I have over Mr Williams? He won't even understand my signals."

"You could perhaps lend him a midshipman as signal officer?"

"Yes, I might do that. I don't mind admitting, Delancey, that I shall be glad when we have finished with Granville and seen the last of the *Invention.*"

After quitting the flagship Delancey went over to the steam-vessel and made himself known again to Mr Williams.

"Welcome to the Channel Islands. I hope you had a good passage from Woolwich and have had the chance to exercise your guns and mortar?"

"Well, Captain Delancey, the passage was all I could have wished. The *Invention* is a good sea boat. We haven't fired our guns, though, and have only a limited quantity of ammunition. Most of our space below decks is filled with coal."

"In your place, Mr Williams, I should not open fire at all, least of all with the mortar. It is not an easy weapon to handle and you can all too easily blow yourself up. Keep out of harm's way and be ready to rescue any ship in difficulties— that would be my advice. But I am not the Admiral and it will be for him to tell you what to do. Have you studied the chart which we shall be using between here and Granville?"

"I have, sir, and I can't say that it fills me with much confidence. There seem to be rocks and sandbanks all over that part of the French coast and the tides run fast between them. I shall follow the Admiral and hope for the best. He is a local man, I hear."

"We shall be sailing at night, however."

"At *night!* That is news to me, I'll confess."

"But you have a sailing master, no doubt?"

"I have Mr Bateman but he was no more than a boatswain in his last ship."

"Well, I admire your spirit, Mr Williams. In your place, nevertheless, I should take a local pilot. Should you part company from the squadron between here and Granville, you might otherwise be in danger. I used to command a privateer in these waters and may still have old shipmates in St Helier. Shall I ask around and find you a good man who has spent his whole life in these parts?"

"That is very kind of you, sir, very kind indeed. But shall we have time?"

"We have time enough. The *Sulphur,* bomb ketch, is a notoriously slow craft and we are still waiting for her to join the squadron."

Authorised by Williams, Delancey went ashore and visited several taverns which he had known in years past, finding some old friends finally in the Royal Oak. He ended in earnest conversation with a dubious-looking character called Etienne Le Feuvre, who finally returned with him to the *Invention.*

Delancey now explained to Williams that Le Feuvre would be his pilot—for a suitable fee, payable in advance—and that his own ship, *Vengeance,* would keep in close touch. In this way the navigational dangers would be minimised. Even with these precautions, Williams would need to study the chart and keep a sharp lookout. Having thanked Delancey and seen him return to his own ship, Williams looked at the chart again with renewed misgivings. Between Jersey and Granville lay the Grelets Banks, the Minquiers, and Les Sauvages while the actual approach to Granville was flanked by the Chausey Islands to starboard and the Cathcue Bank to port, followed by a nightmare range of obstacles clustered around the actual target. He knew already about the tidal range. Seven fathoms rise and fall! Forty-two feet! The French coast hereabouts was a region of hideous complexity and Mr Williams deeply regretted having come near the place. He had pictured a scene in which the *Invention* would have been the focus of interest, all these sailing-ship seamen watching him with amazement. Mr Williams was an engineer, a friend of Mr Bramah, an expert in his own field. The *Invention* was his masterpiece, affording a glimpse of the future. He was himself no seaman or navigator and he had left the Thames estuary before he realised that Mr Bateman's knowledge did not extend to nautical astronomy. Bateman professed to know the English headlands by sight but was totally unfamiliar with the French coast, which English shipping always avoided in time of war. On a fine autumn day the *Invention,* following the men-of-war, might have made a name for herself despite these difficulties and hazards. But this Admiral, who was plainly out of his mind, proposed to make his attack by night! Whatever the *Invention* achieved would be unseen, unrecorded, unknown to history or legend. If he were to emerge unscathed—and this was now almost the height of his ambition—Williams would owe his safety to the pilotage of the shifty-looking Etienne Le Feuvre, for whom he felt an instinctive distrust. But when he attempted to discuss the problem with Le Feuvre he discovered that his pilot knew no English and could not even understand Mr Williams's few words of French. What Le Feuvre spoke was an obscure local dialect of which no one else on board knew a word. All Williams could do must be to give Le Feuvre the helm and hope that he knew what he was doing. While still at St Helier, with interpreter at hand, the Jersey pilot insisted on the *Invention* having another boat, making room for everyone on board; a pessimistic but not unreasonable stipulation in view of the vessel herself being such a novelty. This boat, her third, was towed astern. Had Mr Williams been a man of wealth he might at this time have withdrawn from the current operation—and few would have blamed him—but the hull, engine, rigging, equipment, and provisioning of the *Invention* had cost him his entire fortune. If he failed to prove the usefulness of the steam-vessel on this occasion he might have no second chance next year or ever. He had gambled for high stakes and doubted now whether he could win. He stood in fact to lose both his fortune and his life.

Sir James Saumarez sailed from Jersey on the morning of 13 September, the *Invention* astern of the men-of-war. Lagging in the column were the two bomb vessels, whose presence was essential to the bombardment's success, and the *Invention*—under sail only—was slower even than they were. Night fell and Williams lost sight of the squadron, his last glimpse giving him the impression that Le Feuvre was steering a more westerly course. Had they possessed any language in common, Williams would have pestered his pilot with queries as to their position. Thwarted in that way, he could only bite his nails with anxiety and peer into the darkness of a moonless and cloudy night. He half expected to hear gunfire and see flashes from the gun muzzles but all was silent as the hours passed and as a light westerly breeze brought them nearer the place they were to attack. Going below to his cabin, Williams studied the chart afresh and looked with horror again at the tangle of obstacles into which they were heading. He knew that they were on a rising tide and that this was the main reason for the attack's timing, and there was some small consolation in believing that they might re-float the vessel if she ran aground. In that sense the sandbanks opposite Granville might be thought relatively harmless but all the other hazards from the Minquiers to the Little Etat were rocks, whether exposed or tidal or normally hidden. Le Feuvre had the leadsman in the chains and had his eye on the compass but must otherwise depend on some sort of instinct. If that were so, his instinct failed him for the *Invention* crashed into a rocky obstacle at about 1:40 A.M. on the 14th. The sails were immediately struck and a hasty inspection was enough to show that the vessel was lost. She was held forwards by the rocks themselves but had been badly holed below the waterline. The water was pouring aft from there, ensuring that the vessel would sink by the stern. Had she been in ballast an effort could have been made to pump the water out and the rising tide would have lifted her clear, but the water was going into the coal bunker and the pump had been choked by coal dust. The only possible course was to abandon ship, thanking heaven (or Le Feuvre) for the extra boat which was already in the water. The other two were quickly launched and about ten minutes were available in which people could save their gear, together with the ship's papers and navigational instruments. The *Invention* went down as the boats stood by. There was some discussion at this point as to the direction in which the boats should go but the problem was solved for them dramatically. Far to the east and south there was the light of a starshell, followed by the rumble of gunfire. The bombardment of Granville had begun and an estimate of distance and bearing made it fairly clear that the *Invention* had been lost on Les Sauvages, about twelve miles west of the squadron's route. Mr Williams ordered his men to row in the direction of Granville and his boats were picked up before daybreak by the cutter *Carteret* which had been sent back to look for them. On board the *Cerberus* the rescued men had the privilege of watching the bombardment of Granville which finally ended towards the evening of the 15th.

Chapter Nine

THE RAID

FIONA did not land at Dover. It seemed to Delancey, on second thoughts, that a better plan would be to put her ashore at Deal. He recalled that this was a common resort for naval officers' wives and that she might care to remain there until such time as *Vengeance* might sail again. When he paid his respects to Rear-Admiral Edward Knight, he found that Mrs Knight was on board the flagship for the day. When Delancey was presented to her and mentioned that Fiona was with him, Mrs Knight was instantly helpful.

"You must bring her ashore at once and she shall stay with us until a proper lodging can be found. She should on no account stay in Lower Deal where the common folk live, nor even in Middle Deal where some married lieutenants put their wives. Good lodgings are hard to find these days but vacancies occur when ships are posted to a foreign station. Did I hear something about the *Europa* quitting this station, Admiral? That would mean a vacancy when Mrs Barnett leaves, as I suppose she will, and in the better part of Upper Deal."

Delancey accepted this kind invitation on Fiona's behalf and promised to bring her to the flagship that afternoon. Only after these matters of moment had been settled could the Rear-Admiral begin to explain the functions of his squadron. He did so as he and Delancey paced the quarterdeck in the autumn sunshine.

"We lately looked upon ourselves as very much in the front line of defence, and indeed we are still, save that the season for a possible invasion is past. We may take it that the French will stay ashore now until the spring of 1804. That does not mean that they are inactive or have given up the attempt. We know from intelligence reports that they are still building flat-bottomed boats and similar craft. We also know that they have considerable forces in camp around Boulogne. We assume, therefore, that the invasion is planned for next summer. All we can do in the meanwhile is to patrol the French coast and prevent them gaining much sea experience. We shall harass them until the end of October and then keep them under observation. The inshore work is done by sloops and gun-brigs, of which I have eight, backed up by two smaller frigates—yours being one—and these again supported by my flagship *Antelope*, a 50-gun ship, as you see. If and when the invasion is attempted my squadron is ready to be sacrificed while larger forces are assembled to meet the threat, some from the Nore and some from Portsmouth. You will find, when you go ashore, that our military preparations are on a vast scale, with regular and militia regiments everywhere. Our generals are very confident but few of their units have been in battle. The government's policy is to meet the French on their own coast, not on ours."

Rear-Admiral Knight, a small man with protuberant eyes and impatient gestures, impressed Delancey as an officer of great resolution and energy, eager to do his best with rather meagre forces devoted to a rather unpromising task. He supposed that Knight had been unlucky in the past, never present in any general engagement and never perhaps in action at all. This was the fate of many a good officer, through no fault of his own, but Knight's over-eagerness was a little too apparent.

When the briefing was over, Delancey went to fetch Fiona and sent his boat to take her and Mrs Knight ashore.

"We live here," explained Mrs Knight, "in an atmosphere of perpetual excitement, with drums and bugles and shouted words of command. Lower Deal is especially noisy and we shall have to pass through it on our way to Middle and Upper Deal, which are quieter and more respectable. I have a carriage of sorts to take us up the hill, which is otherwise a tedious walk indeed."

The quayside, where they came ashore, was a scene of great activity and Mrs Knight pointed out the handbills on every wall, one of which particularly amused her:

THEATRE ROYAL ENGLAND
In Rehearsal
and meant to be speedily attempted
a *Farce* in one Act
called
THE INVASION OF ENGLAND
Principal Buffo
MR BUONAPARTE
being his FIRST
(and most likely his last)
appearance on the stage

"There are a score of these handbills and a great many patriotic songs roared out every evening, some with words which no lady should hear. The officers' great rendezvous is the Hoop and Griffin Inn, near the landing place in Beach Street. Very senior officers stay at the Three Kings and there are numerous taverns for the seamen and soldiers. We have our Assembly

Rooms and even a small theatre in High Street. The troops are here in great strength, both regular and militia. The militiamen are all very warlike and few of them realise that the Navy is our true means of defence. The Admiral is sometimes quite vexed to hear how the soldiers talk, just as if their bayonets were all we had to depend upon. What a nice man your husband is, Mrs Delancey, and very much the gentleman if I may say so. That once went almost without saying in the Navy but there have been great changes in time of war. Some officers are a very good sort of people but not at their best in a drawing room. I should suppose that Captain Delancey has been much at Court and that you yourself have moved in the highest circles. Here in Deal we have to amuse ourselves as well as we can, our highest ambition being to have an occasional invitation to Walmer Castle. Mr Pitt is much in residence there, you know, and is very active with the Volunteers. It was his notion, I believe, to have the cavalry barracks built between here and Walmer."

With creaking springs and behind a weary horse, the old carriage made its way up the hill. Passing it on the way down came a column of infantry, singing a version of the popular song "Britons strike home" followed a little afterwards by the tune of "Brighton Camp" or "The girl I left behind me."

"Fine fellows, I'll allow," said Mrs Knight, "but where would they be without the *Antelope* and the *Vengeance?*" Fiona had to agree that Britain's wooden walls were the country's only sure defence.

It was early evening when Mrs Knight showed Fiona to her room which was small but which offered a splendid view over the sea, a prospect which showed literally hundreds of ships at anchor, lit by the setting sun. The house was on the crest of the hills which overlook Lower Deal and afforded a view over Sandwich Flats towards the North Foreland.

"It is difficult to realise," said Mrs Knight, "that all these ships, both merchantmen and men-of-war, are in a sort of harbour. They are protected on the seaward side by the Goodwin Sands, some part of which are even above water at low tide, but which form a breakwater, whether visible or not. The main entrance at the Downs is from the north by Gull Stream opposite Ramsgate. The tradespeople of Lower Deal do a great business in supplying ships with provisions and will be much the poorer, I think, when the war ends. I do hope that you will be comfortable here."

"I could ask nothing better, Mrs Knight, but could wish that the house would cease its motion as the waves pass under it!"

"I know that feeling so well! It will have ceased, I promise you, by morning."

Delancey dined on board the flagship on the following day, his fellow guests being Captain Harding of the frigate *Lizard* (28), Captain Miller of the sloop *Plover,* and Captain Wallingford of the sloop *Cynthia.* For Delancey's benefit, the Admiral explained that active service for the year was not entirely finished.

"The French build many of their gunboats and similar craft at places like Dieppe, Calais, or Le Havre but it is their plan, it would seem, to collect them at Boulogne, perhaps because they are more easily protected there. When they attempt any such movement we try to intercept them. The French have lost several craft in this way, usually driven on shore and wrecked. It may serve to lower their morale or even convince them that the invasion of England is not really possible."

"Do we know, Admiral," asked Delancey, "what types of craft the French are building?"

"We have identified gunboats and gun-brigs, some of considerable size, able to embark a hundred soldiers, we are told, or fifty horses. There are smaller craft, each mounting a single gun and there are, finally, large flat-bottomed rowing boats. We assume that those last-mentioned craft will embark the bulk of their infantry. They can be built, of course, in the smaller ports or fishing villages. Nor need their construction take more than a week or two. There must be a thousand of them at Boulogne by now."

"But we have captured none?"

"None so far."

"A pity. What I mean, Admiral, is this. If and when the invasion is attempted, it would be useful to infiltrate one of our own craft, unrecognised, among theirs."

"But is Boney really going to attempt this invasion?" asked Harding. "He must see by now that it is suicidal."

"In the words of the ballad," said Miller:

'When and O when does this little Boney come?
Perhaps he'll come in August! Perhaps he'll stay at home.'

My guess is that he will cancel the invasion plan as something too hazardous to attempt. Yes, as something quite impossible."

"Well, gentlemen," replied Delancey. "I beg to differ from you. He will not think it impossible because he has already done it. He invaded Egypt with an army of thirty-six thousand men embarked in four hundred transports, and Nelson failed to intercept him—he could have ended the war had he been successful. There is a difference, I grant you, between thirty-six thousand men and, say, one hundred thirty thousand but pray consider the comparative distances involved. How far is it from Toulon to Alexandria? Over fifteen hundred miles, I should guess. From Calais to Dover is about twenty and other crossings about thirty. When Bonaparte's admirals say 'Impossible!' he can reply 'Fiddlesticks! I did it over a much greater distance and avoided one of Britain's best admirals on the way!'"

"But consider the difficulty of embarking such a vast army!" said Harding.

"I know more about the difficulties than he does but he could easily shout me down in argument. I think he may make the attempt next summer and I hope, for my part, that he does. I should like to meet him in mid-Channel!"

"Amen to that!" said the Admiral. "Better that he should tangle with us than with the Sussex Militia. But where does your captured gunboat come into the plot?"

"To come near Boney himself without him seeing the danger."

"It's a good idea, Delancey, I grant you that, and I'll give it some thought. But these craft of theirs are seldom beyond the cover of their own batteries. When would you make the attempt? Next year?"

"No, sir, in October; after they are snugged down for the winter."

"I see what you mean. Yes, that would be the time. Put your proposals in writing and I'll study them."

The conversation became more general and there were frequent references to dinners attended ashore. The troops were numerous, both regular and militia, the volunteers were all in arms and local patriotism found vent in numerous banquets at which loyal toasts were drunk and belligerent choruses were thundered. Delancey gained an impression that Knight's squadron was too often at anchor and his captains too often ashore with their wives. He found next day that Fiona had come to the same conclusion.

"There is a regular society here of naval officers' wives, who play whist and drink tea together. They are nice people and Mrs Knight has been kindness itself. But it is not the sort of life I care to lead. I think I shall do better to make a home and garden for you at Anneville. I would rather do something useful, and while it is delightful to see you from time to time, I have a guilty feeling that I am distracting your attention from the war. If you will agree, dearest, I shall go back to Guernsey now."

"After spending one more night with me aboard the *Vengeance*."

"That goes without saying! But I hope that you will see what I mean—that you will not think that I am deserting you?"

"I know exactly what you mean but could never have made the same proposal myself. You are perfectly right about the squadron. We spend our time between the North and South Foreland, with an occasional glance at Dieppe. But it is all wrong. We should be constantly at sea between Calais and Le Havre, we should know the French coast better than they do themselves. We should patrol up to the high tide mark. Should the French attempt an invasion next year we should be the men who know every inch of the battlefield. You are right, dearest. The moment has come to part."

On board the frigate and sharing a double cot, Richard and Fiona were very close together.

"You are not the wild girl I married."

"I know and I have been wondering why. I now have a part to play as a post-captain's wife, junior to Mrs Knight, senior to Mrs Wallingford. There is a naval society here into which I have to fit. But, apart from that, we are at war and I have been and am still a part of it. I have heard gunfire in the distance, I have seen wounded men, and I have tried to say kind and useless words to women whose husbands have been buried at sea. I met Mrs Travers—but you met her too—it was only three weeks after her wedding, poor woman. Lives are being lost each month, each week. I have grown older since I came to Deal."

"You look no older, my love."

"I could wish that were true. I hate to leave you but I do no good here. Some day we shall be together with no frigate to come between us. Now there are too many nightmares."

"Dream, love, of better times to come when the French have been beaten and Napoleon locked up in the Tower of London."

"Sharing the lions' cage . . . I am glad to see that Teesdale looks after you. The new curtains do something for your day cabin, don't they?"

"Not as much as you do for my night cabin. No, they are stately and luxurious. I believe the Rear-Admiral is envious!"

"He does envy you, in fact, but for a different reason. You have seen more active service than he has. In everything but rank you are his superior and he knows it. All things considered, he has been nice to you—more so than some flag officers I could name—and Mrs Knight could not have been kinder to me."

"I do better than that. I adore you."

"Do you, love? Tell me about it!" He told her and resumed the tale at daybreak when it was almost time for her to go ashore.

As the gig disappeared shorewards Richard stared sadly after it wondering how he could combine such happiness and such grief. She was a grown woman now and with the airs, on occasion, of a great lady. But then he remembered her actual age.

If she was a child when he met her first—when little more than a child himself—she was no longer a girl when he saw her at Drury Lane. The fact was that she was playing a young girl's part and played it even when off the stage. She had been as full of vitality and fun as a kitten. Then they had become lovers and there was still so much of childhood about her—the teasing, the laughter, the mischief. Had he been wrong to bring her to Deal, to the fringes of war? No, she could not, in any event, have avoided the distant rumble of the cannon, nor the blood-stained bandages nor the widow's grief. She had to grow up but he could have wished, all the same, to see her innocent expression for a little longer. It is man's fate to destroy what he values most. He was glad, in a way, that she was not with child. Or was that a selfish thought? Would she not be happier if expecting her firstborn? Would he not himself risk his life more willingly in the belief that he had transmitted something of himself to the next generation? No, he wanted to keep her as she was, the girl who had scampered about the stage and laughed at him. In short, he wanted the impossible. . . . He gradually became aware that someone was trying to attract his attention and might indeed have been doing so for several minutes. It was Wetherall, with a touch of anxiety in his voice.

"Sir . . . Sir . . . A signal, sir, from the flagship!"

It was high time for him to turn to the matter in hand. Fiona had set off for London, Southampton, and Guernsey, and Richard, for his part, was still at war. More than that he was presently allowed to make a close inspection of the French coast, never turning seaward until he had drawn the fire of every battery. Where was the weakness? His interest finally centred upon Epineville and St Valery-en-Caux, neither a place of much importance but both with a few fishing boats to be seen. He dared not linger over these places for fear of attracting attention but he noted that the reaction to his appearance was belated, the gunfire sporadic and inaccurate. Returning afterwards to the squadron's anchorage in the Downs, Delancey was cheered up by the appearance of Mather and his other followers who now joined him at last. He was thus able to say goodbye to Atkinson, who had done his best, and look forward to having a well-trained crew again. He noticed a change of atmosphere when Mather came aboard and he was almost as glad to welcome the young gentlemen, Northmore, Topley, and Stock; Luke Tanner, his coxswain and—not least—John Teesdale, his steward. He would make something of the *Vengeance* yet.

Delancey had decided by now that the capture of a French gunboat or landing craft would involve an indirect approach. He must capture a French fishing boat first and use that for his attempt on the gunboat, convincing the French at the same time that the fishing boat had been destroyed. His first move, with the Admiral's approval, was to acquire an old and worthless fishing craft which lay on the beach near Walmer. His carpenter undertook to make the vessel more or less seaworthy for a single short voyage. She was then equipped with an old mast and a lug sail. When *Vengeance* sailed for Epineville the old fishing vessel was taken in tow; an odd procedure but the rumour ashore was that she was to be used as target in a gunnery exercise. The approach to the French coast was in darkness and Delancey gave Northmore his orders after the frigate had sailed, all officers being present so that all would know the plan in detail.

"We are going to raid Epineville, gentlemen, a small French port which we recently inspected. You may recall that its defences appeared to be weak. My guess would be that such cannon as they have mounted there are manned by fishermen volunteers—men like our Fencibles—people who are slow to assemble and whose aim will be indifferent. I have no doubt that there are some troops there but not, I suspect, very impressive or numerous. Our object is to capture a fishing vessel and I have made a sketch to indicate the craft I want. When we looked at Epineville I counted seven fishing boats of a reasonable tonnage, two of them much larger than the rest, and all beached at low tide. The two bigger ones were the third and fourth from the left. My impression was that the third was in better shape than the others, but this might be due to a recent coat of paint. I want the better of the two, anyway, and I want her undamaged if possible. The other should be set on fire, which will add to the confusion and help cover your withdrawal. I fully realise, of course, that these vessels may have been moved or may have changed places—I could give you only the latest information we have. For this service, Mr Northmore, you will have the launch and a picked crew, well armed, together with eight marines commanded by Sergeant Blake. It will be the task of the seamen to bring away the fishing vessel. It will be the task of the marines to capture a prisoner or two—some fishermen and, if possible, a soldier. It is my hope that Mr Northmore can perform this service with the men he is to lead. Should he need help, however, Mr Topley will follow in the cutter with a further detachment. Should that assistance prove insufficient I shall bombard the town. It will be a moonless night and our approach must be silent. High tide should be at 2:00 A.M. and I shall launch our assault at 1:30 A.M. with the tide still rising but with some possibility of bringing the captured vessel out on the ebb. It may occur to you that a fishing boat is a small prize to show for the effort we are to make. That is indeed the truth. This is not an affair of prize-money but an effort to secure a French fishing boat for a special purpose. When she has been secured and is well out to sea we shall burn the old craft we have in tow. Seeing this, the French will conclude that we are disappointed in our capture and that the fishing boat has been destroyed. She will not have been destroyed but will presently be anchored at the head of Trinity Bay, unseen by such enemy agents as there may be in Deal."

"Forgive me for raising the question, sir," said Mather, "but this raid would seem to justify the employment of a commissioned officer."

"So indeed it would, Mr Mather, but it is the preliminary to a more important raid and I am not risking my lieutenants in the meanwhile. I have every confidence in Mr Northmore, who has seen a great deal of active service. Any other questions? No? Then be so good, Mr Mather, to see that the boats are properly manned and armed. That will be all, gentlemen."

The frigate hove to in darkness about half a mile from Epineville. Delancey had decided not to anchor because of the noise that would be made by the cable. He kept under sail while the launch was manned and then gave Northmore the order to go in. With muffled rowlocks the launch pulled away and with no sign of alarm from the shore. With Mather, Delancey paced the deck, talking quietly about the problems Northmore would have to face.

"There are bound to be sentries on the beach, whose muskets will give the alarm. The French batteries will be manned in ten minutes but will have no target until somebody remembers to fire starshell. It remains to be seen what troops will counter-attack the beach but it is the more rash of these who may end as our prisoners."

"May I ask you, sir, why the taking of prisoners should be of such moment?"

"It is chiefly their uniform clothing I want so that we can afterwards man the captured fishing boat with men who will pass as Frenchmen. The costumes must be exactly right. Infantry uniforms we shall need later on—specimens, merely, that we can imitate. If our efforts succeed we shall have, in the end, a French gunboat which will be exactly like any other save in the one respect that it will be on our side. Such a craft might be the origin of vast confusion and might even—who knows?—do some considerable damage."

In the sternsheets of the launch Northmore was holding to a compass bearing, the scattered lights on shore affording him no clue to his target. His oarsmen rowed steadily, and no one spoke a word. After twenty minutes or so he could just make out the line of the breakers but the sea was calm and nothing could be heard. Then, at long last, he could make out the position of the fishing craft and altered course so as to head for the third from the left. As the launch neared her, he could see that she was moored, head on to the beach, by the bows and stern. There was nobody aboard her, seemingly, and no one near. So the launch was brought quietly alongside her and he as quietly climbed aboard. His difficulty was now to assess the value of the craft without seeing her in daylight. He had brought a lantern with him, however, and lit it when he was below decks. She was a common type of vessel with a central hold for the fish, a forecastle for the men, and two small cabins aft for the skipper and mate. She would probably measure about eighty tons. Her state of repair was good but she was plainly an old vessel and the smell was horrible. He extinguished the lantern, came on deck, and dropped quietly into the boat. Without a word he motioned the oarsmen to push off, steering the launch towards the next vessel, the fourth. She, too, was deserted and he was able to inspect her in the same way. She was rather bigger than the first and was not so old. He came to the conclusion that this was the better one and was only sorry that he could not inspect her rigging. Anyway, his choice had been made and it remained to see how to free her from her mooring. It could be done in one of two ways, but both were relatively noisy. To unbitt the cables would make a prolonged rumble. To cut the cables with an axe would be quicker but noisy enough to wake the dead. As against that, the alarm must be given at some stage if prisoners were to be taken. Making a quick decision he decided to leave six men, under Bailey, boatswain's mate, to look after the fishing boat and make her ready for sea, while he led the remainder ashore; the shore party comprising six armed seamen and nine marines including the sergeant. Within a few minutes they were on the beach, still unchallenged and Northmore began a cautious approach to the village. Any sentries posted must have gone to sleep for the landing party met with no resistance of any kind. It was all very well to land with orders to take prisoners but how was this possible when no opponents presented themselves? That cannon were in position to defend the place was known, for they had themselves been engaged by them, but they were evidently sited on either side of the village or perhaps on rising ground behind it. There must surely, however, be some sort of headquarters or guardhouse in the village itself? There was and they fairly stumbled across it. Of the two sentries outside, one threw his musket down and put his hands up. The other did the same but fired his musket in the air first. The alarm had been given and a bugle sounded from some point farther inland. The time had come to withdraw.

With his two prisoners secured, their wrists tied together by spunyarn, Northmore marched his men back the way they had come. He could feel that, so far, all had gone according to plan. It could only be a matter of minutes, however, before the men from the guardhouse should be on their heels. It would mean a running battle back to the beach with darkness to cover their retreat. He quickened the step but resisted the impulse to run. While their entry to the village street had been in almost total darkness, lights were now coming on in the cottages, windows were being opened, and neighbours were calling to each other, asking what was amiss. Owing to all these glimmering lamps and candles, the street was becoming clearly visible and they themselves were no longer hidden by darkness. A skirmish in the village street was the last thing that Northmore wanted to bring about because his opponents would know the ground and he had only just begun to see it. He had reached a point where there was a white painted garden wall on his right faced by three or four shops on his left. At this moment he heard the sound of troops on the march, the noise of boots on shingle coming from some point ahead of him. He realised at once what the situation was. The French had no sentinels on the beach because they were relying on a system of patrols. A patrol had been out when the landing took place, probably at the far end of the beach. It was now returning and had heard a shot fired. It would fall back on the guardroom in the village where the other men, who had previously been on patrol, had been caught off their guard. He now had opponents both in front and rear. With a decision which did him credit, he gave out his orders: "Sergeant Blake, an enemy patrol is coming this way from the direction of the beach. Draw your men up in line, with the two prisoners in rear, and advance until you can see the enemy. Then fire a volley and attack with the bayonet. Fight your way back to the launch and be ready to cover the embarkation of my party. I intend to fight off the men who are following us. Is that clear?"

"Yes, sir. Good luck, sir. Marines, form line by the right. Quick march!"

On the left a shopkeeper in his nightshirt, holding a lantern, had opened his front door, ready to protest against the noise other people were making.

"Follow me!" said Northmore to his seamen and made straight for the shop door. In a minute the shopkeeper had been bundled inside, bound hand and foot, and gagged. His lantern was left outside the door, faintly illuminating the street, and Northmore drew up his men inside the darkness of the shop, two opposite the door, three opposite the window, and one told to find an escape route by the back. "Watch your front," said Northmore. "Take aim and be ready to fire." The sailors were no marksmen but they had a position of advantage. They were facing a whitewashed wall. What light there was came from their side of the street and they were themselves invisible. Perhaps a minute passed before the approaching footsteps could be heard. Northmore drew his own pistol and levelled it. The tramp of army boots came nearer accompanied by a great deal of undisciplined chatter, punctuated by the leader's voice calling for silence. Then the dark figures were silhouetted against the white background and Northmore called out "Fire," his own pistol being aimed at the leader. Three of the enemy fell, the leader included, and the rest took to their heels.

"Re-load," shouted Northmore. At that moment the seaman returned from the back of the house and reported, "I've broken down the back door, sir. It leads into a lane."

"Thanks, Willis. Give me your musket." Stepping into the street, Northmore fired a shot in the enemy's direction and then handed the weapon back. "Re-load, Willis," he said, "and then follow us out at the back and along this lane to the right." To the rest he said, "Follow me!" and resumed his withdrawal but now in the lane and no longer in the street. Over somewhere to his right he heard Sergeant Blake shout, "Fire!" and then "Advance!" The marines' volley was answered by a volley from their opponents and then came the sounds of hand to hand fighting. All depended now, as Northmore realised, on the strength and resolution of the French patrol, which might, for all he knew, outnumber Blake's men by three to one.

He quickened the pace and heard Willis somewhere behind him, running to catch up. Then he found what he was looking for, a gap between the cottages on his right, not a lane but a vegetable garden. Charging through the cabbages, he found himself in rear of the enemy, who had not given ground before the marines' attack. As his men came level with him he gave the order "Half right, aim. Fire!" He then led his party in a loud cheer. "Hurrah! Come on! Charge!" There were only seven of them all told but their sudden appearance was too much for the French, who now fell back in disorder, leaving a number of killed and wounded. The marines followed in good order, less two casualties, and Northmore told his seamen to re-load. Then he headed again for the beach and was guided to the

launch by the shouts of the man who had been left to guard
it. He was nearly there when the French attacked again.

    That the French should have returned to the attack did them
great credit. By doing so, they turned Northmore's reembarka-
tion into a difficult rearguard action. Sending his seamen back
to the launch, Northmore led the marines into action again with
a further volley and another attack. Then they fell back towards
the launch, firing as they went and suffering further casualties,
two wounded and one killed. "Embark!" shouted Northmore
finally and everyone ran for the boat, from which the marines
continued their fire while seamen pulled for dear life. The
enemy's musketry was now sporadic as they lost sight of their
target. Then the launch reached the captured fishing craft and
Northmore, first aboard, gave orders for cutting the cables and
making sail. A few minutes later the scene was lit by starshell
and the shore batteries opened fire. Their aim was wildly inaccurate and no shot came anywhere near their vanishing target.
Within half an hour Northmore was back on board the frigate,
reporting his capture and his losses. "I have two prisoners and
some French clothes removed from one of their shops."

    "Well done, Mr Northmore, I'll hear your full report later.
You may now take command of the vessel you have captured,
for which I'll allow you a crew of eight seamen under a petty
officer of your choice. Take with you all you will need, not forgetting your navigational instruments and a chart. Make sail
after the frigate and take station at a distance of two cables
astern. We are on course for the Downs, where you will anchor
the prize at the head of Trinity Bay. Mr Topley, take the launch
alongside this other old craft and set fire to her, then return on
board and resume your normal duties. Mr Mather, prepare to
heave anchor and make sail. Our little operation is finished."

Chapter Ten

INVASION PLANS

THE WINTER of 1803–4 might have been spent mostly ashore but Rear-Admiral Knight now thought proper to maintain a show of activity. Addington's government was tottering under heavy attack and Lord St Vincent had to prove that its naval side was unmatched for vigilance. So Knight kept his squadron busy although with little to show for it. On the French side the sole activity was in slowly assembling the invasion fleet at Boulogne and the adjacent ports. Many of the landing craft were built at small harbours to the westward. When completed they were sent to Boulogne in batches of four or five, keeping close to the French coast and running for shelter whenever a British man-of-war appeared. Under the guns of the nearest battery they would wait until the coast was clear and then resume their voyage. On rare occasions they were caught too far from harbour and were driven ashore and wrecked. Something could be made of this in the Gazette but Delancey, for one, thought that these efforts were useless. He had been in favour of an active policy in summer but these efforts in winter involved too much wear and tear. Apart from that, he preferred to see the landing craft full of troops before he attacked them. All he wanted, in the meanwhile, was to capture a specimen gunboat for future use. The Rear-Admiral was sufficiently impressed by this idea to place two sloops, *Cynthia* and *Plover,* under his orders and allot him a cruising area between Cherbourg and Le Havre. Attached to this small force was the captured French fishing vessel *Pauline* manned by Lieutenant Le Couteur of Jersey with a partly Channel Islands crew, all clad as French fishermen. The hunting ground was the Baie de Seine, the stretch of coast where the landing craft would be tempted seawards, partly to shorten the distance from Barfleur to Le Havre and partly because that coast is particularly dangerous. Delancey thought that a capture might be made off the Plateau de Calvados. Assuming that the landing craft came from the coast of Brittany, they would round the Cap de la Hague and so eastwards. If pursued off the coast of Normandy they would make for Le Havre by going close inshore around Trouville. In that area an innocent-looking French fishing boat would snap up the last of them and the others would be too conscious of pursuit to turn back and attempt a rescue. They would all have crews for the passage only, signed on for the one voyage, not men craving for a place in naval history or national legend. The success of the operation must depend upon placing the fishing boat between the gunboats and their possible place of refuge. It was also essential that the capture should be made without damaging the prey.

Delancey's plan was sound enough but it depended for its success upon the enemy doing what they ought to do. For weeks they failed to play the part assigned to them, there being no movement of landing craft at all. Then the traffic began again but the craft pursued made straight for the shore and beached themselves under cover of a shore battery before they could be captured. Delancey later moved his forces nearer to the Seine estuary and was finally rewarded by a useful capture near Trouville. A group of five landing craft were chased by his two sloops towards Le Havre and the last of them was snapped up

by *Pauline* off Les Vaches Noires without a shot fired on either
side. It was neatly done and Delancey recognised the vessel as
a Peniche or large flat-bottomed rowing boat. He soon had her
under a tarpaulin in the Naval Storeshed at Deal, not as a matter of preservation but in order to avoid reminding the French
that there was such a craft in British hands. Delancey had only
a vague idea of a plan for her use but he could at least imagine circumstances in which she might be the ace in the pack.
With her he was able to store a small collection of French uniforms and seamen's clothing, items which could be copied as
necessary. Rear-Admiral Knight congratulated Delancey on his
coup but was only mildly interested in its possibilities.

For Delancey the campaign of 1804 began with a conference held at Dover Castle on 3 April. It was presided over by
Admiral Lord Keith, whom Delancey now saw for the first time.
He was a rather handsome man aged 58 who had been in the
Navy since 1767 but who had never been present in a general
action. He it was who suppressed the naval mutiny at Sheerness, having had a generally distinguished career in many parts
of the world. George Keith Elphinstone, ennobled in 1797,
was a Scotsman of known ability to whom the naval defence
of the English coasts had been largely, but not entirely, entrusted. He was chiefly famous in the service for having
probably made more prize money than anyone else. His flag
was in the *Monarch* but he had called this conference on shore
so as to have the generals present, together with Rear-Admirals
Montague, Thornborough, and Knight, Commodore Sir Sidney
Smith and such of his captains as were available, Delancey
being one of them. The castle courtyard was filled with horses
and orderlies, junior officers and grooms. Outside the precincts,
Dover itself was a scene of frantic activity, with large garrisons

in the Castle and the Citadel and vast tented camps stretching inland as far as the eye could see. It was a fine spring day in early April and the French coast was in full view and was obviously the scene of similar activity but with a more aggressive purpose. British agents had been active on the French side of the Channel and it was one of the first objects of the conference to acquaint all present with the French order of battle. The one civilian at the conference, introduced as Mr Xenophon, was clearly the master spy for the Calais–Boulogne area. Lord Keith opened the proceedings by addressing his senior military colleagues on the subject of co-operation between the services, never more important than it was going to be during the present year. If Bonaparte was going to invade England it would have to be between June and September. They would hear evidence that his preparations were well advanced. Against his designs our first lines of defence consisted in the men-of-war which constantly ranged the French coast. Our second line lay in the main fleets based on Portsmouth and Chatham. Our third line lay in the troops which defended our shores, our fourth in the armies which are concentrated at points further inland.

"Let me say, Sir Charles," he concluded, "that I am greatly impressed by the good order and discipline which is evident among the military formations I have seen in both Kent and Essex. That they will give a good account of themselves, should the enemy land, I am wholly convinced. Before we discuss practical measures of defence, however, I thought it appropriate to hear the latest intelligence about the enemy forces. If you agree, Sir Charles, I shall ask Mr Xenophon to address us on this subject, about which he is better informed, I believe, than anyone else on this side of the Channel. I think that we shall learn from him that our preparations, which some people think excessive, are in fact barely sufficient. Mr Xenophon."

Mr Xenophon was a lean, hawk-faced man dressed in dark clothes which were intended, no doubt, to be inconspicuous. Carried beyond a certain point the effort to avoid notice is apt to make anyone the centre of attention, and this could have been said of Mr Xenophon. He spoke, however, with great confidence and clearly considered his own efforts as central to a war effort of which Lord Keith and the rest knew only the fringes.

"I shall arrange the intelligence we have collected under four general headings: the harbours on which an attempted French invasion will be based; the landing craft available; the troops to be committed; and the time of year at which the attempt will be made. As regards the harbours, it is now sufficiently clear that they are all between Etaples and Dunkirk. Boulogne, Calais, and Dunkirk are all important but Boulogne is the port from which the main effort will be made. Other places like Dieppe may have a part to play but it is not from there that the flotilla, or any part of it, will sail. Our concern is with nine harbours in all, centred upon a headquarters at Boulogne. Now, as regards the craft available, we estimate that there may be about nine hundred designed for the purpose and up to five hundred requisitioned fishing boats, tonnage enough for some seventy thousand infantry but with the total numbers still increasing. I come now to the troops actually in the area. I would not myself put the number at more than forty thousand men, but the engineers are laying out additional camps, perhaps doubling the accommodation now available, not all these camps being on the coast. What is significant about the Army of England, as it is called, is not its present strength but the presence there of some crack units which would never be used in a mere diversion or feint. Last of all, I should assume, as you do, Lord Keith, that the invasion attempt must be made between June and September. I have no actual information on that point but I should judge that arrangements cannot be completed within eight weeks and that October would be too late in the year. In Bonaparte's place I should choose the month of July and would prefer the period leading up to the full moon. I should be made to realise, however, that embarkation of a large army would depend upon a week of calm weather, more than the Channel will usually offer."

"Thank you, Mr Xenophon, for a very useful and clear summary of the facts known to us. Do you suggest, in effect, that the Army of England is to number seventy thousand to eighty thousand men?"

"No, my Lord, that would be too small a force to serve the Corsican's purpose. To embark less than a hundred thousand would be to risk immediate defeat on landing."

"Thank you, Mr Xenophon, I agree with you." After a short pause he addressed the senior army officer: "Sir Charles?"

"Well, my Lord, I was surprised to hear no mention of cavalry or artillery."

"We can assume, General," said Mr Xenophon, "that Bonaparte will not have forgotten either, he himself being a gunner. We know, in fact, that some of the larger craft are fitted to carry up to fifty horses. But no cavalry regiments have yet appeared. My agents are all clear on this point."

"Nor need it surprise us," said another general. "If cavalry were now there in force they would have used up all the local forage long before July. The same would be true of the artillery.

When they appear it will be because the invasion is imminent."

"I am sure you are right, General," replied Mr Xenophon.

"Agreed," said Sir Charles, "but I question whether a force of a hundred thousand could be thought sufficient. I should be surprised to hear of less than a hundred and fifty thousand men being deployed."

"The total may well exceed that number, Sir Charles, for all we know."

"If it does," said Lord Keith, "Bonaparte must be relying on using the same craft for a second or even a third trip. If that is so, he must choose the shortest sea passage."

"We have no intelligence on that subject, my Lord," replied Mr Xenophon.

"From Boulogne the nearest point would be Dungeness," continued Lord Keith, "and I would assume that the invading army must land between Folkestone and Hastings."

"Our assumption has been the same," said Sir Charles, "but we have included Dover and Brighton among the points we must be prepared to defend."

"Very rightly, Sir Charles. If Bonaparte should change his mind about this hazardous campaign—and it is my opinion that he will eventually cancel it—your military preparations will be a principal cause of his discouragement."

"Your naval vigilance, my Lord, will give him still greater pause for thought."

"Thank you, Sir Charles. But I should myself consider that his hesitation, when the time comes to give the order, must arise more from the inherent difficulties of the task. One consideration which led, I believe, to my present appointment is that I commanded, on the naval side, at the invasion of Egypt in 1801. My problem was to sail from Malta and to land about sixteen thousand men at Aboukir from over three hundred boats. I thus have actual experience of a large-scale conjunct expedition, more perhaps than most of my fellow flag officers. This Egyptian affair was an opposed landing under heavy fire but the presence of the enemy was, in truth, the least of my worries. To embark and disembark an army is no easy task at any time and the whole operation can be disorganised at any moment by a change in wind direction or a patch of mist. When confronted by the sort of difficulties I have met with, Bonaparte may well conclude that the thing he means, at present, to attempt is not even possible."

A short silence followed, broken by Rear-Admiral Thornborough, who asked whether Bonaparte was likely to use any secret weapons. There were rumours, it seemed, of vessels driven by steam-engines, of new explosive devices, and even a boat able to travel below the surface. Had Mr Xenophon any facts on the basis of which these rumours could be supported or denied?

"All we know for certain, Admiral, is that the American inventor Fulton gave a demonstration of steam navigation at Paris and that his invention was rejected. His underwater boat was similarly demonstrated at Brest and judged to be impracticable. He is now in England, offering these and other devices to the Admiralty."

"And if he has a sympathetic hearing from Lord St Vincent," remarked Sir Sidney Smith, "I for one will be astonished." There was some laughter at this.

"And I would share your astonishment," said Lord Keith. "While remembering, however, that his lordship's period of office may not be eternal." This comment produced a murmur of subdued conversation, all being aware that the government's fall was expected within weeks. "There are others aspiring to high office who may be less sceptical of innovation."

Some further discussion followed but the general conclusion, summarised by Lord Keith, was that Bonaparte might be expected to attempt his invasion of England in July, that his army centred on Boulogne would number no fewer than 150,000 men, and that he would aim to land at points between Folkestone and Hastings. "Whether he will really make the attempt must remain to be seen and I have my doubts about it. These are nevertheless the assumptions on which we must act. If he comes, we must be ready for him."

The conference came to an end and its members dispersed, Lord Keith and other flag officers going to dine with the Governor of the Castle, less senior officers dining together at the Dover Stage Inn. With them was Mr Xenophon, as conspicuous as ever in wearing no uniform. Delancey found himself next to Captain Denham of the *Eagle,* who was inclined to ridicule the scale of military defence.

"What is droll to me, sir, is that Bonaparte has never understood the importance of our commerce. Success against us means, to him, his marching into London at the head of his army. But Lord St Vincent and his advisers have never been worried about that. Their fears have always been that the French would find means to intercept our East and West India convoys. London could be ruined without the entry of a French army. Fortunately for us, he never seems to have realised that we are more concerned about our trade than about his troops. I question myself whether our regiments here can serve any useful purpose."

"I am much of your opinion, sir," replied Delancey, "more

especially regarding Bonaparte's ignorance of where we are most vulnerable. But I think myself that our troops do more than add colour to the scene. Their strength will be known to Bonaparte and he is thus compelled to reinforce his Army of England. Granted that his men are veterans, he must have numbers at least equal to those that will oppose him. But each additional division or brigade makes his embarkation problem more difficult. His plan, so far as I understand it, is a staff officer's nightmare."

"I must confess my ignorance of conjunct expeditions," replied Denham. "Wherein is the special difficulty to which you refer?"

"Well, sir, our conjectures as to the French strength range from one hundred thousand, minimum, to one hundred fifty thousand. Whichever figure we accept, we know that such an army must have room to camp and room to exercise. I have made inquiries about the Duke of York's expedition to the Helder in 1799. I have even a note of the numbers and dates. He led thirty-five thousand men in all but where were they encamped? Not at Deal, not on the beach. Here at Dover? Impossible. All the accommodation and all the space is taken up by the garrison, by the men who are to stay here; and the same applies to Folkestone or Ramsgate. No, the bulk of the force was camped at Barham Downs, about twenty miles from Deal or two days' march. Embarkation began during the second week in August and the first division sailed on the 12th. The second division sailed on the 26th. The head of the third division reached Deal on 7 September—five thousand strong—and embarked on the 9th. The Earl of Chatham, Commander in Chief, sailed on the 10th and the last brigade did not embark until the 12th. Using the sheltered anchorage of the Downs,

employing ships as transports, and not mere rowing boats, and
with the help of the Deal boatmen—probably the best boat-han-
dlers in the world—it took Lord Chatham's staff about four
weeks to embark thirty-five thousand men. You cannot have
men drawn up on the beach for days. You cannot keep them
for weeks on board transport ships at anchor. They must assemble where there is grass for the horses and room to exercise.
But Bonaparte's problem is infinitely worse. Boulogne has some
sort of shelter from the Bassure de Baas and there is a useful
basin a mile up the river and another at Wimereux. But he has
no proper transports and must rely on the flotilla of small craft.
How long will it take him to collect one hundred fifty thousand men from the encampments up to thirty miles away? How
long to embark them and how long before they can sail? At
Lord Chatham's speed of embarkation it would take him over
four months; four months free of bad weather and free from
interference by us!"

"I beg leave to suggest, sir, that Bonaparte is an abler commander than Lord Chatham."

"What—abler than our future Prime Minister's brother?
Surely you cannot be serious? But even were Bonaparte four
times as good—an almost seditious idea—his embarkation
would still take four weeks of fine weather with the British
taken completely by surprise. But what surprise is possible?
Boulogne is the place and July is the month. No one at today's
conference is going to expect the attempt to be made from
Toulon in December."

Before the dinner ended, or at least before the party dispersed, Delancey managed to have a word with Mr Xenophon.
Inquiring further about the *Nautilus*, he asked whether anything had been heard about her or a similar craft at Le Havre.

"I *have* had a report about that," admitted Mr Xenophon, "and have not known what to make of it. There can be no doubt that the *Nautilus* herself is at Brest and has been rejected. If there is another such device at Le Havre she must be another vessel, similar in design but possibly an improvement. With Fulton in England, any other such craft must be the work of someone else—probably someone who worked with him on *Nautilus*. Do you think that such a vessel poses a serious threat?"

"I don't know, Mr Xenophon, but I shouldn't dismiss it as fantastical. There are three ideas under current discussion: the steam-vessel, the boat which can travel under the water, and the explosive device used at sea. Each has certain possibilities but what would be really dangerous would be a combination of the three. I suggest, sir, that Le Havre should be watched with care. We need to know of any plot that is hatching there."

Chapter Eleven

WHEN WILL BONEY COME?

REAR-ADMIRAL Knight's squadron was at anchor in the Downs when news came on 11 May that Addington had resigned and that William Pitt had formed a new government with the Duke of Portland, Lord Eldon, the Earl of Chatham, Canning, Huskisson, and Spencer Perceval. Replacing Lord St Vincent at the Admiralty was Lord Melville. News of the event reached Deal in a matter of minutes by telegraph, the semaphore system which had connected Deal with the Admiralty since 1796. If there was lingering any prejudice against Delancey at the highest level, it went with the removal of Troubridge and Markham. He had no claim on Lord Melville for any special favour but he could at least hope for a better frigate than the *Vengeance*. By reputation he was still the man who had destroyed the *Hercule,* a French ship of the line, and he might at least hope to be treated as well as anyone else. Knight signalled for all captains and gave them the news at once.

"Politics apart," he concluded, "I think this a change for the better. Lord St Vincent is an excellent man, as we all recognise, but he was so intent on preventing corruption in the dockyards that he almost brought work to a standstill. Melville will wish to fight Bonaparte rather than the shipwrights and caulkers at Portsmouth and Chatham. He will also expect to see early results, the actions which will prove that a new energy is being

applied to the war. Facing the French invasion flotilla we shall
be relied upon to harass it. It is for me to make a plan but I
am open to consider proposals from any of my officers." There
was an awkward silence, broken at last by Captain Harding of
the *Lizard,* the senior captain present.

"I must confess, Admiral, that I am somewhat at a loss. We
might claim, I think, that we have done all that is possible. We
have no means of forcing an entry into Boulogne harbour. Lord
Nelson himself planned the attack in August 1801, achieving
nothing but a heavy loss of life and the loss of Captain Parker.
He also discovered, at great cost, that the enemy gunboats are
secured by chains, not by ordinary cable. Few of us would hope
to succeed where Lord Nelson failed and the French will have
strengthened their defences since his attempt was made. We
could bring bomb vessels to a point within range of their
defending gunboats but their fire would be wildly inaccurate
as it always is. My own view, Admiral, is that we should let
them alone until they actually embark their troops for the invasion. Then we shall catch them at sea."

"Delancey?" said the Admiral.

"Were the decision left to me," replied Delancey, "I should
agree with Captain Harding. Encourage them to attempt their
invasion of England. Keep out of sight and allow them to think
it the easiest task in the world. Then catch them in mid Channel! But that decision, which I believe to be correct, will not
satisfy our Members of Parliament. They will ask their lordships of the Admiralty why nothing is being done and that same
question will then be passed on to you, Admiral. What are we
doing against the French flotilla? What do we plan to do? I
submit, sir, that we cannot reply 'Nothing.' As against that, I
am utterly opposed to any plan which occasions a great loss of

life. We can sacrifice men in order to defeat the enemy. I would never incur losses in order to placate the ignorance of Parliament. My idea, sir, is to make noise enough to merit a column in the newspapers, give all the appearance of energy but take the least possible risk."

"An admirable solution in principle, Delancey," said Harding. "Perhaps you will now go into more detail?"

"Now, sir," protested Delancey, "you must be fair. I have given you the broad outline. I had expected you to contribute the rest."

"Be damned to you! What do you take me for? A confounded magician?"

"Well, Admiral, failing help from Captain Harding, I will add one further idea. The enemy defences can be penetrated in one way only; by the entry into their harbour of a vessel they recognise as one of their own."

"Ah, your captured gunboat?" asked Knight.

"No, sir. By the entry first of all of another gunboat which my gunboat will have captured."

"Well, let's have the rest of it."

"I have not drawn up a plan in detail, sir. We were not told beforehand that our views would be invited."

"That's true, I'll allow. Who else has an idea to put forward?"

There was a prolonged silence, the other captains looking embarrassed.

"Well, gentlemen," said the Rear-Admiral at last, "I accept Delancey's plan in principle. We have to do something to give proof of our activity. It is not a cause in which we are justified in taking a great risk with our men's lives. It must rest, as a plan, on deception rather than mere force. With all that we agree. It remains to be seen whether Delancey can translate a vague idea into a real plan of action. How long do you need, Delancey?"

"I can do it by tomorrow, sir, if I can do it at all."

On the following day Delancey had an interview with the Admiral alone. He was now able to explain his plan at length.

"Boulogne is the centre of the French invasion effort and that, to my mind, is the place we must attack. There are gunboats which form a defensive line in front of the river mouth and these are covered in turn by coastal batteries. The town itself, on the right bank, is a mile up the river with the new basin facing it on the left bank. Boats specially built to form part of the invasion flotilla are crowded into the basin. Requisitioned fishing boats are moored in the river higher up. At regular intervals the gunboats in the new basin are taken to sea as an exercise, heading north or south so as to remain covered by the batteries. Should there be any threat of attack some movement of these boats is certain; they would move to meet a threatened landing. The chief danger they must provide against is that their gunboats may be fired upon by their own shore batteries. They provide against this by distinctive flags in daylight, by distinctive lights after dark. These arrangements are frequently changed. We know from past experience that any frontal attack on Boulogne will meet with fierce resistance."

"Agreed, Delancey. All this is generally known."

"So my first conclusion, sir, is that an actual raid, with the landing of troops—were we contemplating such a raid—would take place at Wimereux, three miles further north. There is another basin there for landing craft but it is nearer the sea, the defences are weaker and the shoreline to the south is sand rather than rock. A feint attack on Wimereux would be credible and the noise would be heard in Boulogne. I should myself assume that a division of gunboats would emerge from Boulogne and sweep northwards to meet the apparent threat. All would have hoisted the appropriate recognition lights. Agreed, sir?"

"Yes, agreed."

"When it becomes apparent that the raid on Wimereux has come to nothing—due, of course, to the skill and courage of the defending artillerymen—the division of gunboats will return to Boulogne."

"No doubt."

"The gunboats will be the same in number but we shall have intercepted the last one and added to the column another boat—a flat-bottomed craft now at Deal—and an ordinary French fishing boat, just such a craft as we have at anchor in Trinity Bay. Both will by then have hoisted the correct recognition lights. The flat-bottomed boat will enter the crowded basin, packed with explosives to be ignited by a half-hour fuse. The fishing boat will then take the boat's crew on board and make for the harbour mouth, escaping in the panic caused by the explosion."

"And you think that such an explosion will destroy much of the flotilla by fire?"

"No, sir, I don't. The explosion vessel will have kegs of gunpowder underneath a top dressing of incendiary devices and hand grenades. It could do a great deal of damage but I doubt if many vessels would be actually destroyed. Its biggest effect would be on enemy morale. It would be, in effect, a slap in the face. If that can happen in their own fortified harbour, what might happen at sea? Our publicised account would be proportionately good for our own morale. It would look well in the newspapers."

"I agree. I think, moreover, that your plan is a good one,

with the possibility of doing much damage at a minimum risk. I shall need permission from Lord Keith and I shall need two bomb-vessels for the dummy attack on Wimereux. You will need French-speaking volunteers—all seamen from the Channel Islands that you can collect. Now, as to command, I shall direct the feint attack on Wimereux, you will direct the raid on Boulogne. Who is to lead the raiding group?"

"I planned to do that myself, sir, speaking French as I do, or at least Norman French, like a native."

"Nonsense. You shall do nothing of the sort. The task is one for a lieutenant, not for a post-captain. He must be fluent in French, that I allow. He must be senior enough for promotion should he succeed. Within those limits, take your pick of what we have. Say nothing of this to anyone until I have the Commander-in-Chief's permission. In the meanwhile I am grateful to you for putting forward an ingenious plan and one which might well succeed. I shall see to it that you have full credit for your part in the planning and execution. Supposing we succeed in the raid, how will the French react?"

"They will deny that any damage was done. They will report that we were driven off with heavy losses. Then, to restore morale, they will plan a raid on, say, Brighton, hoping to pick a day when the Prince of Wales is there."

"That would please the Prince, anyway. He longs for active service but is forbidden by the King, who will not risk the life of the heir apparent. A battle at Brighton would suit him very well."

"It would be worth a knighthood for somebody, sir."

"Do you really think they would risk any such attempt, Delancey?"

"I don't know, sir. It would be what I would do in their place. But Bonaparte and I may not always think alike. I should not, in his position, have formed the Army of England at all."

Lord Keith's permission arrived quite promptly. He was at the Nore and Knight's messenger went by road from Deal to Sheerness, returning with his lordship's approval and the promise of two bomb ketches on temporary loan, sailing immediately for the Downs. Informed of this, Delancey took Mather into his confidence and asked his advice. "We need someone to command the fishing vessel *Pauline,* someone to command the flat-bottomed boat, and a lieutenant to direct the raid. The lieutenant cannot be you."

"Why not, sir?"

"Your French is not good enough, Mr Mather. I need a Channel Islander and the Admiral suggests that he should be fairly senior. The two junior officers must also be fluent, a necessity which rules out both Northmore and Topley. I also rule out our own lieutenants, Weatherall and Seddon—the one too fat, the other too stupid and neither able to speak any language but his own. Who else is there?"

"Well, sir, there is Le Couteur and the Jerseyman who manned the *Pauline* when she captured the peniche. They came from the *Cynthia.*"

"Yes, there is Le Couteur. . . . The trouble is that we are on the horns of a dilemma. To go straight into Boulogne harbour we need a man of exceptional resolution. He will know that his failure, should he fail, will not bring him to a prisoner-of-war camp but will place him before a firing-squad. Such an officer I could find and you might well be the man chosen. We need, on the other hand, a man who can pass himself off as a Frenchman. Such an officer I can find but does he have the other qualities needed—coolness, courage, seamanship, and determination?"

"I beg pardon, sir, but I should have said that you are the only man who could do it."

"And I have been told that I mustn't. What is your opinion of Le Couteur?"

"I know very little about him, sir. He captured that peniche quite neatly."

"I know he did but he does not strike me as a man of more than average resolution. I shall consult with the other captains and ask their help."

Many fruitless conversations followed, names being put forward, discussed, and rejected. In general, the good linguists were good at nothing else, known courage going with an appalling accent. They came back to Le Couteur in the end, with Northmore in the *Pauline,* accompanied by a midshipman called Renouf from Alderney to do the talking, and a master's mate called Syvret from Guernsey to command the captured gunboat. Delancey was not satisfied with this leadership but he reported to the Rear-Admiral that these were the best men he could find. There followed a period of feverish preparation, the peniche being brought out of store and caulked and repainted, the *Pauline* being checked and repaired, the explosives being shipped, and the volunteers interviewed. Much trouble went into the making of clothes and uniforms which would pass as French. All thus disguised would have their British clothes at hand, ready to do a quick change if there should be risk of their being captured. Delancey doubted whether it would save them but knew that this was a precaution that had to be taken.

It was impossible to make these preparations without

rumours being current on the quayside at Deal. Delancey therefore leaked the information that a raid was being planned on Wimereux—a story which had the merit of being partly true. That the rumour would reach France was fairly certain, and was desirable, indeed, as concentrating all last-minute defensive efforts on the wrong place. A great deal of technical expertise went into the loading of the peniche, the kegs of gunpowder being carefully packed with stones wedged between them and a tarpaulin lashed over all to keep them dry. Half-hour fuses were laid under the edges of the tarpaulin and each of these covered with its own tarpaulin flap picked out with a touch of white paint. On top of the tarpaulin were rows of hand grenades, half explosive and half incendiary, all held in position by rope grummets. Over the grenades went another tarpaulin, to be removed at the last moment, and the fuses for all these missiles were set for 32 minutes. The fuses were not really that accurate and the lighting of them was going to be a nerve-racking task for the men on board who were to tumble into a boat and be outside the inner basin before the vessel exploded. Could all this be done before the French became aware of it? That was a question which Delancey often asked himself. He knew too well that the plan could be foiled by a single brave man and a few buckets of water. As against that, the instinct of most men, seeing fuses alight (and not knowing whether they might not be set for five minutes) would be to run for cover. Once the explosion vessel was in the basin at Boulogne—and God knows whether that would prove possible!—the odds on its detonation were probably about even. Granted it went off, the French invasion attempt would not be delayed by as much as a day. It would be French morale that would suffer, and morale (Delancey told himself hopefully) is half the battle. In odd moments of depression he could see only the prospect of utter confusion and disaster.

The squadron sailed on the afternoon of 27 May 1804, the occasion marked by the Rear-Admiral's recent promotion. Flying the white ensign instead of the blue, the frigates *Antelope, Lizard,* and *Vengeance,* followed by the sloops *Cynthia, Plover, Gannet,* and *Heron,* followed in turn by the bomb vessels *Terror* and *Volcano,* as also by the *Pauline* and the flat-bottomed boat now renamed *Panic,* made an impressive array, beginning well but somewhat tailing off. Course was laid for Wimereux but a prearranged signal at dusk led to *Vengeance* quitting the line, followed by *Pauline* and *Panic,* and heading for Boulogne. Delancey had Le Couteur, Northmore, Renouf, and Syvret with him in the *Vengeance,* using this opportunity for a final briefing.

"High tide will be at two in the morning," Delancey explained, for perhaps the third time. "So the bombardment of Wimereux is timed for midnight, with two hours of the flood-tide still to go. Fire from the sloops will make considerable noise but they will be out of effective range. We calculate, on the other hand, that some of the bombs from *Terror* and *Volcano* should reach the basin where the French landing craft are concentrated."

"Will they do much damage?" asked Le Couteur.

"I shouldn't think so," replied Delancey. "There will be little moonlight at best, too little for any accurate direction of the mortars. The bombs that don't miss the basin altogether will mostly fall in the water. The French may think, however, that we are planning to land—"

"What!" exclaimed Northmore. "With the whole confounded

French army encamped on the beach?"

"That wouldn't prevent a raid," replied Delancey in mild tones. "It would merely throw doubt on the landing party's chances of survival. However, there will be noise enough to bring a diversion of their gunboats out of Boulogne—anyway, that is what I am counting on. That is your moment to move in, Mr Le Couteur. What is your first task?"

"To observe the French recognition lights and hoist the same in *Pauline* and *Panic*."

"Right. You have the lanterns and coloured glass. You are then to close with the French gunboats, placing yourself within sight but out of hail. By 2 A.M. the cannonade will cease and the squadron off Wimereux will have the Admiral's signal to withdraw. With the cease-fire the gunboats out of Boulogne will return to base. Assuming that they do this in line ahead, as they will need to do for passing the harbour entrance, the *Pauline* will capture the last of them, the *Panic* instantly taking her place in the formation, followed a little afterwards by *Pauline*. The captured gunboat will stay with us, less her crew."

"What shall we do with the French seamen, sir?"

"Send them ashore in the *Pauline's* launch. We don't want to be bothered with prisoners."

"But won't they give the alarm, sir?"

"Yes, they will but too late to serve any purpose. It will take them at least an hour to reach Boulogne on foot, and then they will have to explain themselves and wait in the outer office. It will be two hours before any senior officer is informed. *Panic*, meanwhile, will follow the other gunboat into the basin. Having lit the fuses, Mr Northmore, you and your men will escape by boat and join the *Pauline*. I shall cover the withdrawal of both craft from a position on the flank of the moored gunboats. I can go in no further on a falling tide. I have described the plan in some detail and I have drawn a diagram—here it is, on the table—from which you will see what we have to do. In actual practice, things are apt to go wrong in detail. If and when they do so, we must all remember the essential aim—to explode the *Panic* in the midst of the French gunboats, doing the maximum damage and creating the greatest confusion and alarm."

"What I can't understand, sir," said Le Couteur, "is why we have to capture the French gunboat. Why not simply follow her in?"

"Because the number would be wrong," replied Delancey patiently. "Fifteen gunboats put to sea—or twenty, or whatever the number is—and sixteen return to port. What will their signal stations make of that? What will their shore battery commanders conclude? A stray fishing boat they should accept, provided she is obviously French, but an extra gunboat—no, that won't do. It does not matter if the last one should lag behind—she could have sprung a leak or broken an oar—but the total must be correct."

"Are we to suppose, sir," asked Northmore, "that the *Panic* explosion will do a great deal of damage?"

"No," said Delancey. "My own estimate would be two gunboats destroyed, six or eight damaged, a hundred windows broken, and a thousand housewives given a terrible fright."

"Is it worth the trouble, sir?" asked Le Couteur.

"No," answered Delancey. "In terms of damage I should say not. Our plan is aimed at French morale. All this is to happen on their own doorstep, with a whole army as audience. If Boulogne is not safe, where can they feel secure? We shall leave them in no mood for battle, and our own morale will be correspondingly raised. You need not think that our efforts will be wasted."

"I assume, sir," said Le Couteur, "that I am to direct from the *Pauline* and that Mr Northmore will go ahead of me in the *Panic*. I take it that we shall be under easy sail?"

"That is correct. From the start of the bombardment, allow an hour for the gunboats to come out and move towards Wimereux. I should assume that they will be in line abreast. You must not be in the area ahead of them. When the bombardment ceases they will presently go about and head back to base, probably in line ahead. That will be when you move in. Make the success signal, Mr Le Couteur, when the target gunboat has been captured. I cannot offer you close support because the sight of the frigate would put the French on their guard. They might even guess that the Wimereux affair is a feint and that Boulogne is the place actually threatened. We could never succeed after that. Remember—we want that gunboat without a shot being fired. Once she is taken, Mr Syvret will bring her back to me while Mr Northmore and Mr Renouf will take her place with the *Panic*. Is that all clear?"

There were no further questions and the group dispersed, Le Couteur going to *Pauline* with Syvret, Northmore to *Panic* with Renouf. Delancey turned to Mather and asked him what odds he would offer.

"About even, sir, at best. We know too little about the officers, one of whom will need to have exceptional courage and resolution."

"We know that Northmore is a good man. Of the others I liked best the eagerness of Renouf."

"I agree, sir. That youngster was full of fight, to judge from his looks. But he has probably never been in battle and may change his tune when under fire. What will you do, sir, if the French gunboats remain in harbour?"

"I shall cancel the operation. I can order Le Couteur to follow the French back to base. I could never order anyone to go in alone. That is asking too much."

Chapter Twelve

"PANIC"

VENGEANCE was still under easy sail at midnight when the bombardment of Wimereux began. The noise was impressive and the distant scene was lit by occasional flares. Delancey trained his night glass on Boulogne and watched for the expected reaction. Nothing happened for half an hour and then, after what seemed a lifetime, the French gunboats were glimpsed as they left harbour. There were only six of them, however, under sail but in no apparent haste.

"They are merely out to reconnoitre," said Delancey to Mather, "but there are enough to serve our purpose. Signal *Pauline* and *Panic* to make more sail."

When *Pauline* drew abreast of the frigate, Delancey hailed Le Couteur.

"Go in now but don't close with the gunboats until they begin to withdraw. Good luck!"

The *Pauline* and *Panic* drew ahead and the noise of the bombardment intensified, probably because the bomb-vessels had opened fire. Flares were being used by both sides and it seemed that the Rear-Admiral was attacking with vigour. It could be assumed (or at least hoped) that the French gunboat commanders were looking towards Wimereux and would take no notice of *Pauline*, a stray fishing boat.

"I can make out their recognition light," said Mather at last. "Red over two white."

"And our craft," said Delancey, "have now hoisted the same. I could wish now that a shorter time had been allowed for the bombardment."

"Yes, sir, but bomb-vessels always take an hour to find their target."

"That's true."

At long last the distant thunder of gunfire died away and a man in the foretop reported that the gunboats were on their way back to Boulogne. Now the flares became infrequent and it was more difficult to see what was happening. Delancey decided to give Le Couteur some closer support.

"Make more sail, Mr Mather," he ordered, and the *Vengeance* heeled a little before the westerly breeze. The decks were already cleared for action but now the men stood to their guns and Delancey made his tour of inspection. He foresaw no immediate action but took the routine precautions. When he returned to the quarterdeck he was unable at first to see what was happening. Then a flare lit the scene and he could see, for an instant, that his plan had miscarried. It looked as if *Pauline* had taken the last gunboat but the other five had gone about and were going to the rescue. There was the sound now of gunfire and musketry and Delancey realised that *Pauline* was no match for her opponents and might be taken in another twenty minutes. The time had come to intervene and he did so by lighting a flare and firing a gun, enough to show his presence. In the light, however, of a second flare he could see that *Pauline* was still under attack, the French evidently hoping to recapture their gunboat before the frigate could come within effective range. The only consolation was that *Panic,* which could be glimpsed well north of the *Pauline,* had sensibly kept out of the firing and might not even have been seen by the enemy. The next obvious move in the game was for the *Vengeance* to steer so as to cut off the gunboat's retreat. But this would have attracted the fire of the shore batteries—and, in any case, the capture of gunboats was not the object in view. Delancey crowded on more sail and opened fire with his bow chasers. Although the range was still extreme the effect was immediate and the gunboats began to pull away from *Pauline,* using their oars rather than their sails to facilitate their escape to windward. The clouds had drifted aside and a half moon lit the scene enough to show that *Pauline* had the captured gunboat close alongside and that *Panic* was tacking towards her. All firing in the area had died away but it seemed, as the distance lessened, that *Pauline* had sustained some damage, as might seem inevitable. She was hove to and her crew's only visible activity was in attempting to repair her rigging.

As the frigate came within hail Le Couteur, using his speaking trumpet, reported that his craft had been hulled in two places and was leaking. "I submit, sir, that we abandon the operation and return to port."

"Is the captured gunboat undamaged?" asked Delancey.

"Yes, sir," replied Le Couteur. "We have her crew below hatches."

"Very well," said Delancey. "Keep your prisoners on board and return to base. Leave the gunboat with me."

"Aye, aye, sir." The relief was obvious in Le Couteur's tone of voice, backed up as it was by the sound of the pumps at work.

"So that is the finish," said Mather, not without a trace of satisfaction.

"Why so?" asked Delancey, rather coldly.

"Well, sir, we have no means now of saving the crew of *Panic*."

"On the contrary, we have the captured gunboat, Mr Mather."

"Yes, sir, but you said yourself that an extra gunboat—seven now instead of six—would cause alarm at once."

"That is quite possible but it is a risk we must take. The operation will proceed as planned but with this difference. I shall now take command of the captured gunboat, with Mr Syvret as second in command. You will command this ship in my absence."

"But, sir, this is near suicide! Your life is too valuable to throw away on such a hazardous mission. I beg you to send me or another officer."

"I said, Mather, that I could never order anyone else to go in alone. Well, I hold to that. So the task falls to me."

By now the *Panic* was within hail and Delancey ordered Northmore to follow the French gunboats into Boulogne according to plan. "One change, however—you will no longer be brought out by *Pauline* but by the captured gunboat which will be on your heels. Off with you and make all speed you can."

Northmore needed no exhortation and it was left to man the remaining gunboat, hastily arming the seamen as they jumped into her. Syvret followed and then Delancey himself. The moon was now hidden again and it was in almost complete darkness that the gunboat headed after her consort. Both vessels had the correct recognition lights and those borne by the last French gunboat were just visible, at half a mile, from

Panic. The weakness of the arrangements, which there had been no time to remedy, was that all the French clothing which the captured gunboat's crew should have been wearing was on its way back to Deal in *Pauline*. Wasting no lamentations on that subject, Delancey turned to Syvret and asked him abruptly whether their craft had a name.

"I have seen no name, sir, and have concluded that she is merely Gunboat Number 379."

"It is time she had a name. We are both from Guernsey, Mr Syvret. Where is your home there?"

"My father has a house in the new part of St Peter Port—Hauteville."

"The fashionable quarter, eh? Very well, then. We name this craft the gunboat *Hauteville*. Her task is to rescue the crew of the explosion vessel *Panic* after the fuses have been lit. Have you been in battle before, Mr Syvret?"

"No, sir."

"Then your future will depend a great deal on your conduct tonight, above all on your presence of mind. Should I be wounded, you will find yourself in command with many lives depending on your skill and timing. What about your own pistols, to begin with? Have you checked their priming?"

"Yes, sir."

"Good. Do you think we have lessened the distance between us and *Panic*?"

"I think we have, sir, and I think we should. *Panic* has a cargo and we don't."

"Correct. Unluckily, we lost time at the beginning, owing to the damage sustained by *Pauline*. Never mind, we are going to succeed."

To find the entrance to Boulogne harbour was unexpectedly easy even on a dark night, the pierheads being marked by lights. The *Panic* headed confidently for the gap and *Hauteville* followed, but now at little more than a cable's distance. Where things went wrong was in the very harbour mouth. Delancey heard a confused noise—with shouts and two or three pistol shots—and guessed at once what had happened. The French had detailed some boat to row guard and *Panic* had fairly collided with her. He had known all along that there could be a guard boat, but hoped that the French might have forgotten what was, in fact, an obvious precaution.

"Pull for your lives!" Delancey rapped out the order and then added, "*Panic* is in trouble. Pull!"

Adding to the sense of urgency, he drew one of his pistols and saw to it that young Syvret did the same. Ahead in the gloom *Panic* seemed to be more the centre of argument than conflict. His guess was that she had already been taken. She looked the part at any distance but not at close range, with her bulging tarpaulin amidships and her reduced number of oarsmen. He wondered how young Renouf's Alderney French was being accepted. The boy was fluent enough but his accent would be peculiar. The babble of voices grew louder as *Hauteville* closed on the scene and Delancey could see now that the guard boat was alongside *Panic,* both vessels motionless. He guessed that *Panic*'s men had been heavily outnumbered. Wrapped in his boat cloak, he stood up as the gunboat swept alongside the explosion vessel, the coxswain telling his men to back water. Without hesitation, Delancey jumped on board *Panic* and thundered (in French):

"What is going on here?"

It was Renouf who replied in the same language:

"We have been stopped, Captain, by this officer, who evidently knows nothing of our mission."

Renouf was facing a young but burly French officer whose sword was drawn. Just beyond them lay Northmore, perhaps knocked unconscious (or perhaps dead?) as a result of the first encounter.

"What is this, young man?" roared Delancey. "What do you think you are doing? Why have you attacked a French gunboat? Why have you wounded a brother officer? What will the Emperor do when he hears of this? Are you insane? Have I to put you under arrest?"

Taken aback, the French enseigne de vaisseau began to explain that the gunboat looked suspicious, was not typical of her class.

"She is different, you say? Of course she is different! We have just captured her from those English pigs, these murderers and madmen! Try to stop us and you will face a court martial! Take your sacred boat to hell out of this before I ram the craft down your throat! The English are up to some filthy trick with craft like this, made to look like ours. There may be a whole flotilla of them! Can't you see that the Admiral must know of this at the earliest possible moment? Can't you understand that our mission is of the utmost importance? Can't you understand anything? Stand to attention, imbecile! Put your hat on straight. Try to look like an officer even if you have to behave like a fool! Go back to your miserable boat and look out for the enemy. Take yourself off before I shoot you for mutiny."

The Frenchman was overwhelmed by mere force of personality, muttering apologies and scrambling back into the

guard boat, followed by his men. Delancey gave him no time
to recover his dignity but yelled after him: "Don't just sit there
in your sacred boat! Back to your proper place! Move! If I so
much as see you again I shall have you back on the lower deck."

The boats had drifted to a point within hail of the pierhead
on the starboard side and a voice could be heard from overhead, someone (an artillery officer?) asking what the
disturbance was about. Delancey bawled a reply which seemed
to serve its purpose:

"Some half-wit son of a fishwife has tried to prevent our
return to base. All is well now—no cause for alarm. I think the
enemy have been driven off. Their attack on Wimereux came
to nothing."

Speaking now to Renouf, Delancey told him to proceed up
harbour and then, shouting to Syvret, told him (in French) to
take command of *Hauteville*. Northmore, it was obvious, was
in no state to command *Panic*, the crew of which had been
weakened by the loss of two men wounded in the recent skirmish. This made the task no easier but they were past the main
defences and it remained to enter the inner basin with the non-
chalance of seamen who were based there. There were many
craft anchored in the river but *Panic* attracted no further notice,
the oarsmen rowing steadily and the coxswain holding close to
the starboard side of the channel. *Hauteville* followed at a
respectful distance and the boat being towed by *Panic* seemed
to be in good order, with one man in charge of her. Renouf
assured Delancey that flint, steel, and tinder were all ready but
that they planned to light their linstocks from a lantern which
they had concealed but lit. The youngsters were excited but
seemingly unafraid.

Several hazards remained, the first being the possibility— perhaps the likelihood—of there being some sort of guard set on the entrance to the inner basin. There might even be a watchword. Granted that difficulty were overcome (supposing it existed) the other hazards would follow the lighting of the fuses. There might be men at hand who would extinguish them. There would certainly be a hue and cry after the explosion took place. What were their chances of escape? Remote? One of the worst risks would be from their own grenades. If they survived all that, the escape down the river would be aided by the ebb tide and the general confusion. Watching for the expected opening to starboard, Delancey wondered whether he had ever been involved before in such a mad enterprise. It was his own plan and events—the loss of Le Couteur and Northmore—had finally left him to execute it himself. This was just as well in one way. No one else from the *Vengeance* could have bluffed his way past the guard boat. But would another such bluff bring him safely back to the frigate? After the explosion the French would be in a very different mood, furious with themselves and with each other, ready to shoot anyone at sight. To reach the target had not, so far, been too difficult. To withdraw after the blow had been struck might very well prove all but impossible.

Just when he had begun to wonder whether he had over-shot the entrance the quayside to starboard suddenly ended and two lights could be seen marking the passage, which was all too narrow from the British point of view. Glancing back, it was just possible to glimpse the faithful *Hauteville*, keeping her distance. Reassured on that point, Delancey told his coxswain to steer for the middle and then, as the *Panic* went in, the challenge came from the starboard side.

"Qui vive? What gunboat is that?"

"Numéro 379, damaged after an encounter with the enemy."

"Bring her in closer."

"What was that? I can't hear you."

"Bring her in so that I can check the number."

"I can't hear you. I'll report back when the gunboat is safely moored."

"I must see her first."

"What's that? Who am I? I am Delacroix, frigate captain."

All this time the gunboat was drawing away from the sentry post and she was actually out of earshot before the discussion ended. Ahead lay the mass of gunboats, moored, as Delancey had heard, to mooring chains stretched across the basin and supported by buoys. To reach the centre of the flotilla seemed at first impossible, the craft being so close together. Heading to port, Delancey hoped to find an empty berth. There was none but there was space at the end of the line and *Panic* proceeded slowly along that side of the basin. Once more there seemed to be no room between the crowded vessels. When the gap appeared Delancey had almost given up hope of finding it. There had to be a passage somewhere, however, if only to allow the French to row guard, and there it was, narrow but sufficient.

"Starboard—hard over!" said Delancey and the *Panic* passed into a sort of corridor, with gunboats moored on either side. He looked again for a gap and in vain. One thing clear, however, was that all the craft were unmanned, the guards being all on the quayside. So the opportunity existed to make a gap where there was none. Bringing *Panic* up to a gunboat which seemed to be in about the middle of the line, Delancey jumped on board and presently was able to study the system of moorings. There were chains, as he had expected, but each individual gunboat was moored to its chain by an ordinary hemp cable which went round her foremast before being bent to a solid cleat in the vessel's bows. To unbend the cable was a simple matter and Delancey, having freed one gunboat, returned to *Panic* and told his oarsmen to back water. With the ebb tide's assistance they pulled that gunboat out. Repeating the manoeuvre with a second one, beyond the first, Delancey set both of them adrift and fastened *Panic* by the same means to the chain where the second gunboat had been moored. After bringing the boat alongside, Delancey gave the order to remove the tarpaulin and throw it overboard. When that had been done he gave Renouf the order to light the fuses. Four men lit their linstocks from the hidden lantern and scrambled along the gunboat, lighting the fuses with all the speed they had gained in rehearsal. It was quickly done but the French took alarm at this moment. Some sentry may have seen the pinpoints of light or heard the drifting gunboats bump into each other. A shot was fired in the air and this was followed, within a minute or two, by the sound of a distant bugle.

"Man the boat!" said Delancey, and followed the others only after he had seen the half-conscious Northmore helped aboard.

"Give way—and *pull!*" was Delancey's next order and he told the coxswain to steer to port, his aim being to return by the other side of the basin, the far side, that is, from his line of entry. This was partly on principle, partly because the bugle call had come from the other direction. With the alarm already given, escape was going to be very difficult indeed.

Delancey's boat, a cutter, reached the end of the passage and turned to starboard when the far quayside was reached. There was no challenge so far and, looking back, Delancey could see nothing of the pinpoints of light which they had left, flickering, on board *Panic*. That did not mean that they were invisible from the higher level of the wharf. Assuming that these had been seen, the French would react by sending an armed boat into the basin with orders to investigate, and Delancey felt a moment of sympathy for the young officer to whom this duty would fall. There might be twenty minutes to go (give or take five minutes either way) but who was to know that? Another and more distant bugle sounded and then the noise could be heard of men running at the double on the far side of the basin. Delancey was about to tell his oarsmen to put their backs into it but he realised that they were doing their best, knowing the situation as well as he did. Their bow wave was smacking against the stonework as they passed. Now they were at the corner of the basin and turned sharply to starboard.

It was while they were approaching the entrance to the basin that Delancey, who was listening for it, heard the approach of the guard boat. A young officer's voice could be heard, accompanied by the creak of the rowlocks and the splash of the oars. Both boats were nearing the entrance, although from opposite directions, and Delancey guessed that the French boat would be there first. That he was right about this was confirmed when the French boat hailed the men on guard. He could distinguish no actual words but could imagine some youngster asking, "Which way did they go?" or words to that effect. With any luck words and gestures would induce the guard boat to turn left. Consulting his watch by the light of the hidden lantern, Delancey saw that it was fifteen minutes since the fuses were lit. In theory at least the guard boat might be there in time.

"Vast pulling!" he whispered, and his boat glided silently towards the entrance. As he did so he glimpsed the French boat rounding the far side and pulling away from him. "Pass me a musket!" he muttered and was handed one which he checked and found to be loaded and primed. "Hard a-port!" he whispered to the coxswain and the boat drifted slowly towards the entrance. Before the corner was fairly turned and while the guard boat was still in sight he aimed at it carefully and fired. It may be doubted whether he hit his target but the result was very much what he expected. The boat turned sideways, his fire was returned, and then the boat swung back towards him. The musket balls spattered the quayside harmlessly and he knew that *Panic* was now pretty safe from interference. At the same moment he became aware of another French boat approaching the entrance from the river. To avoid an encounter with her—and hoping that this boat would be fired upon by the other—he told the coxswain to creep close to the stonework to port, hoping thus to be less visible. These tactics were successful up to a point, the newcomers being distracted by the recent sound of firing within the basin.

"Pull for dear life!" Delancey whispered and his boat headed for the river. He glanced again at his watch—about five minutes still to go. At that moment a solid object—presumably a round shot—was dropped from the quayside above him and crashed through the bottom of the boat. Whipping off his boat cloak he stuffed it into the hole, which was just beyond stroke, and held it in position.

"Starboard!" he shouted, and the next round shot fell clear of the boat, splashing the oarsmen but doing no other damage.

They had taken a lot of water on board, however, and would do well to keep afloat for another ten minutes even with bailing. But now there was a new danger. As they drew away from the quayside, avoiding the cold shot, they became a better target for musketry. He heard an officer giving the word for a volley and the muskets fired together. Most of the shots missed but two men were hit and the boat was holed again somewhere forward.

"Pull!" he shouted. "Hard a-port!"

Still under fire, the boat turned the corner and was safe, more or less, from the other danger; the one the French did not know about. The range was lengthening for the marksmen on the quayside but the second guard boat was in full pursuit. Delancey's boat was likely to sink in another five minutes and his only consolation lay in the fact that *Hauteville* could be seen and was coming their way. Help was at hand but would probably come too late for the wounded and the non-swimmers. Turning to the coxswain, Hemsley, Delancey said, "I want you and Sapworth to save Mr Northmore when this boat sinks. You are both good swimmers and he is too good a man to lose."

At that moment *Panic* exploded with a noise like the end of the world. For an instant the whole scene was light as day. Then it was dark again but with grenades bursting all over the basin and some of them falling harmlessly into the river. It was impossible to judge what damage the gunboats had sustained but there was a dull flickering light which suggested that at least some of them were on fire. Watching, fascinated, Delancey suddenly found that he was up to his knees in water. The boat was sinking beneath him.

"There is the *Hauteville!*" he shouted to his men, pointing.

"Swim for it!" The swimmers obeyed at once, Hemsley and Sapworth supported Northmore with an oar under each arm, and Delancey told the non-swimmers to use their oars to support them. Then he threw off his coat and swam after Northmore, cursing meanwhile, to find the water so cold. In the ordinary way all the swimmers could have been overtaken by the pursuing guard boat.

What saved them was the French attempt to save the remainder. By the time the last of these had been rescued (and only one was drowned) those who could swim were on board *Hauteville*. Nor did it immediately occur to the Frenchmen that *Hauteville* was anything but what she seemed, one of their own gunboats showing the correct recognition lights. As the guard boat came within hail, Delancey shouted in French "Well done! We have the other prisoners on board. They must all be raving mad! Did they expect to escape? Anyway we have them now." Going about smartly the *Hauteville* began to drop down river on the ebb. Shivering and wet through as he was, Delancey had still to save the rest of his men. For the moment, it would seem, the French were stunned by the explosion. They would react later and look with immediate suspicion on any vessel seen leaving harbour. By tomorrow incidentally, half a dozen officers, naval and military, would be under arrest and facing a court martial. Delancey had a passing moment of pity for the youngster who commanded the first guard boat to appear. He had turned back when fired on—well, who wouldn't?—but he doubted whether the French were in the mood to accept excuses.

Proceeding down river among all the anchored fishing boats, *Hauteville* was repeatedly hailed by men on harbour watch who wanted to know what had happened. His teeth chattering, Delancey shouted to each in turn that there had been an explosion in the new basin and that nobody as yet knew the cause. Were the English responsible? To this question, when it came, Delancey replied that they could never have penetrated the defences. The explosion must have been an accident due to someone's carelessness. *Hauteville's* passage down the river was surprisingly uneventful. If she ran into trouble it would be in the harbour mouth and perhaps with the same guard boat. The trick, he knew, was to seize the initiative. As they drew near the entrance he could see that a guard boat was fairly in their way. When within hail he asked questions first.

"Has any vessel left harbour since that explosion was heard?"

"No, Captain, and we have been here since nightfall."

"No craft has passed you, not even a rowing boat?"

"No, Captain. What has happened though?"

"We don't know. We think, however, that the explosion was probably accidental. Supposing it were an English crime, typical of these treacherous pigs, we mustn't let the criminals escape. We have been sent to give you support. Tell the gunners ashore that you have been joined by Gunboat Number 379."

Hauteville hove to while the guard boat ran its errand. After some shouting in the distance Delancey made sail again and presently took up position just outside the harbour mouth, an obvious menace to any craft attempting to escape. His position was impeccable but the ebb tide slowly carried him seawards and he was presently out of sight in the darkness. An hour later he was on board *Vengeance* and heading for base.

"Thank God that's over," he said to Mather. "Our losses are small and Northmore is recovering well from a knock on the head. We did all we set out to do. Renouf and Syvret behaved very properly in a situation of peril. I am not sure what I am going to say about Le Couteur."

"Well, sir, you would hardly question that *Pauline* was damaged."

"Yes, but how seriously? Or were a couple of shot-holes being used as an excuse?"

"We shall have the carpenter's report, sir."

"So we shall. I never thought that Le Couteur was a particularly active officer. I am glad to think that he is not one of mine."

"What havoc, sir, was caused by the explosion?"

"I have no means of knowing. It took place as planned, in the middle of the basin and we saw the grenades scattering in all directions. Half of them will have been wasted but some of the incendiaries may have found a target."

"And the flames would spread, surely, from one gunboat to another?"

"I doubt it, Mr Mather. Seamen, dockyard workers, and soldiers should have been there in ten minutes. All fires would be extinguished in twenty minutes after that. No, we have shaken their self-confidence. The actual damage done will be small, perhaps negligible."

"I hope, nevertheless, that your own leadership will be recognised."

"It won't even be made public. I was under orders to direct the attack, leaving the operation to Le Couteur and others. I don't even know how to word my report or to whom credit should be given. Through no fault of his own, Northmore was out of it. I shall have no words of praise for Le Couteur. Renouf and Syvret are mere children, neither of them ready for a commission. As for me, I had no business to be there at all."

"It is a miracle, sir, that you are alive."

"Alive, yes, but very exhausted and very wet. I shall go below and turn in. Take the frigate back to the Downs but call me, of course, in case of need."

Delancey went to bed but failed at first to sleep. The purpose of his raid had been mainly political, to show Parliament and public that the government recently returned to power had introduced a new vigour into the waging of war. Rear-Admiral Knight would have gained approval and perhaps even some official sign of recognition. Pitt and Dundas would be pleased. But what of the French reaction? Napoleon would be furious. The explosion had been in the presence of the French army or a large part of it. Its importance could, of course, be minimised. It could be described as a mere pinprick. But the fact remained that the British had gone into the inner harbour at Boulogne and it was quite useless to pretend that their attempt had failed. French soldiers, who were to embark under the protection of French seamen, would begin to regard the planned invasion as suicidal. The seamen who would be responsible for transporting the Army of England could not even keep the British out of the gunboat basin at Boulogne. If the British could do that at the main point of embarkation, what would they do to the invasion craft in mid-Channel? If the Emperor were to restore morale he would have to strike back quickly not with propaganda but with action. What would he do? Putting himself in Napoleon's place, Delancey tried to think of a counter-stroke, an exploit for which the resources existed and which would overshadow recent events at Boulogne. It was no easy problem but Napoleon was no ordinary man. What was Britain's most vulnerable point and how could it be reached?

Delancey fell asleep before he could answer either question, nor did he solve it before breakfast next day. He had many other things on his mind, incidentally, not the least of them the wording of that confounded report. He was to claim afterwards that while he had not known the answer to his question, he had known—and was perhaps alone in knowing—what question to ask.

Chapter Thirteen

WALMER CASTLE

D ELANCEY looked about him and thought there was something to be said for the life of a flag officer. Rear-Admiral Knight's cabin was furnished in a civilised style, no doubt at his wife's instigation. The sunlight streaming through the stern windows was reflected from mahogany and silver, from glass decanters and gilt picture frames. The *Antelope* might be of an obsolete class but she was at least a two-decked ship with room for a flag officer in addition to the captain. Would he ever achieve his flag? It seemed most unlikely. The promotion would come on his deathbed if it came at all. But what had Fiona said? "You are a legend, while Knight has nothing more than a command." That was nonsense but there was something uneasy about Knight's show of authority. He asserted himself but with an obvious effort as if apologising for his lack of distinction. But the Rear-Admiral had nearly finished reading Delancey's report. He was about to make the inevitable comment.

"Considering the brilliance of the exploit—and I use that expression deliberately—your report, Delancey, is not very informative. It is carefully worded but the effect is—what word do I mean?"

"Laconic, sir?"

"Exactly! Laconic. You give credit, moreover, to Mr Syvret, master's mate, to Mr Renouf, midshipman, and to no one else.

What about Le Couteur? He took that French gunboat, after all."

"He did that and then found an excuse to take *Pauline* back to the Downs."

"An excuse which you accepted."

"I did not accept that *Pauline* was badly damaged. I accepted the fact that Le Couteur lacked the courage to take her into Boulogne."

"You say nothing about Northmore."

"What can I say? He was badly hurt at the outset and was rescued with some difficulty. He is an excellent young man but he was unlucky on this occasion and could do nothing to add to his reputation."

"Your story is that Syvret placed the explosion vessel in position and lit the fuses, he and his men being rescued by Renouf, neither of them being fit for promotion. How could they do what they did without a more senior officer, to direct them? What part did you play, Delancey?"

"How could I enter Boulogne, sir? I was under orders to remain outside."

"And you would never disobey an order?"

"I have been taught from my youth that orders must be obeyed."

"So we split the credit between two mere children, neither of whom had been in battle before."

"But, surely, Admiral, the raid on Boulogne would have been impossible without your distracting the French by the bombardment of Wimereux. As for me, I might claim the credit for drawing up the plan which these youngsters were to execute."

"Both plan and execution were brilliant. I give you full credit for both. I shall add—since we are alone—that I also give you credit for being an accomplished liar. I know what happened, having other sources of information. You may be laconic but some of your men are not. Very well, then. Your report shall stand and my covering letter to the Board of Admiralty will fill in some of the gaps, making sense of what you omit. Have you any idea of the damage you did?"

"None at all, sir. The explosion took place in the middle of the inner basin. It should have destroyed the nearest gunboats. A few others may have been damaged by grenades but many of these fell in the river or on the quayside."

"Starting some fires?"

"Maybe, but they would have been extinguished within the next ten minutes. The French were all over the area before I— I mean, before Mr Syvret—had gone."

"Yes, they would be."

"The damage we did was to French morale. It seems to me that the Emperor must order his men to retaliate."

"But what can they do, in heaven's name? They have no men-of-war in the Channel, nothing bigger than a gun-brig. Their sail of the line are all blockaded in port from Brest southwards. What retaliation is possible?"

"Well, Admiral, I know what I should do in Napoleon's place, although I have no reason to think that his ideas and mine are the same. At the conference held at Dover in April—or was it on some other occasion?—I remember someone suggesting that the French might raid Brighton when the Prince Regent is there. Were I the Emperor I should rather raid Walmer Castle when the Prime Minister is there. Pitt's capture would be a master stroke, a brilliant preliminary to an invasion attempt. It might not seriously affect our strategy—some people would say that our subsequent conduct of the war would be improved—but it would shake our confidence. To have the Prime Minister in such an exposed position has always seemed to be a mistaken policy."

"He sees himself commanding his volunteer battalions in battle. But we indeed run a risk in having him so often at Walmer. Luckily, their lordships are aware of this. I have orders to station a frigate off Walmer whenever the Prime Minister is in residence, and the *Lizard* is already there."

"So the French can see at a glance whether he is in residence or not?"

"That idea did occur to me. But the *Lizard* could beat off any force they have available in the Channel and the sound of gunfire would alert every garrison for miles round. Our preparations seem to me tolerably complete. What more can we do?"

"Why, sir, we can send for Mr Xenophon and ask him for the latest news from the French coast. If they have a plan he is likely to know about it."

"Their lordships had the same idea. Mr Xenophon is to be in Deal tomorrow and we shall have supper together at the Three Kings. I should like you to join us."

The Admiral had secured a private room but nothing was said about secret matters until the servants had withdrawn. Mr Xenophon, who looked as sinister as ever in his rather theatrical way, then opened the discussion before the Admiral could call upon him. A decanter of Madeira was on the table and the candles were reflected in the polished mahogany. It was good to be ashore.

"You should know, Admiral, that your recent raid on Boulogne gave great satisfaction to all members of the Cabinet.

Your conduct was highly approved and Captain Delancey's name has been brought to the attention of the Prime Minister. I have been at pains to discover what you actually achieved. Seven gunboats were destroyed, five others more or less damaged. Two soldiers were killed by grenades and three seamen wounded. These losses are trivial but the Emperor's wrath has caused other casualties. The Captain of the Port has been dismissed. Five naval and military officers are to face a court martial. One junior officer, commanding a guard boat, committed suicide, before the Court of Inquiry was even convened. Everyone concerned is trying to ensure that the blame shall fall on someone else. Defensive precautions have reached a crescendo of inconvenience and several harmless civilians have been shot by sentinels anxious to show their vigilance. There is greater friction than ever between army and navy. The only way to restore confidence is to plan some counter-stroke before the Emperor appears at Boulogne. There can be no doubt that such a counter-strike is being planned or prepared. On the assumption that the invasion itself may be planned for July, this preliminary raid must take place in June."

"During the month which has now begun," added the Admiral. "But the French have no men-of-war in the Channel."

"Just so," replied Mr Xenophon. "We can assume therefore that some secret weapon will be used. The new weapons of which we have information are three: the steamship, the catamaran, a floating box filled with gunpowder, and the *Nautilus*."

"And the *Nautilus* was last heard of at Brest," commented the Admiral. "She underwent her trials there."

"That is perfectly true," said Mr Xenophon, "but we are now informed that an enlarged and improved vessel—call her

Nautilus II—was built at Paris to Fulton's design and is now undergoing trials at Le Havre."

"So that the French plan must probably depend upon that vessel?" suggested the Admiral.

"Not necessarily," replied Mr Xenophon, "it could depend upon the steamship or the catamaran."

"It would, in any event," said Delancey, "depend upon good weather and a dark night."

"Which points to the third or fourth week in June," replied the Admiral. "Could we persuade the Prime Minister to stay in London for those two weeks?"

"I doubt it," replied Mr Xenophon. "The Prime Minister has spent nearly his whole life at his desk, but he now sees himself as a man of action. Talk of danger and he will move towards the sound of guns. He takes very seriously his role as an amateur soldier. Some crisis might keep him in London but he would prefer to be on the invasion coast, ready to sell his life dearly, sword in hand, at the head of his troops."

"I sometimes think," sighed the Admiral, "that war is better left to the professionals."

"As I claim to be one of them," said Delancey, "may I be allowed to suggest a possible way of meeting this threat?"

"I should be more than grateful," replied the Admiral. "Tell us what you have in mind."

"My proposal, sir, is that you relieve me of other duties, detaching *Vengeance* to deal with this one threat—as advised, of course, by Mr Xenophon—and trust me to frustrate the enemy's design. I am no genius, sir, nor do I pretend to have any exceptional abilities, but some success might be achieved by an officer who had no other duties to distract him. You,

Admiral, have a dozen other things on your mind. If we are to defeat the enemy's scheme we shall do it by thinking, not by force."

"I incline, sir," said Mr Xenophon after a pause, "to support Captain Delancey's proposal. Considering his recent success at Boulogne, I think him as likely to succeed as anyone else. I would promise to give him all the information I have. I can myself think of no better plan."

"Very well," said the Admiral, after a minute's inward struggle, "you may consider yourself detached, Delancey, on a particular service in which you can count on every assistance from Mr Xenophon. The nature of your task will not be disclosed to anyone outside this room. Refill your glass, Mr Xenophon, and we'll drink to Delancey's success."

That ended the meeting, Delancey going back to his frigate but agreeing to meet Mr Xenophon on the following day. Immediately, he wanted to be alone and he wanted to think. In previous ships and during other campaigns he had acted as the leader of a team, relying on Mather's support and discussing each problem with his officers or with some of them. On this occasion he was in a strange position, isolated by the need for secrecy, unable to consult anyone but Mr Xenophon. He had often been in battle before but this was a battle of wits, a war to be waged while he paced his cabin or scribbled notes which he would afterwards destroy. When he finally summarised his notes he found that they comprised a tentative outline of a possible French plan, reading as follows:

Object: To capture Mr Pitt alive. Once this were done the return voyage would present no problem. No one would fire on a ship with so eminent a prisoner on board—one the French could hang if their vessel were attacked.

Means: Steamship, catamaran, *Nautilus II.* The French would use *all three* in the one operation, the steamship to cross the Channel in a dead calm (if possible), the catamaran to remove the *Lizard, Nautilus II* to carry out the raid on Walmer Castle, assisted perhaps by spies already in the area.

Date: Latter half of June, on moonless night for preference.

Command: No obvious name, but spy ashore could be Fabius, once active in Ireland and quite ruthless enough for such an operation as this.

Possible plan

I To intercept the steamship near Boulogne or any other point of departure.

II To intercept the steamship at sea.

III To intercept the raiding party near Walmer Castle.

Because of the recent raid Plan I must be deemed impossible. Plan II would not be feasible on a dark night. So we must adopt Plan III, with possible sacrifice of *Lizard.* Can Mr X provide the shore party?

When Delancey went ashore again next day in the forenoon, he was in civilian clothes. He did not want Mr Xenophon to be seen with a naval officer. Why had the man to look so obviously a secret agent? Vanity? Of his real ability there could be no doubt at all. He was, in any case, the man with whom

Delancey had to work. They met by arrangement at the Three Kings and Delancey at once proposed a walk in the direction of Walmer Castle.

"If we are in the open air, sir, the day being fine, there is no danger of anyone listening at the keyhole."

"Very true, sir. Secrecy is vital—so much so that we had best defer anything of moment until we are clear of the town."

They walked along the coast, keeping to a path trodden mainly by preventive men or foot patrols of infantry. It was a fine day with cloud patterns chasing each other over the sea. From their left came the sound of the breakers and all around them was the cry of the gulls. Delancey was enjoying his day ashore and said as much.

"You will hardly understand the pleasure I feel in treading the turf and smelling the mere scent of trodden grass."

"And yet," replied Mr Xenophon, "the enemy is there, almost in sight, planning the destruction of all we value."

"Very true. How far is it to Walmer?"

"About two miles."

"I propose we rest at the half-way point. We can talk then and I will give you the conclusions to which I have been led since our last meeting."

They were presently seated on the grass and Delancey produced his page of notes. To seawards of them lay the frigate *Lizard* at anchor, showing that Pitt was in residence. When Delancey had finished reading there was a minute's silence. Then Mr Xenophon asked his first question:

"Can you describe the man you call Fabius?"

"Easily, sir. He is of medium height, rather fat, with a white flabby face, sometimes wears spectacles, often disguised as a priest or a clergyman. He is a foreigner but his English is perfect or almost so. He was the man who tried to organise a revolt in western Ireland, supposed to coincide with the French landing in 1798."

"An impossible task," commented Mr Xenophon, "but I know the agent you describe. He passes under a variety of different names but the code-word, Fabius, is new to me. I agree with you that he will be involved in the present French plans, supposing there is one. He is the best agent the French have ever had in Britain. If your suppositions are correct—and I must remind you that they are no more than suppositions—he will be in Deal at this moment. Where else could he be?"

"But do you accept my reasoning?"

"It is logical enough but based on little but your assumption about what the French will do. They may have some totally different plan. I'll admit, however, that there is one reason for supposing that your guess is right. I know from recent and reliable intelligence that the *Nautilus II* is now at Boulogne, having arrived there two days after your visit. I have no news of any steam-vessel."

"Your agents in Deal should be able to recognise Fabius, if he is there."

"I wouldn't be too certain of that. He is a master of disguise and probably wears the uniform of a British army officer."

"Unless he is employed as a gardener at Walmer Castle itself."

"Just so. I am not too sanguine about his being identified, I have greater reliance on hearing of any steam-vessel which appears on the French coast opposite us. There are Deal fishermen who give me the news from Boulogne."

"They daren't put in there, surely?"

"No, they meet with French fishermen in mid-Channel and exchange information."

"So they work for both sides?"

"Of course. They are paid by both sides. It is some compensation for the way in which their ordinary business is interrupted in time of war. If a French steamship were to move from Le Havre to Boulogne I should hear of it. I should accept it, moreover, as evidence that a plan such as you describe—or something like it—is about to be put in execution, and almost certainly before the end of the month. Tell me this, though. If we surmise that your supposition is correct, what do we want to do? Do we want to destroy the enemy vessels on sight? Or do we want to catch their men ashore?"

"We want, surely, to catch them ashore. If we do that we might catch Fabius as well."

"You should be employed in intelligence work, sir. You have too good a brain to be pacing the quarterdeck."

"I leave all that undercover activity to the Duke of Bouillon. I doubt, however, that he can help us in Kent. I suspect that his agents cover the ground between St Malo and Brest."

"An able man, the Duke, and I say nothing against him but his bailiwick, as you say, lies further to the westward. I shall let you know at once if I hear tell of that steam-vessel."

"Thank you. Now it seems to me that we have to make a plan. I shall remain at anchor in the Downs for the time being and I can at any time provide a landing party of armed seamen and marines. I should like to warn the captain of the *Lizard* but am under orders to say nothing to him or to anyone else. I want to look at Walmer Castle this morning and study the ground between it and the beach. From the map it looks extremely vulnerable."

"It is vulnerable and Mr Pitt resists all special measures of defence. He will have no troops in the immediate vicinity because they would disturb the game. He takes out a gun from time to time and occasionally bags a wood pigeon or rabbit. He takes very seriously his role as Warden of the Cinque Ports, with responsibility for defending the shores of Kent. This position carries with it a salary and this he feels he should earn. So far as security goes, Mr Pitt is not, therefore, an easy man to assist. As for Walmer Castle, it dates from the time of Henry the Eighth, has been modernised as a residence but not as a fortification. We shall see it in a few minutes."

Walmer Castle, as they approached it, seemed anything but formidable; a low squat building with embrasures, planned for four rounded bastions and in the general form of a four-leafed clover. It was oddly unimpressive but comfortable, it was said, as a country house. It had a dry moat and a flag fluttered from the flagpole, indicating that Pitt was in residence. The castle was clearly more of antiquarian than military interest. Nor was there anything to prevent strangers from inspecting it, as Fabius had probably done. Mr Xenophon had learnt that the drawbridge was raised at night and the path they were treading was obviously patrolled. There was no guard in the castle itself, probably because the accommodation was wanted for Pitt's servants and guests, carriages and horses. It was quite close to the shore, being originally sited so that its artillery would cover the beach.

"From the French point of view," said Delancey finally, "the place is ideal."

Mr Xenophon agreed that the French could have done no

better had they planned it themselves. There was nothing between the beach and the ramparts apart from the moat and there did not appear to be a sentinel, even, on the gate. Pitt's Cinque Port Volunteers or Fencibles were said to number about three thousand but they all slept at home in their beds. It might be thought probable that some of Pitt's servants were enrolled in this corps and suitably armed but they would amount to little more than a corporal's guard. His retinue must be limited in number by the circumstance that he was, as it was rumoured, almost bankrupt. There were troops and to spare within a mile or two in three directions but Walmer itself was undefended. The nightly raising of the drawbridge was due not to Pitt's vigilance, said Mr Xenophon, but to the insistence of colleagues in the Cabinet. The Castle's security depended almost entirely on the *Lizard,* still peacefully at anchor within perhaps a mile of the shore.

"Not an easy problem," concluded Mr Xenophon.

"No," agreed Delancey, "but we've already gone some little way towards a solution. Were the *Lizard* removed from the chessboard, the *Vengeance* is ready to take her place. She will remain in the Downs after the squadron has sailed."

"So you could land your marines and patrol the grounds?"

"What—without the Prime Minister coming to hear of it? I should be relieved of my command. I should never be employed again. You can reject that possibility from the outset."

Delancey met Mr Xenophon again in three days' time, once more at the Three Kings. By this time the secret agent had more news from Boulogne, news which he revealed as they paced the lawn.

"The French have a steam-vessel in the inner harbour, just

arrived from Le Havre under sail. My informants can tell me
nothing about her speed or the distance she can go or the fuel
she can load. She is schooner rigged, unarmed, and could measure about eighty tons."

"My guess," said Delancey, "is that she can travel at about
four knots in calm weather, more than that with a following
wind. She will have coal enough to cross the Channel but
might, in any case, tow a barge or lighter with a further supply, enough for the return passage. I have been aboard a steamer
called the *Charlotte Dundas* and would surmise that this French
craft has much the same performance. Tell me, how many
agents have you in Deal?"

"I have five in all."

"And have they heard or seen anything of Fabius?"

"Nothing at all but that need not surprise us. In time of
peace our informants might tell us of a stranger recently staying at the Hoop and Griffin, a man never seen before in these
parts and not landed from any ship in the Downs. But in
wartime there are too many strangers all the time. The Inn servants can tell us nothing. If we assume that Fabius wears a
uniform, that of a naval lieutenant or an army captain, who
will notice him? There will be twenty others of his rank, all
demanding attention at the same time, and the servants too
busy to remember any of them. His disguise will be good,
remember, but for which I might have identified him myself.
Since hearing of this steam-vessel I am convinced that he is
here, probably with other agents, and I am sure moreover that
the French do intend some sort of raid."

"Which can only be a raid on Walmer Castle. How simple
it would be if Pitt were a little more reasonable."

"He is a sick man, sir, headstrong, difficult, and irritable, impossible to advise."

"So we must meet this threat without his help. The crisis will come on the first calm day or, rather, night, after 15th June. What is the name of that steam-vessel—did your informants discover that?"

"She is called the *Corsican*."

"Boulogne harbour dries out with the tide. The *Corsican* will sail when there is water enough and reach the target area in about six hours, well before daylight. We shall be there before her. She will be visible, I should add, because of the sparks from her funnel."

"And that," muttered Mr Xenophon, "is something I never thought about."

Next day Delancey came ashore again but accompanied this time by his marine officer, Lieutenant Bartlett, by Northmore and Topley. He walked again to Walmer Castle and took these officers over the ground between its ramparts and the sea.

"Your men will be deployed on the seaward side of the path and your task will be to intercept any landing along this shore. The marines will be in the centre with the seamen, in two parties, on either side of them."

He defined their areas of responsibility and warned them to memorise every feature of the terrain. They would be in pitch darkness when the time came. They were to say nothing, incidentally, about this present exercise. "I should like to have brought the men along or the more senior of them, but I dared not risk their talking about it."

At supper ashore that evening with Mr Xenophon, Richard Delancey described his arrangements and then added: "The actual grounds of the Castle I leave to you and your men. I think, however, that I should come with you."

"Why, sir?"

"I have the best chance, I think, of recognising Fabius and he will approach the place, I take it, from the landward side."

"Yes, I think that his task will be to kidnap the Prime Minister, delivering him to a boat crew landed from the *Corsican*."

"But what about *Nautilus II*? That craft must have some role to play in the drama, but I can't at the moment see what her part is to be."

"Nor can I. Agreed, however, that you join my group. In dark civilian clothes, please, and armed only with pistols."

Chapter Fourteen

"NAUTILUS II"

O N 15 JUNE it was blowing a half gale from the south-west which was still a stiff breeze on the 17th. It fell calm on the evening of the next day with only a faint easterly wind. There was no means of knowing that the raid would take place on the night of the 18th/19th but the weather at least was suitable and the French could have no certainty that it would be as favourable again before the nights were moonlit once more. Delancey sent his men ashore and then landed so as to meet Mr Xenophon at the Three Kings. If all their calculations were right, the *Corsican* would already have left Boulogne and might be expected off Walmer any time after three in the morning. Mr Xenophon had a private room where he had provided supper for his five agents. If he was flamboyant in manner and dress, his men were quite the reverse. They were as carefully unremarkable as could be wished, medium in height, colour, and age, nondescript in clothing and expressionless in face. They were not introduced to Delancey by name but were described vaguely as "my friends." They each carried a walking stick and Delancey having occasion to move one of these, found it unexpectedly heavy. Seeing his look of surprise, Mr Xenophon explained that such a stick was called a pacifier. "We drill it partly hollow and pour in molten lead . . ."

From Mr Xenophon's final orders it was obvious that his men had been over the ground very carefully, certainly inside the castle ground and probably within the castle itself. They referred to a sketch-map of the place in which various points were marked A, B, C, and D. It appeared that Mr Xenophon would be at A, with Delancey and one of his men. Two other agents would be at B, two more at C, and all would close on D at a given signal. Delancey assured Mr Xenophon that seamen and marines were under strict orders to keep to seaward of the coastal path.

"I have introduced only one change into my plans as previously agreed. Two of my ship's boats will patrol the area beyond the line of the breakers, each commanded by a lieutenant. We have thus three lines of defence shoreward of the guard frigate. For an enemy landing party to reach the castle is all but impossible."

"I wouldn't say that," said Mr Xenophon. "You forget that Fabius and his men may be in the castle already."

"What, without your knowledge?"

"Conceivably, yes. We should be wrong to underestimate our opponent's ability."

"So the Prime Minister could have been murdered by now?"

"To murder him would not be very difficult. The present plan, if we have guessed aright, is to secure him as a captive and hostage. That is no easy task."

"Well, they have been fortunate so far. What little wind there was has died away to nothing. There is a flat calm and a dark night. From the French point of view it is now or never."

"We should be on our way," said Mr Xenophon, and led his party into the street. There his men separated and disappeared into the darkness. The night's adventure had begun and Delancey cursed inwardly about having sent his boats out on patrol, involving the risk of their clashing with boats from the guard frigate. But what else could he have done? He could not leave his commissioned officers without a role to play, useless as he thought them to be. Nor did they present the only hazard for the garrison commander at Deal knew nothing about the expected danger. One of his patrols could clash with the marines. Secrecy is essential and yet, he reflected grimly, there can be too much of it.

When *Corsican* appeared, just before 3 A.M., Delancey was sitting on top of Walmer Castle's boundary wall, looking fixedly seawards. Beside him, Mr Xenophon was looking towards the castle. They were both well concealed by a tree which grew against the wall on the landward side. Keeping still and maintaining silence, they were immensely thankful for a warm night. Saying nothing, Delancey touched his companion's arm and pointed seawards. Through his night glass he could just make out the trail of sparks as the steam-vessel approached, after passing the southern end of the Goodwin Sands. The guard frigate lay at anchor about one mile offshore, to the north of the enemy's course and so well to the left of the picture. Delancey handed his night glass to Mr Xenophon who presently handed it back again. "So you were right," he whispered, "and the frigate lies motionless in a dead calm." In another half-hour the steam-vessel was abreast of Walmer but no longer headed in their direction. She was steering almost directly towards the frigate but would probably pass her on the far side. At this point the *Corsican* signalled to the shore, a light flashing four times and then, after a pause, twice more. Contact with Fabius had evidently been made.

Delancey felt sorry for Captain Harding of the *Lizard*. What could he make of this spectacle, he who had never seen a steam-vessel before and who had been given no warning that one might appear? All he could see was a trail of sparks in the night. All he would be able to hear, as this apparition approached, was the unfamiliar noise of the engine. Harding reacted, predictably, with a flare which lit the whole scene for half a minute. Through the night-glass Delancey made out the *Corsican* as a schooner-rigged craft, with no sail set, flying the American flag and towing something astern. Ensigns are not flown at night and this one had obviously been hoisted in anticipation of that flare. As Fulton's name was well known the American flag might not be unexpected. Delancey could imagine Harding's voice on the speaking trumpet, telling *Corsican* to heave to or whatever you do with a steam-vessel, dammit, so as to bring her to a standstill.

The Frenchman responded by altering course so as to pass under the frigate's stern. Then he altered course so as to reach a position on her starboard beam. Watching helplessly, Delancey remembered that the catamaran was a possible threat, a floating box packed with gunpowder, triggered off by pulling a lanyard. If this was the thing being towed, the two sharp changes of course would swing the devilish device against the anchored frigate. If only Harding had been warned. But what, anyway, could he have done? A few minutes later the scene was lit again by a bright flash, quickly followed by the thunderclap of the explosion. It seemed to Delancey that the frigate's stern had been blown off. There was another flare and the sound of a gun but the steam-vessel was now directly ahead of the frigate and there was hardly a gun that could be brought to bear. The *Lizard* must in any case be sinking and all efforts would now go towards lowering her boats. She was on fire aft and there was light sufficient to see the activity amidships. By the same light Delancey could see that his own boats were coming to the rescue. The fools! But he could hardly blame his officers. Anyone else in their position might well have done the same. But there was the enemy in sight and his own first line of defence had gone! Now the frigate was settling by the stern, her bows in the air, and only a single boat in the water. Most of her men would clearly be drowned and there was nothing he could do to save them. Harding, he knew, would go down with his ship. Now the fire was extinguished by the rising water and darkness closed in upon the scene of the tragedy.

"Poor devils!" muttered Delancey. "How many of them can swim a mile?"

"Only a handful, I should guess," replied Mr Xenophon, "but boats should come out from Deal."

A blue flare was lit by one of the boats belonging to the *Vengeance* doubtless to facilitate the rescue operation, but the light also showed that *Corsican* had lowered two boats which were now pulling towards the shore, one directly towards Walmer Castle, the other towards some point further south. All being well, these two parties would be dealt with by Topley and Bartlett respectively, leaving Northmore's men without opponents. But where did *Nautilus II* come into the French plan? Resistance was expected and the purpose of the two boats must be to draw our fire and keep our men occupied. Meanwhile on a flank (probably the left from the enemy's point of view—the flank further from Deal and its garrison) *Nautilus II* would land a small party, perhaps four or five men, to make contact with Fabius, who by then would have the Prime Minister as captive. Delancey whispered his conclusions to Mr

Xenophon and added that he would now lead half of North-more's men along the path to the far side of the castle.

"All is quiet on this side," he explained, "but I'll leave North-more here all the same."

He scrambled down from the wall and was presently strid-ing down the path behind where Northmore's men had been posted. His worry was lest he should be fired on by his own seamen, but Northmore, as he soon realised, had his men well under control.

"Who goes there?" came the challenge, to which he replied with the password, "Vengeance." He was then allowed to pro-ceed, the sentinel adding "Beg pardon, sir. You'll find Mr Northmore a hundred yards down the path."

"Thank you, Cowling."

Delancey was challenged again by Northmore's orderly and was presently able to tell Northmore that he wanted twelve of his men and a petty officer. "All is quiet on this flank," he explained. "There may be an attempt to outflank us on the other side."

"May I come with you, sir?"

"No, you mayn't."

"Very good, sir. I'll collect the men."

It took ten minutes to assemble the party, by which time there was a distant sound of musketry, probably from Topley's sector. So Delancey led his party on with what speed was pos-sible in the dark. The seamen followed him, cursing under their breath, and Yates, a boatswain's mate, brought up the rear.

"Halt! Who goes there?"

"Vengeance."

The next challenge came from Mr Bartlett's orderly. The

marine officer himself was too occupied even to look round.

"I'm holding my fire, sir," he explained in a whisper, "until the enemy reach the shore."

There was a pause and Bartlett said, "Ready with the flare, Calvert."

After another minute came the sound of a boat, being beached.

"Flare!" A blue light revealed the beach, the boat and the enemy.

"Fire!"

There followed a scattered volley and the figures on the shore collapsed, one of them however trying to get back into the boat.

"Corporal Samson's party—advance at the double!" Came the sound of the marines' boots crashing through the shingle.

"Well done, the marines!" said Delancey, and led his own party away. When he made contact with Mr Topley he learnt that the other boat had already been dealt with and that there would be no prisoners. He hurried on and was finally rewarded by the glimpse of a distant lantern on the beach itself. As he came near it he was challenged "Qui vive?" and replied by telling the Frenchman that he was a prisoner. There followed the sound of a musket falling to the ground and Delancey, advancing, found a French seaman standing guard over a beached fishing boat. Just beyond the boat the light from the lantern revealed *Nautilus II,* a strange-looking vessel with a glass turret on top. Abaft the lookout turret was a tube which rose another three feet or so—probably the means of ventilation. Looking inside with the lantern he found, as he had expected, that her crew, apart from the one man, had gone ashore. She was driven, he could see, by a screw and this was propelled by crank handles on which three men could work at the same time. She would be manned by a commander, who would also be the helmsman, and probably six men, allowing three to rest while three worked. She had been cast off by *Corsican* which had towed her across Channel, probably at about the time that the steam-vessel had been sighted, and then had made her final approach while submerged and invisible. The plan would be to rejoin the *Corsican* with Mr Pitt a prisoner on board. It would soon be daylight but no one would dare to intercept *Corsican* with such a hostage at risk. Her fuel would all have been used up but she could have sailed home at leisure with the first breeze. It had been, he admitted to himself, an ingenious plan. Looking wonderingly round the small interior of the sub-mersible craft, Delancey found much to admire. To begin with, she was perfectly dry without any sign of even the smallest leak. She had been coated with pitch and he guessed that this coating had been repeated and thorough. The screw shaft had admitted no water at the point where it pierced the hull. All the workmanship appeared to be excellent. Admitting this, Delancey was still very certain that a brilliant idea may be less important, in practice, than the technique essential to translate theory into practice. Anyone with a lively imagination could devise, on paper, a flying machine or a balloon driven by some sort of engine. The real difficulty lay in making the thing, apply-ing a watchmaker's expertise to a bigger task and one on which one's life might depend. The *Nautilus II* was ahead of her time. An underwater boat should not be built of timber but of some metal—copper perhaps—and it would need a steam engine. Was that possible though? How could the vessel carry enough coal? And how was the explosive charge to be pinned on the enemy? Had Fulton really solved that problem? It seemed to

Delancey that *Nautilus II* was well designed to carry out the sort of mission on which she had been sent but ill-suited for any other type of operation. The practical difficulties were immense and all the available resources in brains, money, and vision were committed to the direction of the present war. For use in some future conflict there might be all sorts of elaborate machines but they would have to be developed during a previous period of peace.

Dismissing these thoughts, Delancey returned to the matter in hand. What had happened at the castle? For all he knew the Prime Minister might have been killed by now. Lantern in hand, he scrambled off the underwater craft and sent his prisoner off under escort. Then he collected his men and prepared to follow the path inland which the Frenchmen would have taken and which led, as he knew, to the castle. Hardly had the march begun, however, when Delancey's party was fired upon from the sea. The volley was, luckily, inaccurate, but musket balls flew overhead, hitting the rocks beyond and whining off on ricochet. Delancey could guess what had happened. Wetherall and Seddon had landed their rescued seamen and were now back on station, eager to prove their vigilance. Whichever of them it was now lit a blue flame and Delancey, jumping on board the fishing boat, waved a white handkerchief and hoped to God that he would be recognised. There was no more firing and Mr Wetherall presently came ashore to offer his apologies. "Beg pardon, sir, I took you for the enemy."

"Very well, your apology is accepted. Your next task, Mr Wetherall, is to tow this queer vessel into deep water. You will find fifteen fathoms south-west of the Sand Head. When you have depth enough, sink her. Is that understood?"

"Sink her, sir?"

"Yes, knock a hole through her bottom. Do it quietly and then take your boat back to the ship. Say nothing about this to anyone else and tell your men to say nothing about it to their messmates. Your story will be that you tried to tow this experimental craft back to the Downs but that she sank on the way, being quite unseaworthy. Is that clear?"

"Aye, aye, sir."

Delancey assembled his men again—they had scattered to take cover when fired upon—and resumed his march inland after ten minutes wasted. Whatever had happened in the castle, he would be too late to play any part in it unless it were to cut off the retreat of the enemy survivors. He did in fact capture three in this way and brought them back to the castle. The drawbridge was down, the gate open, and Mr Xenophon met him in the courtyard which was well lit by lanterns.

"The skirmish is over, sir. We have seven prisoners, two of them still unconscious. You have brought in three more. The rest escaped."

"And Fabius?"

"He escaped as of course he would. He or his men killed a footman and strangled a young chambermaid who must have tried to raise the alarm. The poor child could not have been more than eighteen years old. She could have been tied up and gagged. There was no need to kill her. Oh, yes, Fabius was here all right. One can recognise his handiwork."

It was a strange scene, with Pitt's servants collected at windows and doors and just a hint of the coming daybreak. Mr Xenophon went off to make another search of the grounds and it was Delancey who now had to face a tall and imperious woman, one he recognised as Lady Hester Stanhope, niece of the Prime Minister, who had been Pitt's hostess and chatelaine since the summer of 1803. She was aged 27, he had been told, past the ordinary age for marriage, and Pitt was her only hero. She was not beautiful and at that hour of the morning was not even attractive. She was formidable, however, and her sarcasm had made her enemies or so he had heard, one of them being the Earl Stanhope himself. When Pitt was briefly absent, as must happen fairly often, she held sway over the Cinque Port Volunteers—Delancey had glimpsed her reviewing them—and she was honorary Colonel besides of the 15th Light Dragoons and the Berkshire Militia. At the present moment she was fuming over the disturbance and over the fact that she had not been called and asked, presumably, to take command at least until the Prime Minister should appear.

"Permit me to ask, sir, what you are doing here? How do you and your followers come to be within the castle? Explain your presence, sir, and understand, pray, that I shall call for the fullest investigation into the incident."

"I regret, Lady Hester, that you have been disturbed. The French have landed here and two of your servants have been killed. We have captured most of the enemy and are hunting the rest."

"Am I to understand, sir, that the Emperor Napoleon is leading his whole army ashore?"

"No, Lady Hester. There has been a raid, no more than that."

"And what, may I ask, would have been the object of this extraordinary enterprise?"

"The French have not so far explained their plans in any detail, or not at least to me. I should myself surmise that they were attempting to capture the Prime Minister."

"The man on whom all our efforts must centre! They could

do worse, I must allow. You say that two of our servants are dead. Do you know their names?"

"I understand that one was a footman called Thomas, the other a chambermaid called Dorothy. I should suppose that they were trying to warn you and call generally for help."

"Dorothy? A nice child and quite a favourite of mine. And who, sir, are you?"

"I am Captain Delancey, commanding the frigate *Vengeance*."

"And why had you to land with your seamen? Where were the Cinque Port Volunteers?"

"Still in their beds, Lady Hester. There has been no general alarm or there was none at least until the danger had passed."

"I take a serious view of the affair, Captain Delancey. The navy should keep to the sea and leave the French soldiers to be opposed by the forces we have so painfully raised, accoutred, and exercised."

"Very good, Lady Hester. Should Napoleon land here I shall point out the castle to him and will then respectfully withdraw."

The lady glared at him for an instant. Then her expression abruptly changed and she laughed helplessly. Delancey now saw her as quite an attractive woman, high-spirited, blue-eyed, and evidently able to see the comic side of things.

"Very well, Captain," she said finally, "I have been talking nonsense and you have told me not to be silly!"

"Far from it, Lady Hester. I have been telling you, in all but words, how much I admire your spirit."

"Flattery seldom fails. So the affair is over and I can go back to bed?"

"Yes, indeed, unless you would wish to reassure the servants and tell them that they have nothing more to fear. I have spoken to them myself but it is to you they look for guidance and protection."

"I must write to Dorothy's mother, poor woman. How strange to think that a mere girl should fall victim to the enemy when all our armed menfolk are asleep."

"It is often the innocent who suffer, Lady Hester, but not all the French escaped and a number were killed."

"What sort of men were they?"

"Not men we should despise."

"I should imagine not. When that French gunboat was taken I went with the Prime Minister, Lord Camden, and Mr Charles Stanhope to inspect her. There were thirty soldiers on board, with two cannon, and there were four sailors. They were well clothed, well supplied, and well fed. In my opinion they were all picked men."

"I should not doubt it, Lady Hester. I hope that the Prime Minister is not more active than his physicians approve."

"He is more active than I approve. He works harder than anyone living, with people coming to see him all day and papers to read all night. I could wish he were out of office but what then would be the fate of our country? He is killing himself and I know no way to save him. All this is, of course, between ourselves . . ."

"You can trust me, Lady Hester, and I shall never forget the privilege I have had to meet you."

Parting with this great lady, Delancey took the opportunity to walk on the ramparts and see what happened to the *Corsican*. She was at anchor, he could see, in the position where last seen. There were boats alongside, evidently his own, and her deck was lit by lanterns. She had been taken by his officers and he could just glimpse the white ensign hoisted over the tricolour. With nearly all her own men ashore, her two or three men on anchor watch would have made no resistance. Hurrying down to what had originally been the guard room, now evidently the steward's office, he found pen and paper and wrote a brief note to Mr Wetherall or Mr Seddon.

You are hereby required and directed to remove everything of value from the captured steam-vessel, together with any documents found, send your prisoners to the *Vengeance,* and then blow her up with a keg of gunpowder. Her loss will be described as accidental, so prevent your men knowing exactly how it came about.

Signed,

Richard Delancey,

Captain, Royal Navy

Having scribbled this note and given it to a petty officer for delivery to Mr Northmore, who would send it out to the schooner, he went out into the courtyard where he found Mr Xenophon in conversation with a young army officer who had just ridden over from Deal to ask what was happening.

"There has been a French raid on Walmer Castle," he was explaining, "but we shall probably decide against making the fact public. We shall make it known locally that it was an exercise."

When the young officer had gone Delancey asked Mr Xenophon what had happened to the Prime Minister. "He can't be asleep, surely, after all this noise?"

"Mr Pitt? He is not here but went to London yesterday afternoon. Dear me, didn't I tell you? How remiss of me. I can only offer my sincere apologies. I do hope you will forgive me."

"But how astonishing that the Prime Minister should leave so unexpectedly at the very time we had reason to want him out of the way!"

"Well, not exactly astonishing. He received a royal command to come to Windsor immediately."

"How very fortunate!"

"It was not a coincidence. I have reason to believe, you see, that the King's letter was a forgery and that His Majesty knows nothing about it."

"But how can you be sure of that?"

"I forged the letter myself."

Chapter Fifteen

DEVILISH DEVICES

THE PUBLIC never knew anything about the raid on Walmer Castle—as was agreed, indeed, on both sides, for the French were just as reticent about the affair. As for their lordships of the Admiralty, they did not want it to be known that the enemy could set foot in England even in small numbers and by outlandish means. For people in Deal who had heard the firing, the explanation was that there had been a naval exercise, of which the garrison, by some mischance, had received no prior warning. Taken as a whole, the defensive measures had been highly successful.

Thinking of the affair afterwards, Delancey doubted whether the elimination of William Pitt, had it happened, would have been any serious loss to the war effort. Pitt was resolute, indeed. He had not thought of making peace on the enemy's terms. As against that, it was a question whether he really understood the art of war. His reputation rested upon his knowledge of finance as revealed in time of peace. That he or Dundas, his previous mentor, had any grasp of strategy might seem more than doubtful. It would seem, moreover, that Pitt was now a sick man, and one addicted to playing soldiers. As against that, had Pitt been taken by the enemy—his amateur soldiering having the chief result of exposing him to capture—the morale effect would have been tremendous. What encouragement it would have given the French and what alarm it would have spread in

Britain! How could our soldiers dream of attacking Napoleon when our forces could not even defend Walmer Castle? It had been a desperate attempt, Fabius being the mastermind who had devised it, and Delancey was glad to think that he himself had played a significant part in parrying the threat. He wondered whether Fabius would be blamed for the failure and discredited. On further consideration he concluded that Fabius would be given some other task but at lower level. Had it been a British failure the officer responsible would have been sent to some colony or other, to Jamaica, perhaps, or New South Wales. The French had less scope for this sort of promotion but there were places to which their less outstanding men could be sent. There was Mauritius, for example, where Decaen had been sent as penalty for being a follower of Moreau who had been Napoleon's rival at one time. Were there to be any revived plan for the invasion of England, Fabius, he concluded, was unlikely to have any hand in it.

Unfortunately, members of the Cabinet, accepting Delancey's word for it that *Corsican* was a suicidal vessel (the boiler of which had blown up) and that *Nautilus II* was quite unseaworthy, were greatly impressed by the effectiveness of the catamaran. Here was a British frigate destroyed in the Downs. Could not the same device be used against the invasion flotillas? Delancey, had he been consulted, would have pointed out that *Lizard* was sunk in very unusual circumstances. She had been a sitting duck in a dead calm. She had been deceived by the American flag. Such a situation might never exist again. Nor did the French landing craft present the same sort of target. Above all, the fact that the catamaran had been used successfully by a steam-vessel did not mean that a sailing ship could do the same thing. Delancey had dire misgivings about the catamaran which he thought useless as a weapon and highly dangerous to those who might be ordered to handle it. Were any of them entrusted to him he resolved to sink them in deep water and report that they had proved ineffective. He would accept risks where the object was worthwhile. He would not sacrifice lives in pursuit of mere nonsense.

The Walmer Castle affair took place in June 1804. By July, it was obvious from their troop movements that the French attack on Britain was to take place in the immediate future. The Army of England, said to be over 160,000 strong, was now deployed between Etaples and Ostend and was organised into the several corps under the command, respectively, of Marshals Ney, Soult, Lannes, and Davoust. Signal for the invasion would be the appearance at Boulogne of the Emperor himself, an event which would be known in Deal within 48 hours. Rear-Admiral Knight, being joined by another frigate, the *Sparrowhawk,* as replacement for the *Lizard,* sent for his captains—less the captain of the *Gannet,* which was off Boulogne—and told them that the crisis was impending.

"Our defence against the invasion flotilla rests, in the first instance, upon this squadron, which may well be sacrificed at the outset. If and when the flotilla sails I shall attack it immediately without counting the cost or making plans for withdrawal. In the meanwhile it is the government's policy to discourage the attempt, showing the enemy that it must end in disaster. Movement of enemy landing craft must increase as the chosen date becomes more imminent, partly as the vessels concentrate and partly as the crews are exercised. We shall take every opportunity to press home our attacks, knowing that the resolute handling of our ships might well be witnessed by Napoleon himself. Even a mere skirmish may have its effect on

Napoleon's mind, illustrating on a small scale what confusion and defeat might result from a later attempt on a larger scale. Ours will be a task of the very greatest importance."

The Admiral paused at this point, anxious to judge the effect of his words. The officers were unhelpfully silent and he went on:

"Some members of the Cabinet are anxious for us to make full use of a recent invention to which its supporters have given the inappropriate name of catamaran. I need hardly tell you that a catamaran is, properly speaking, a native craft with an outrigger used on the Coromandel coast of India. This is, however, the official name for this device, which is no more than a floating box of explosives, triggered off by the jerk of a lanyard. We have all expressed our doubts about the utility of this contrivance but ministers are aware that the frigate *Lizard* was destroyed by a catamaran and they can see no reason why the French flotilla should not be destroyed in the same way. We know, as others do not, that the device which destroyed the *Lizard,* tragically ending the distinguished career of Captain Harding and causing the death of so many of his men, was towed by a steam-vessel, able to move in any direction against wind and current. Ministers do not appreciate that a steam-vessel was essential to the success of the French attack. So we are ordered to see what the catamaran can achieve."

"Might I ask, Admiral," asked Flag Captain Saunders of the *Antelope,* "whether we are to make similar use of steam-vessels?"

"No, they have been ruled out. Remember also that the steam-vessel which sank the *Lizard* blew up soon afterwards. This is not generally known but ministers are aware of it and realise that the steam engine is unreliable at any time and would be hazardous in battle. May I ask, gentlemen, whether any of you have experience in using the catamaran?"

At this point the newcomer to the squadron, Captain Moffat of the *Sparrowhawk,* spoke up for the first time. He was a thin-faced man with a rather pedantic manner, eager to show his expertise.

"Yes, Admiral, I am familiar with the catamaran and believe that it can be used with great effect. It is true that results have been disappointing, but I attribute past failures to the ignorance and obstinacy of the officers concerned. Some of them began with a prejudice against this mode of warfare and were resolved to discourage it. The catamaran is useless—more, it is dangerous—when handled by men who are nervous and inept."

"May I ask, Admiral," inquired Delancey, "how these catamarans are to reach the enemy? What form of propulsion are we to use?"

It was Captain Moffat who replied:

"They are propelled by the tide. Having towed them by boat to a distance just out of range of the enemy's gunfire, we cut them loose, jerk the lanyard, and withdraw. The explosion takes place after half an hour, the catamaran having been carried by the tide into the midst of the enemy's flotilla."

"But don't the enemy see them coming?" asked Delancey.

"Not if we distract their attention," replied Moffat patiently. "The catamaran barely shows on the surface and could be mistaken for a piece of wreckage. It is thought advisable, nevertheless, to give the enemy something else to think about. I would myself recommend the use of Congreve rockets. I should remind you, Admiral, that tidal currents run fast on the French coast round here. Catamarans can drift at five to six knots. Apart from the damage they may do, their morale effect can be decisive."

"No doubt of that," was Delancey's comment, but he added, more quietly, "the French, besides, may die of laughing."

"It is easy to sneer," said Moffat sharply. "I have no doubt that laughter greeted the first man who wished to replace the bow and arrow by the musket. There must be progress, sir. We cannot reject all that is novel because it is new."

"I crave your pardon," replied Delancey, "and I am sure that we shall all benefit from your experience. I wonder, however, whether it might be possible to use a captured French gunboat to tow the catamaran?"

"Others have had the same inspiration," said the Admiral. "It seems that we have recently captured one of their craft, complete with crew, near Ostend. I have had instruction to make use of her if the opportunity should offer."

"What type of craft is she, sir?" asked Moffat.

"She is of a class the French call their bateaux cannonières, a lugger armed with two guns. She is smaller than what they call a prame, bigger than a peniche. Strangely enough, the men on board her, seamen and soldiers, were perfectly convinced that they had all but conquered England already. They saw themselves as prisoners for a few weeks, due for release by the Emperor himself."

"Is it true, sir, that Napoleon is now at Boulogne?"

"We have heard that," replied the Admiral, "and we are inclined to believe it. If he plans to direct the invasion in person—as he surely must—this month would be the best time for it. If he is not at Boulogne now he must be due there very shortly."

There was further discussion and it soon became clear that Moffat was to direct a catamaran attack on the Boulogne flotilla with Delancey to cover his withdrawal. The craft captured would tow the catamaran, flying the French flag, to a position just out of range of the French guns, after which the deadly device would drift further inshore on a rising tide. The chosen date was 19 July, on which day the squadron appeared off Boulogne, *Vengeance* hovering three miles offshore and *Sparrowhawk* going in to cover the approach of the captured bateau cannonière, which was to come round the headland to the south. The plan seemed to Delancey hazardous in the extreme and especially so in daylight. Would the bateau cannonière be accepted as friendly by the shore batteries? She was not fired upon, as things turned out, but the situation was complicated that afternoon by a rising wind and a heavy sea. The French flotilla in Boulogne roads was gradually dispersed as the smaller vessels ran for Etaples or St Valery-sur-Somme. The launching of a catamaran had become extremely difficult but, apart from that, the target vessels were insufficiently concentrated. With great reluctance Rear-Admiral Knight cancelled the attempt by a signal from *Antelope* to *Vengeance* which was repeated to *Sparrowhawk*. The volunteer crew in the bateau cannonière began to head seawards again, having presumably left their catamaran where the French might possibly trip over it. Watching the fiasco through his telescope, Delancey wondered whether a catamaran would explode on collision or only after a jerk of the lanyard? What he was never to realise until long afterwards was that the 19th/20th was actually a turning point in the war.

It was, in a way, a horrifying scene. It was blowing hard from the north-north-east and big seas were crashing on the shore with spray tossed high against the dark land and leaden sky. The gusts of wind rose to a shriek and the *Vengeance* pitched and rolled in sickening fashion as Delancey focused his telescope on the French landing craft. All order among these had been lost, some of the larger vessels working to windward, most of the smaller craft running down wind for Etaples, others again running to anchor off Boulogne. At Delancey's elbow, Mr Mather was studying the scene.

"And all this happens to the poor devils before we have even come to close range."

The French craft were in fact under distant fire from three gun-brigs which were able to go further inshore than the *Vengeance*. It did not appear that much damage was being done by this desultory cannonade but it was enough to discourage the movement to windward.

"Those gun-brigs afford no sort of a gun platform," commented Delancey. "This weather does not suit them."

"It doesn't suit me either, sir," replied Mather. "I keep thinking that our masts will go over the side."

"We'll ride more easily when we anchor."

The motion did improve after the anchor had been dropped but the wind rose, if anything, towards evening. A passing gleam of light revealed a bay in which the storm-tossed landing craft numbered 27. With the flood tide Delancey stood in closer and saw that several of the craft were ashore west of Boulogne. Three others were wrecked near Portel, others being dismasted with heavy seas breaking over them. The wind whistled through the frigate's rigging and the scene was generally dismal.

"Boney must be watching this from the headland," said Delancey. "I wish we were near enough to see him."

"He might have stayed indoors, sir," objected Mather as a

rainstorm beat down on the quarterdeck. "Who would blame him?"

"No, he would have to be on the headland," said Delancey. "He must have had reports last night and earlier today, so many craft wrecked, so many men drowned, so many craft reaching St Valery-sur-Somme. He would have to come and look for himself. He would need to show, moreover, that he, for one, is not discouraged. He is there at this moment, you can depend upon it, and he must be wondering whether his invasion plan is practicable. What if it blew like this on the chosen day? He will have lost hundreds of men today. With actual invasion ordered he would have lost thousands and all this with little interference by us."

"He will realise now, sir, what the Channel can be like."

"This he must have known, Mr Mather. What he has learnt is what the weather can be like even in July. If there can be a gale like this in the height of summer, what could he expect in spring or autumn?"

"He has chosen, sir, to think again."

"But he will not panic on hearing about the catamaran we have launched!"

Chapter Sixteen

CATAMARAN

OFF BOULOGNE, Delancey, firmly braced between the gunwale and the shrouds, was watching the bateau cannonière struggle seawards in a wild sea with spray breaking over her. That she was in British hands was perfectly obvious to the French and Delancey saw that a three-masted prame was heading to cut her off. With twenty guns to the two mounted by her intended prey, the prame ran little risk of defeat. Accurate gunnery between relatively small vessels in such a sea was, of course, impossible, but here again the prame had the steadier gun platform of the two. The time had come to intervene and Delancey ordered Mather to make more sail and steer towards the prame. To rescue the bateau cannonière was really the *Sparrowhawk*'s responsibility but that frigate seemed to be in difficulties with a broken spar. The depth of water was shoaling from nine fathoms to seven, from seven to five, and Delancey knew that he must allow for the lessened depth in the trough of the wave. Once in four fathoms he would be in range of the coastal howitzers, firing shell, and soon beyond that he might be fired upon by the coastal guns.

"We shall soon be under fire from the shore, sir," warned Mather.

"It will not be effective at extreme range," replied Delancey, "and we shall try to keep the prame between us and the nearest battery."

"We may expect some help from the *Sparrowhawk,* sir, enough at least to make the batteries distribute their fire."

"I can't make out what Moffat is doing."

"He will be greatly disappointed, sir, to see the signal of recall. I fancy that he may have some idea of doing some damage before he withdraws."

"But the bateau cannonière will have cut its catamaran loose, surely?"

"Do we know that, sir?"

"No, we don't. Who is in command?"

"I gathered, sir, that the launching of the catamarans has been left to a lieutenant from Jersey called Le Marquand—sent here specially from Plymouth."

"I never heard of him."

"I know of him by reputation. He is said to be especially keen on economy with naval stores."

"Very praiseworthy. He has no previous experience, perhaps, of such an operation as this?"

"Probably not, sir. He is moving very slowly and that French vessel is overtaking him."

Delancey studied the scene with a growing impatience. There seemed every likelihood of the bateau cannonière being taken before he could interfere. He was not yet within range and closing the distance would bring him under fire from the shore batteries. Moffat appeared to be fighting a war of his own and Le Marquand seemed to be paralysed. There was every likelihood of severe damage and casualties with nothing to show for it.

"*Sparrowhawk,* sir, has lowered her longboat."

"Why, for heaven's sake?"

"They may have had a man overboard."

That no such emergency had arisen was soon apparent. There was a muffled report and a faint line climbed skywards from *Sparrowhawk's* longboat. It reached its apex and then plunged downwards towards the French prame, falling into the sea perhaps half a mile beyond her.

"Congreve rockets!" exclaimed Delancey. "Moffat's plan for distracting the French! Children playing with a new toy . . ."

"But why fire rockets from an open boat, sir? With the boat tossing as it is, any effective aim must be impossible."

"You can't fire them from a ship, Mr Mather. They would be caught in the rigging and fall on your own quarterdeck. They never, in any case, hit the target. I wish Congreve were here to see that for himself."

The wind was rising from the north-north-east, there was a threatening grey sky and the *Vengeance* pitched and rolled, shipping seas over her forecastle and lashed by the icy spray which flew over her decks. Delancey could see now that he was too late. The bateau cannonière was under fire and would have to surrender in a matter of minutes. Le Marquand was defending his craft with some obstinacy, using small arms as well as cannon, but he was heavily outgunned and outnumbered. Had he surrendered at the outset, as many a man might have done, he would have lost all chance of his boat being retaken by *Vengeance*. This he evidently knew and the resulting action was one that did him credit. His position would have been hopeless had other gunboats joined in the battle but they were intent on finding shelter. The prame closed with him, as Delancey could see, but the heavy seas made boarding impossible. At last the firing died away as the flag was struck. A few minutes later another sighting shot from the *Vengeance* went through the prame's sails, to be followed almost immediately by the frigate's broadside. The prame would have to surrender both herself and her prize.

The capture of a prame was not important in itself but none had been taken before, so far as Delancey knew, and Lord Keith would probably be interested to see a specimen. Once fairly to leeward of the frigate's broadside, the prame duly struck her colours. A minute later the shore batteries opened fire, having been restrained so far by fear of hitting their own vessel. They had less compunction, it would seem, about hitting a French craft that had surrendered. The guns were firing at extreme range but they were correcting their aim, the shots coming nearer. They also had howitzers in action, far less accurate but more dangerous with a shell which sometimes, not always, burst on impact. Through his speaking trumpet Delancey told the French skipper (in French) to steer out to sea. By the same means he ordered the Frenchmen on board the bateau cannonière to surrender. He watched while they gave up their arms to Le Marquand and his men and then ordered the bateau to follow the prame. The splashes from the falling shot had crept nearer during the last few minutes and the frigate was presently hit by a plunging shot which went through the main deck and lodged finally in the hold, causing only minor damage apart from the shot hole. A shell burst somewhere astern and Delancey realised that his ship was in considerable danger. It was unnerving, he found, to watch the trace of the shells and guess where they would fall. He found that Mather was doing the same thing.

"Do you observe, Mr Mather, that these shells drift to leeward at the height of their trajectory?"

"Yes, sir. I would guess that the wind may blow even more strongly at that level."

"So we might do better to edge into the wind?"

"But the Frenchmen will allow for the drift and may even allow too much."

"You are right. All we can do is lengthen the range. I shall waste no time in replying to their fire."

"We should be clear, sir, in about ten minutes."

This was probably a good estimate but ten minutes can seem a very long period of time. The frigate was hit again, this time on the forecastle, and two men were wounded by splinters. No considerable damage had been done but at this moment a shell narrowly missed the bateau cannonière. Le Marquand soon afterwards made the signal that his craft had been damaged and was leaking.

"Make more sail, Mr Mather," ordered Delancey. "Put the frigate to windward of the prame." As the frigate passed the bateau cannonière, Delancey took up the speaking tube and gave a terse order to Le Marquand:

"Board the prame with your entire crew. Then set the bateau cannonière alight. I'll shelter you as you do it."

It was at least relatively easy to board the prame from the bateau cannonière under the frigate's lee but it meant bringing all three vessels to a standstill and close together, making a perfect target for the shore batteries, which were not themselves under fire. From further seaward the Sparrowhawk's rockets were now directed against the French emplacements but seemed to be perfectly harmless as they flew beyond the target. Le Marquand's men were maddeningly slow in boarding the prame and Le Marquand took what seemed hours to set the bateau cannonière alight. His men had to fetch combustibles from the prame and he himself could be seen fiddling with flint and steel. Now the prame was hit and then the frigate again, this time with several casualties, two killed and three wounded. It was immediately after this last hit that Mather suddenly shook Delancey's arm and pointed to the bateau cannonière. She was dragging a rope astern and Delancey had a shock, realising the full horror of the situation. The catamaran was still there at the end of the tow-line—a box about twenty feet long packed with about twenty kegs of gunpowder—and it could be detonated at any moment (as he supposed) by the shock of an exploding shell.

"Make sail!" he shouted to Mather but it was already too late.

Two more shells burst on impact at sea-level, clear of their target but fatally near the catamaran. There was a blinding flash, a deafening thunderclap, and a feeling as if the frigate had been hit by a giant hammer. The catamaran had been somewhere between two and three hundred yards distant, not near enough to set the two ships alight, and Delancey could see, as the smoke blew away, that the prame and the bateau cannonière were also still afloat and without visible damage.

As the people about him collected their wits, Delancey repeated his order: "Mr Mather—*make sail!*" To his signals officer, a midshipman, he added "Signal the prame to follow this ship." To another midshipman, acting as his A.D.C., he said "Tell the carpenter to sound the well and report back to me."

There was a bustle of activity as the frigate got under way. The bateau cannonière was now fairly alight, its smoke drifting downwind, and *Vengeance* now steered a course which would place the smoke between her and the French batteries. The smoke-screen was far from complete and the masts probably showed above it but it would do something to confuse the artillerymen. The ship was not actually hit again although the splinters from one bursting shell destroyed the port quarter gallery. The *Vengeance* presently headed seawards, followed by the prame, and the firing died away. The bateau cannonière had sunk by that time, fired on by the enemy as she went down and notched up, no doubt, as an enemy sloop destroyed by the gunners ashore.

After dropping anchor in the Downs Delancey went aboard the flagship, having collected Le Marquand on the way. The *Sparrowhawk* was already in the anchorage and Captain Moffat was already with the Admiral. Le Marquand had begun some explanation in the boat but Delancey cut him short, saying quietly "Not before the boat's crew." The Rear-Admiral greeted Delancey with a few words of congratulation. "I thought at one time that your ship had gone. You did well to escape without material damage. I fear you will have had some losses." Delancey and Moffat greeted each other without much cordiality and Le Marquand looked thoroughly distressed. They all sat down at the Admiral's invitation, the flag captain and flag lieutenant completing the group, the latter making rough notes as the meeting went on.

"Well, gentlemen, I was ordered to carry out an experiment with the catamaran and made my plan accordingly, with Mr Le Marquand to head the attack in a captured French craft and under the French flag, with the *Sparrowhawk* to cover Mr Le Marquand's withdrawal and the *Vengeance* to cover the withdrawal of the *Sparrowhawk*. A high wind sprang up and a heavy sea and I felt obliged to cancel the operation. To that extent the experiment has proved nothing. For success we needed a light wind and a smooth sea. On the other hand, we have gained some experience of this new weapon and I shall need to summarise what we have learnt. It is not my purpose this evening to blame anyone for a failure which was essentially due to bad weather. All I intend is to complete the story for the purposes of my report. I myself saw what happened up to the time when I signalled the recall. As the flagship withdrew I saw less of what followed and I need to know the facts. Mr Le Marquand, I shall begin with you. What happened after you turned back?"

Reports followed from Le Marquand and Moffat, the first explaining his dilemma with the catamaran, the second claiming to have had success with his rockets.

When called upon, Delancey described the action from his own point of view and was then invited to draw his conclusions.

"I have many doubts and uncertainties, Admiral, and am not as prejudiced as Captain Moffat may suppose. On three points, however, I have formed a tentative opinion. First and foremost, I cannot see that a catamaran has any real advantage over a manned vessel packed with the same, or a greater, quantity of powder. Second, I think that an attack using explosives should always be staged in darkness. Third, I have come to question whether an explosion at sea is as dangerous to the enemy as to the ingenious and intrepid men who trigger it off.

"Earlier today I survived the explosion of a catamaran at a distance of about two cables. I could not claim that I ignored it. I must admit, indeed, that I was greatly alarmed. I will admit, further, that my frigate sustained serious damage the extent of which has still to be established by survey. As against that, we are still afloat and could still give battle.

"The fact, as I see it, is that an explosion to be effective needs a confined space, as when a mine is fired beneath an enemy fortification. At sea the force of the detonation is largely wasted on the yielding waters and the empty sky. The noise is impressive but the enemy is still there. A ship can be blown apart by a mere spark in its own magazine but here the explosion is confined within the vessel's hull. Outside the ship the effect is limited and may even be negligible. Some would argue that the catamaran is useless or worse than useless. I do not say that. I thought that Mr Le Marquand made a good point in observing that it could be used by a ship when closely pursued and so it might provided that the pursuer were in the exact wake of her prey—hardly perhaps an everyday event but not theoretically impossible. As a method, however, of attacking the French flotilla, I doubt its effectiveness. I feel that more could be achieved by the same effort applied in a different way."

"Thank you," said the Admiral. "Will you also give us your opinion of the Congreve rocket?"

"Well, sir, I have never seen them used except on this one occasion. Forgive me, therefore, if I hesitate over reaching any general conclusion. I was not surprised, however, to hear Captain Moffat confess to his ignorance of what damage the rockets did. When you stand behind a weapon you see less, as a rule, than someone else can see from a flank. I watched his rocket attack with great interest and can assure him that nearly all these missiles went far beyond the target—often to the distance of perhaps half a mile. The French artillerymen may well have been distracted by their appearance and noise—I do not question that for a moment—but I doubt whether they sustained either casualties or damage."

"Thank you, Delancey, and thank you, gentlemen. With your good help I have executed the orders I received. I am particularly grateful to Captain Moffat for testing the rockets and advising me on the use of the catamaran. The decision as to their further use must rest with their lordships. My responsibility ends with my report concerning all that took place on this one occasion. I am grateful to Captain Delancey for rescuing Mr Le Marquand and I am grateful to Mr Le Marquand for undertaking an extremely dangerous mission. Please convey my thanks, gentlemen, to all who took part. I am perfectly convinced that everyone did his best. You all have work to do and I must not keep you from it. I should be grateful, Delancey, if you would remain for a few minutes."

When the others had gone the Admiral asked Delancey whether the *Vengeance* would have to be docked.

"No survey has been made, sir, except by my own carpenter," replied Delancey, "but she was making eight inches of water an hour as from the time of the explosion and I suspect that the rate of intake will increase. We have to keep the pumps going almost continuously."

"Can't you get at the leaks and stop them?"

"No, sir. They are too general. The whole fabric of the ship was badly shaken and strained."

"I am sorry to hear it. You see, I have another mission for you; a task I would not readily entrust to anyone else. It will not wait until your frigate comes out of dock."

"Might I know, sir, what task you have in mind?"

"It is one about which you must say nothing to anyone else. I want information about the so-called Army of England. Are the troops ready to embark or has the Emperor cancelled the whole operation?"

"I see, Admiral. Might I ask whether Napoleon is still at Boulogne?"

"Yes, so far as we know. He is reviewing troops, making speeches, distributing medals. But we don't want to know what he says but what he means to do. As soon as we know for certain that the invasion has been cancelled our troops can be redeployed, perhaps with a view to some offensive operation. Knowing this, it will be the French aim to pose the threat, rattling their sabres, while their Army is actually on the march into central Europe. If they do this cleverly enough, we are still manning our ramparts while they have gone somewhere else. We need to discover whether the Army of England is still there. We can be certain that its ghost will remain after its substance has gone. The bugles will sound, the campfires will be lit, the orderly officers' lanterns will be seen. But are the troops actually there? The reports received by Mr Xenophon are contradictory and confused. His informants do not always know what they are talking about. What we lack is a clear answer to a simple question. My belief is that you can provide it. No one else can."

"You may be wanting more, sir, than I have to offer. I can understand, however, why our intelligence system has seemingly failed us. If the attempt at invasion has been postponed by as much as three weeks, there will be considerable movement which a civilian can hardly interpret."

"What sort of movement?"

"Well, sir, no army can camp on the beach for more than a few days. With embarkation imminent, the bulk of the forces will bivouac within two miles of the coast. They can't stay there, however. They need grass and water for their horses, firewood for cooking, space to exercise, and room to breath. They will go inland for ten miles or more. To one agent this will look like abandoning the whole invasion plan. To another it will look like a move to another camp from which the formation can return in twelve hours."

"I see what you mean and am confirmed in my belief that

you are the man to solve our problem. I am the more regretful that *Vengeance* must go into dock."

"With all due respect, Admiral, I beg leave to question whether the frigate is wanted. It is my private opinion, for what it is worth, that *Vengeance* will probably have to be scrapped. If Mr Mather takes her to Sheerness or Chatham, I can stay here on your orders, retaining a picked boat's crew for a particular service. We still have that French gunboat at Deal, which will be enough for our purpose."

"Look, Delancey, you are not going into Boulogne again!"

"Not into Boulogne, sir. That, I fancy, will be the last place from which the formations will withdraw. I would prefer to test the enemy preparedness at a less central point."

"Where, for heaven's sake?"

"At Ambleteuse, sir, a place I have long wished to visit. It is just north of Wimereux."

"*I know* where it is, confound you. But I'll not encourage mere lunacy. You are active enough, Delancey, but we need caution as well. We want you to come back alive."

"I am just as insistent on that point as you can be, sir. It is always, believe me, my prime consideration."

Delancey did well to keep away from Boulogne, a place where vigilance was now an obsession. Had he gone ashore there, however, by some unimaginable means, and had he gained a hidden position within earshot of a certain detached building above the town, he could have saved himself the trouble of landing at Ambleteuse. There were sentries all round the place but the absence of any spy on the British payroll was further explained by the fact that few people knew to what wartime purpose the old farmhouse had been put. Officers and orderlies came and went but troops were billeted everywhere and that building was no more frequented than any other.

On the evening of the day on which Delancey made his proposals known to Rear-Admiral Knight the farmhouse kitchen, hung with maps and charts, was occupied by four tired-looking officers. One was a General but young to hold that rank. He had with him two staff officers, one a Colonel, older than his chief, and the other a Major, the youngest present. He also had at his side a Captain from the Navy, Chief of Staff to an Admiral. Before them on the table was a chart of the French coast, lit by candlelight, and nearby another, smaller table held loose sheets of paper all covered with lists and calculations. For a few minutes the only sound was from the horses outside, one of which was coughing and another pawing the cobble stones. The Major, finishing a final feat of arithmetic, handed his paper to the Colonel who looked at the totals and sighed deeply before handing the document to the Navy's representative.

"It cannot be done, General," said the Colonel finally, "and the Emperor must be told that the plan must be cancelled."

"Because of the interference to be expected from British men-of-war?" asked the Captain.

"It would still be impossible if all the enemy ships were to stay in port."

"You mean the weather conditions likely . . ."

"It couldn't be done in any conditions. The whole plan breaks down on *time!*"

"But surely," said the General, "with discipline, with staff-work, with sufficient activity?—"

"Look, General," said the grey-haired Colonel, "we have worked on these tables for days. We have done our utmost and we have assumed that everyone else will do the same. But the time-table is still impossible. Embarking the troops, horses, and

guns cannot be done in less than eight days. That means that
those embarking first will have been seasick for a week before
the voyage can even begin. Having landed in England, the
troops first ashore must hold out against superior numbers
until the boats return to fetch the other half of the army which
will take another eight days to embark. We are not being
defeated by our own idleness, still less by the enemy's vigilance.
We are being defeated by mere arithmetic. Look at the figures,
General, and tell me that our calculations are mistaken. I shall
be happy indeed if you could reach a different conclusion,
proving me wrong. The figures are there, sir, however, and I
cannot make them tell a different story."

"But the time allowed for embarkation could be improved
upon. You admit that yourself, Colonel," said the Captain, "and
each exercise led to a better result."

"I know that, but it makes no difference. Suppose we have
allowed five hours for the embarkation of a division under ideal
conditions. By threats and promises we reduce that time to four
and a half hours—more easily said than done, but allow that
to be possible—we can save that thirty minutes and as long,
maybe, on the following day. But what have we then achieved?
What we thought would take twenty-two days can be done,
after all, in twenty-one. Does that really help us? And all our
timing assumes that the sea is calm and the enemy inactive!
Whatever we do with the figures we are brought back to the
same conclusion. The operation is impossible!"

"And I am to tell the Emperor that?" asked the General with
a hopeless gesture.

"He knows it already," replied the Colonel. "After all his
campaigns he knows better than anyone what can be done in
a given time."

"So the camps must be abandoned and the troops sent elsewhere?" asked the Captain.

"Not immediately," said the General. "The Emperor will want to keep the British Army pinned down on the shores opposite us. The withdrawal will be gradual and it will be October before our threat is ended for the year. The British cannot be made to expect an invasion after 1st October."

"The weather could be suitable in October," said the Captain. "It sometimes is."

"Obviously," replied the Colonel, "but then the days are too short. All our calculations depend upon the available hours of daylight. We can't embark artillery by candlelight—we should be fools even to attempt it. No, our threat ends on 1st October. We can renew it, of course, next year. I suspect, however, that the Emperor has other plans. He will explain afterwards that this invasion scheme was only a feint."

"Perhaps it was," groaned the Major.

"It could have been," said the Colonel. "But it seems a bit elaborate. A credible threat could have been posed with fewer diversions and less effort. I don't suppose that we shall ever know the truth. Do you know, General, I seldom read history. After my years on the staff I know that the truth will never be told about anything, and if it were told, nobody would believe it."

"Well, then," concluded the General, "I shall advise the Emperor that the invasion plan should be cancelled. I shall be lucky if he does not have me shot for disloyalty."

"Oh, no sir," said the Major. "I have been counting on his humanity. He will do no more, surely, than reduce me to the ranks!"

Chapter Seventeen

CLOAK AND DAGGER

D ELANCEY brought the captured gunboat ashore at a point below the windmill at Zuphen. With batteries a half-mile in either direction he was fortunate to avoid notice but the landing was timed to coincide with the sloop *Cynthia's* ineffective but noisy bombardment of Ambleteuse. All French eyes must have been turned northwards as the cannon could be heard rumbling in the distance, and as flashes lit the horizon in that direction. Who would notice the sound of a gunboat being dragged on shore over the shingle? Covered by this diversion, Delancey left Topley to hold the beach, placing sentries to cover the flanks and the gunboat itself.

"I shall try to reach a place called Raventhus," Delancey explained, "and then push on a mile or so further to a place called Basinghen. I shall return here when my mission has been accomplished."

"When am I to expect you, sir?" asked Topley.

"In about four hours, with luck. If I fail to return before daybreak, you must assume that I am dead or have been taken prisoner. Put to sea in that event and report back to the squadron anchorage. I shall have with me Northmore and Higgs, all of us in French artillery uniform, as you see, and our mission is secret, not to be revealed even to you. Remember to hoist the tricolour at daybreak and remember to keep silent in the meanwhile."

The guns were still rumbling as Delancey marched inland, following the paths which would lead to Raventhus, passing near Zuphen on the way. All was quiet, the countryside seemingly deserted, and it was a warm summer night, suitable for a country walk. For a seaman coming ashore there was also the pleasure of smell, the scent of wildflowers merging with the scent of trodden hay. If Delancey and his men were nervous at first, knowing that they were on enemy soil, they soon gained confidence, feeling that they were the only people awake. Raventhus they never saw because Delancey made his way confidently to a cottage which stood in an isolated position on the western side of the hamlet. So clear was the description given him that Delancey boldly knocked at the door and knocked as loudly again. There was a long pause as Henri Jacquemard woke, lit a candle and came down from the loft where he and his wife, Marie, slept. When he opened the door it was held merely ajar while he asked who it was. When Delancey gave the password the door opened fully to reveal the cobbler himself in his nightgown, holding the poker. Henri, as Delancey knew, was a Catholic and Royalist, opposed to the Revolution on principle, almost as hostile towards Napoleon and for many years in the pay of Mr Xenophon. When Delancey, Northmore, and Riggs had entered, the door was secured again and Henri was joined by his wife and daughter. Madame Jacquemard was a homely woman, devoted to her husband but plainly terrified at the risks he was running. Henriette, the daughter, was a lovely nineteen-year-old brunette with fair complexion and dark eyes, who attracted the immediate and unconcealed devotion of Mr Midshipman Northmore. After Jacquemard and his family had put on some clothes, bringing in some more candles, Delancey could see that his host was evidently more prosperous than the average peasant and that his cottage was correspondingly well furnished. The kitchen fire was coaxed into a blaze, some wine was produced, and they all sat round the fireplace while Jacquemard explained the military situation as it appeared to him.

"Yes, Captain," Jacquemard was explaining in French, "the soldiers that were here have gone, the last of them six days ago. The infantry were camped in the meadows along the River Selaque, with a brigade headquarters at Parte. The cavalry were in camp around Lohen and there was an artillery regiment north of here on the higher ground, perhaps two miles inland. They all took the main road through Basinghen but told nobody where they were going. Come to think of it, I doubt whether many of them knew—none, maybe, under the rank of colonel. They could have marched ten miles or forty by now and we none the wiser."

Delancey had still to ascertain whether the soldiers had gone for good. Jacquemard answered all questions readily and was at least able to identify the units that had been there. The infantry, he said, had included a famous regiment, the Legion of Elite Gendarmes, the soldiers of which had behaved very well. They had worn a blue uniform with red lapels and cuffs, red epaulettes, yellow breeches, bearskin caps, and leather gaiters. Several of them had come to the cottage with boots for repair and had talked quite freely over a cup of cider. They repeated rumours that the invasion plan had been cancelled but did not pretend to know anything for certain. Few of them had been enthusiastic about the invasion scheme and some of them (the bad sailors) were frankly appalled at the prospect. Jacquemard felt that the final departure of this particular regiment would be proof sufficient that the invasion was now no more than a feint; it was not a unit that any French Marshal would willingly leave behind. It was an elite corps, Jacquemard explained, but formed quite recently. It must be a prime object to ensure that the Gendarmes should have at least one battle honour. They could not, surely, be left out of the coming invasion. This was, surely, a logical conclusion.

While this conversation continued Delancey was observing the daughter, Henriette, who had coloured a little when her father mentioned the soldiers of the Elite Gendarme Regiment. Looking away from her again, he told Jacquemard that he would now go on to Basinghen where Mr Xenophon had another agent called Lebrun. He might learn there what route the column had followed. Further than that he dared not go for he had to be ready to re-embark before daylight. On mention of Lebrun's name Jacquemard became rather reserved, saying vaguely that he knew Lebrun as a very respectable young man. Henriette coloured afresh at this point, looking uncomfortably at the floor, subdued by her mother's glance of disapproval. Guessing what the story had been, Delancey announced that he must be going. As he got to his feet he heard voices outside followed by a loud knock at the door. Drawing a pistol, he opened the door to find Higgs covering another man with his musket, the butt of which had done the knocking. The stranger, who had put his hands up, was impossible to identify in the darkness but there was something familiar about the voice. He explained that he was a friend of Henri Jacquemard. In answer to a question, he said that he was alone.

"Come in," said Delancey, making him enter, covered now by the pistol, while Higgs remained at his post.

Once inside the stranger was recognised at once by Jacquemard, who assured Delancey that this was a friend. A minute later the newcomer to the scene removed his hat, threw back his cloak, and stood revealed as Mr Xenophon. Delancey's first reaction was one of irritation. He had been sent on a mission and it looked now as if he was being superseded. Mr Xenophon's intervention had been no part of the plan.

"This is unexpected," said Delancey rather coldly.

"My apologies," replied Mr Xenophon, who then greeted Jacquemard in friendly fashion, bowing to the two women, and then turning again towards Delancey.

"I had to warn you, Captain. Pierre Lebrun, the agent you were to have met at Basinghen, is ready to betray us. Go nowhere near that place. We are in great danger even here."

"How serious is this expected betrayal?" asked Delancey. "Has this man been against us for long? Has he much information to sell?"

"He knows very little," replied Mr Xenophon, "and I do not think that he was disloyal to us until now. I suspect that he had some personal grievance against my friend Jacquemard." The secret agent made reference to Henri but glanced towards Henriette, who looked more downcast than ever.

"Well, what am I to do?" asked Delancey. "Go further inland but avoiding Basinghen?"

"No," answered Mr Xenophon, shaking his head. "That is far too dangerous. As I said, we are not even safe where we are."

"And you came alone?" asked Delancey.

"No, I have two men with me but I left them out of sight when I approached this cottage."

"I suggest that you call them in and add to our strength."

"Agreed." Mr Xenophon went outside and whistled. Looking over his shoulder Delancey glimpsed two dark and silent figures, who vanished left and right after being given some brief instruction. When Mr Xenophon came back into the kitchen he spoke in English.

"Our friends here, whose guests we are, have no knowledge of English. I shall tell you now what we must do. Do not look in the direction of our host's daughter. To discover what we want to know there is no need to go further inland. The secret is here in the cottage. We shall discover it by interrogating the girl. She has a lover in the regiment that was here. I must assume that she knows where that regiment has gone."

"Are you sure of that, Mr Xenophon?"

"Can we be sure of anything? But consider the situation. She is a beautiful girl, just of an age for romance and perfectly innocent, much admired by our friend Lebrun, to whom she may even have been betrothed. Along comes a crack regiment, comprising splendid young men who are starved of affection and who all fall in love with her. She chooses the handsomest of them—I should guess a sergeant aged about twenty-one. The romance is actually encouraged by her father, much to the fury of Lebrun, who decides on revenge. The regiment marches away, the young sergeant swearing that he will soon return and marry her."

"And will he do that?" asked Delancey.

"I doubt if he will return at all. In the meanwhile, he will have written to her—that is as certain as anything can be—and I want to see the letter. The interrogation I leave to you. While it goes on I shall quietly leave the room, go to the loft, and search the place where she sleeps, returning after I have read the letter."

"But how do you know that she can read?"

"Her father can and he should have taught her."

"I expect you are right. Very well, then. Leave the interrogation to me."

Mr Xenophon now spoke in French again, addressing Jacquemard.

"The captain here wishes to ask Henriette a few questions. Please understand that the situation is extremely serious. You must also understand, however, that we are perfectly convinced of Henriette's discretion and loyalty to you. She is a good girl and intelligent enough to answer a few simple questions. Would you be good enough to come forward, Henriette, and sit at the table opposite Captain Delancey?"

After looking to her mother, who nodded, Henriette sat at the table with obvious reluctance. Looking at the girl with her perfect oval face, a little sunburnt and freckled, Delancey felt for a moment how easily he could himself have fallen in love with her. Who has not felt the same protective urge when confronted by such a picture of innocence? Glancing sideways, he could see that the Honourable Mr Northmore was already her slave. He could not allow his own sympathies to go so far. He could, however, be kind.

"How old are you, Henriette?"

Her voice barely audible, she whispered "Nineteen."

"And you have lived here all your life?"

"Yes," she admitted, nervously twisting the hem of her frock.

"Was it not rather a dull place?"

"I don't know."

"Without too many young men?"

"Very few."

"But there was Pierre Lebrun?"

"Yes" (in a whisper).

"How old is he?"

"Twenty-five, I think, or perhaps twenty-six."

"And living in the next village. Did he fall in love with you?"

"I don't know."

"But surely, Henriette, you must know?"

"He said that he liked me."

"Were you betrothed to him?"

"No, never." She looked to her father for support.

"No," agreed Henri. "But Pierre had made her an offer she had not refused."

"And then all the soldiers came, some of them with boots to be mended, and some of them liked you?"

"They said they did, one or two of them."

"And one of them you liked. Was he a sergeant?"

"Yes, but quite young."

"And what did your father think of him?"

Henri decided to intervene at this point:

"I thought him a fine young man with a gallant record in the war, a better match than Pierre, who was lame from birth."

Looking around, Delancey was aware that Mr Xenophon had disappeared. He resumed his questioning.

"And now all the soldiers have gone?"

"Yes" (with a catch in the voice, a half-sob).

"And did your sergeant say where he was going?"

"He didn't know."

"Did he say when he would return?"

"How could he?" (She was crying now.)

"But you expect him to write?"

"Oh, yes, I know he will."

"Did you talk with any other soldiers?"

"With two or three, one of them in the artillery."

"Camped to the north of here?"

"Camped up there." (She pointed, still in tears.)

"And did any of them know where he was going?"

"No."

"Nor when he would return."

"A soldier never knows that."

"I suppose not. So we must hope that your sergeant will come back to you."

"But he will—I know he will!"

"Of course, Henriette. You wouldn't have Pierre now, I expect, whatever happened?"

"Pierre? Never!"

"He must be disappointed though?"

"I am sorry if he is unhappy, but I wouldn't have him."

"Do you think he might be angry and turn against you?"

"I haven't thought of that. I suppose he might."

"Could he be dangerous?"

"I don't think so. Being lame could have made him bitter though."

"How did it happen?"

"There was an accident, I have been told, when he was a little boy."

Mr Xenophon was now back in the room and Delancey brought his interrogation to an end.

"Thank you, Henriette. You have been most helpful. We all wish you every happiness."

He could see that Mr Xenophon was very pleased with himself and asked him, accordingly, what he had learnt. The reply, in English, was brief:

"I found the letter. It is posted from Bethune and he says in it that he is learning German from a comrade. I think that is all we want to know. He is on his way to Germany."

"That seems all but certain. But what if other regiments come here to replace those that are gone?"

"I should like to be reassured about that. At the same time, I think it improbable. Napoleon would never use mere garrison troops for an invasion attempt. He would want his best regiments. And here we have proof that at least one of these has been sent away."

"Before embarking I must have a look at the camp site north of here, east of Zuphen. Perhaps you would like to come too? You might be able to tell whether a camp site has been permanently abandoned or is to be occupied again."

"Very well, then. I am willing, anyway, to try. I cannot at the moment decide what we should look for, the water supply, the drainage, or what else would signify in the eyes of a military man. It occurs to me—"

At this point Higgs quietly opened the front door and warned Delancey that some two or three men were approaching the cottage from the east, along the road. Delancey told Mr Xenophon and added that he would admit the leader to the cottage, leaving Mr Xenophon and his men to deal with the others, whatever their number. Mr Xenophon went outside at once and Delancey called Higgs into the cottage.

To Jacquemard he said, "Please answer the door when someone knocks. If it is someone you know, admit him. If it is Pierre Lebrun admit him and say 'Good evening, my friend' as you do so. Don't admit anyone else. Tell the women to go up to the loft.

"Higgs, stand behind the door. If more than one man should try to enter, knock the second man on the head with this."

He took the poker from the hearth, and handed it to the petty officer. Last of all, he drew his sword and took up a position on the other side of the front door, motioning Northmore to stand behind him.

The intruders seemed to make an infinitely cautious approach, pausing to listen and then moving nearer with silent tread. It was too dark for Mr Xenophon to identify them but he was able to assure himself that they numbered three. He waited with patience, holding his loaded walking stick. He heard, presently, a whispering near the front door of the cottage which ended when one man went forward, now with an audible tread, and the other two moved left and right so as to remain unseen when the door opened. After pausing again to listen, the leader of the group knocked on the door. Inside, Delancey motioned to Jacquemard who answered the door, calling out "Who is there?" There was no chain on the door but the same purpose was served by a log of wood which he had pushed into position. "Who is there?" he repeated, opening the door by about three inches. The visitor gave his name quietly and Jacquemard replied "Good evening, my friend." Kicking the log aside and opening the door more widely, he admitted Pierre Lebrun, who limped into the lamplight as he returned the greeting. Jacquemard closed the door after him and slid the bolt. Lebrun could now be seen as a stocky man of nondescript appearance in ordinary countryman's clothes. No suitable match for Henriette, thought Delancey. . . .

"Are you alone?" asked Lebrun. Jacquemard nodded and Lebrun continued, "I have brought two friends with me, men on whom we can rely. May I call them in?" At that instant Lebrun glanced sideways and saw Delancey, realising at once that he had been trapped. Before he could move Delancey ran him through with the sword, the point entering his left side near the heart. With no more than a single stifled cry he

collapsed on the floor in a pool of blood. He had been wearing a woollen bonnet and Delancey now used this to wipe his
sword before sheathing it. Then he opened the door more
widely and waited. In a minute Mr Xenophon joined him and
said quietly, "We have taken care of the other two."

"Are they dead?" asked Delancey. Mr Xenophon nodded.

"We could not take prisoners. I see that you are of the same
opinion."

"I was thinking of Jacquemard's safety."

"So was I, and I hope to God that these are the only men
who knew of his association with me. I incline to believe that
they were. Lebrun expected a reward for betraying Jacquemard
but he would not want to share it with more than he had to."

"It remains to dispose of the bodies. I expect that Jacquemard will help us."

Far from being immediately helpful, Jacquemard was
crouched, white-faced, over the fire, trembling violently after
being sick on the hearth.

"B-b-but why? Why kill Lebrun, your own agent? I never
saw bloodshed before. Why?" He made the sound of vomiting
but nothing came. "You are murderers!"

"He was betraying us, Jacquemard," replied Delancey. "He
had come with two men to arrest you. It was to protect you
that we killed them all. What else could we do? But we need
to dispose of the bodies so that the disappearance of these men
will have nothing to do with you. They left their homes in darkness, walking out into the night. No one will know where they
went. No one must ever know. We must bury them where the
newly turned earth will not show, and we must do it quickly.
Let's lift Lebrun outside, to begin with. Then call the women
down."

"But they had best know nothing about it."

"They know already. Do you think they are deaf? Some intruders have been killed. They need not know their names but we need their help to clean up the mess. Not a spot of blood must remain. Quick, Jacquemard, you must be ready by daylight to deny all knowledge of the affair. You have not seen Lebrun for days and cannot imagine why he should have gone out after dark. He will return, no doubt, you will be confident: and your daughter will be sad indeed if he doesn't."

To Mr Xenophon Delancey spoke as quickly and firmly.

"I shall go on to look at the artillery camp site. I suggest, however, that you remain here and attend the funeral. Then keep the rendezvous at the creek below Zuphen. We must be at sea before daybreak."

Chapter Eighteen

THE SOLUTION

DELANCEY set off for the camp site, accompanied only by Northmore. He set a rapid pace, knowing that time was short. As they stumbled and slipped on loose stones he tried to explain the object of his mission. "We know," he said finally, "that the camps near Ambleteuse have been deserted. We do not know whether the regiments which have gone will return or will be replaced by other troops. If the sites have been deserted for good we may conclude that Napoleon has cancelled the whole invasion plan. I think myself that all danger is past but a report to that effect must be supported by some real evidence, of which we have little at the present moment."

"What sort of evidence can we find, sir?"

"I don't know. We shall have to use our eyes and brains."

"I'll do my best, sir, but why should any regiment be sent away and then ordered back?"

"Why, to find grass for their horses. But Napoleon might also want to deceive us about his intentions, pretending to break up his invasion army but meaning to come back after our defending forces have been dispersed."

"But why should they disperse, sir?"

"Again, to find grass for *their* horses. So long as Napoleon's threat remains, our defending army must be grouped round Dover and other possible landing places. That means that the army cannot go elsewhere and raid French territory. So

Napoleon has his motive for leaving us in doubt. We shall perform a valuable service if we can report that this threatened invasion is now a mere feint."

"I understand, sir." The conversation died away as they went uphill. Then, as the ground levelled off for a space, Northmore ventured on the subject which filled his mind.

"What did you think of Henriette, sir?"

"I thought her very lovely. She is the sort of girl one remembers for the rest of one's life. We shall never see her again, however; that much is certain."

"But the war may end and we could travel once more."

"We should find her married to someone else. She will be married within the twelvemonth. You won't marry until you command a ship of your own, and then you'll marry the Admiral's daughter."

"It sounds a dull prospect, sir."

"Maybe I didn't set you the best example."

They were going uphill again and spared their breath for a while, each with his own thoughts. Delancey reminded himself that every man must at one time have dreamt about loving a perfectly innocent young girl, someone who would be affectionate, without artifice or pretence, a flower just ripe for the picking.

He had had that dream himself a lifetime ago in New York. Such a love affair or marriage might, he supposed, prove idyllic. Or would it? Who can tell what a pretty and giggling schoolgirl will turn out to be later on when aged thirty or forty? We might guess that she will be like her mother but who is to know? An attractive girl, too diffident to reveal her true character, can later be petulant, quarrelsome, extravagant, and vain. Henriette might end as a virago. . . . No, she wouldn't. Odd how the whiteness of her hands contrasted with the sunburnt complexion of her face. He himself had married late in life, as his professional career had served to dictate, and no sensible man would at that age have married a schoolgirl. He had been lucky enough to find a woman of the world, beautiful, passionate, and experienced. He wished that he were with her now and in her arms. Instead of that he was pacing the land of France, an enemy or spy, due to be killed on sight or shot after capture. He had best forget about his girl's white shoulders and think rather of his own peril. He looked anxiously at the eastern sky. Was it his imagination or was there already just a hint of the coming daybreak?

Dark as it was, Delancey followed Jacquemard's directions without much difficulty, coming at length to the track which had led from the road to the camp site. A post marked the spot but the sign, whatever it had been, was gone. The ground here was deeply trampled and rutted by the horses and gun carriages. It had been strewn with furze and bracken earlier in the year but now the ground was dry and hardened. A camp site likely to be occupied again would be guarded against trespass, surely, by two or three invalids provided with a tent? Or was that the wild guess of a seaman who, in reality, knew nothing about it? He should have had an army officer with him but the Admiral did not want that. His intelligence of the enemy must come from a naval source. Somewhere ahead of Delancey there was a noise in the darkness which he could not at first identify. He presently realised that sheep were grazing there. Did this provide proof that the camp site had been abandoned? It did nothing of the sort. When a new regiment appeared the sheep could be driven off. Then he came to a gate, flanked on either side by a stone-faced bank and hedge. The gate was new and far narrower than the gap in the earth bank. The space had been filled in with a railing. All the carpentry was solid and well put together, made to last. But the gate was just too narrow for a gun carriage or army wagon. He could see from the ruts that the military traffic had used a wider space. He could also see that the gap in the bank had been widened, no doubt while the camp existed. Now the soldiers had gone and the peasant owner of the field had returned. He had made money out of the soldiers, one might assume, selling them eggs and milk with an occasional rabbit or chicken. Now the artillery had gone and the sheep were back. Had the troops been expected to return, the gap would have been stuffed with uprooted thorn bushes. But the peasant had made a proper gate and fence. His land was once more his own. To be exact, this was the peasant's assumption, based on what information he could get. The peasant could be wrong and soldiers, Napoleon included, have been known to change their minds. But here was as good evidence as he was likely to find and it was strengthened by his discovery of a similar gate on the other side of the field. Beyond that again his way lay downhill through another and rather dirty field which had been too well grazed by horses—it was horse-sick, to use the expression he had heard—and here he came across a barn under construction; another solid and permanent-looking structure, the whole site smelling of sawdust and pitch. Here was something to clinch the opinion he had already formed.

"The peasant was well compensated for the use of his land. He has spent the money on a new barn and new gates."

Delancey was thinking to himself and was hardly aware of saying that last sentence aloud but Northmore replied at once:

"But didn't the peasant need the money to live on?"

"He didn't get it until the troops left."

"Then how did he live, sir?"

"He went to work for somebody else whose labourers had been conscripted into the army."

"It seems likely enough, sir."

"It is still fiction. But I am still ready to report that the camp site has been abandoned, and given back to the owners."

"Is that proof, sir, that it will never be occupied again?"

"No, it is no proof of that. But what proof could we expect to find? We can provide what seems to be proof of present intention. We can never offer our assurance that present decisions will not be reversed. Our task has been performed, Mr Northmore. I can report that the great invasion is not to take place this year, nor probably next year either. To make this report, however, we need to stay alive. We are now heading for the coast and we need to re-embark there in darkness. Time is short and there is just a hint of morning in the sky. On either side of the creek where we landed there is a French battery within half a mile. There will be sentinels posted and patrols going to and fro along the cliffs. We shall have to slip between them, and Mr Xenophon, following a different route to our left, will have to do the same."

"But won't the French patrols have seen the gunboat, sir?"

"She will have been pulled up under those overhanging rocks. We shall be in more danger when we put to sea."

The path lay downwards and they found themselves sheltered from the wind by the rising ground on either side. Somewhere ahead of them, as they knew, the path they were on would intersect with the cliff path which would cross the stream on their right by a footbridge. This was where they were most likely to meet with a patrol. The danger was real enough but Delancey took comfort from the fact that he wore a French uniform and could speak French with fluency, although with a provincial accent. Even Northmore knew enough to say "Oui, mon Capitaine" with reasonable confidence. It struck Delancey that Mr Xenophon, whose mission was an afterthought, was not disguised in the same way.

Descending the path towards the creek where they had landed was not as simple as the ascent had been. It was all too easy to trip over a loose stone and start a miniature landslide. Time was short, moreover, and a cock could be heard crowing at a distant farm. It would soon be morning, their gunboat exposed to the French artillery. How to combine speed with caution? Then, pausing for a minute's rest, they heard the sound they had been dreading: the tramp of a patrol approaching from their left. They must quit the path and find somewhere to hide.

Delancey had hardly reached this decision before there was a musket shot, followed after a pause by two or three more. The patrol had seen or heard some movement but none they had themselves made, for the shots had not been fired in their direction. It was clearly Mr Xenophon and his men who had run into trouble. They were armed only with pistols and loaded sticks and would be at a disadvantage when confronted (and outnumbered) by muskets and bayonets. While Mr Xenophon's two men might well be thought expendable, Mr Xenophon could not be replaced. It would be a disaster if he were killed, a worse disaster if he were taken. To judge from the sound of firing, which had died away for the moment, Mr Xenophon was still on the landward side of the cliff path. He had probably been about to cross it when the patrol appeared. The likelihood was that the firing would attract another patrol from the other direction. Turning away from his own line of retreat,

Delancey reached the cliff path and, telling Northmore to follow, marched towards the area where the patrol must be. He
made no further efforts to avoid noise. Why should he aim at
stealth? He was a French captain of artillery seeking to discover
what the noise was about. He feared at first that he would miss
the patrol but he presently saw that one of the Frenchmen carried a lantern. At least one of the men had remained on the
path while the others had gone uphill to deal with the intruders. As Delancey approached the lantern a young corporal
assumed the "on guard" position and shouted a challenge.

"Friend," replied Delancey, pressing on. "All right, Corporal, all right, all right! Where have they gone?"

"They are somewhere up there, Captain," replied the corporal, pointing.

"That is where you are wrong, corporal. They crossed the
path further back and headed down towards the sea. I just saw
them as they disappeared. Three men in civilian clothes—
smugglers, perhaps. Can you call the patrol back?"

"I can fire my musket. They will think that I have seen
them." The corporal fired in the air. "That will warn the
sergeant." Delancey drew a pistol and fired that in the air, telling Northmore to do the same. "The sounds of a skirmish," he
explained. "That will make the sergeant hurry." All three
weapons were now re-loaded and then Delancey asked the corporal his name.

"Lazareff" was the reply, followed by the information that
he came from Le Mans and had never been in battle before.
Delancey felt the urge to point out that he had never been in
battle yet. He restrained himself, however, and thought quickly
about his next move. It would be useful, he decided, to take a
few prisoners for questioning. These men were the nearest to

hand. He would send them down to the creek where they would run into Topley's men. He himself would follow to prevent their escape. The danger in this was that he and Northmore would be fired upon by their own side. As against this, the chief merit in the plan was that Mr Xenophon would hear the firing, not directed at him, and would make for the beach by some route further to the left. A further merit lay in the chance of taking prisoners but this was very much an afterthought. These men guarding the coast had never formed part of the Army of England and would have no intelligence better than hearsay. He doubted whether young Lazareff, for example, would have much to say for himself. Some minutes passed and then the patrol could be heard approaching, with much stumbling, slipping, and swearing. It comprised a sergeant and four men, all rather short of breath. Following his practice, Delancey did not wait to be questioned.

"These men have escaped you, sergeant. They crossed this path ten minutes ago. I just glimpsed them as they disappeared in that direction. Corporal Lazareff fired his musket as a signal. If we follow up we shall trap these men against the sea. I think they are smugglers rather than spies. They can explain themselves, however, when they are caught. They were unarmed so far as I could see."

Delancey was careful to stand in the light of the lantern, which showed up his uniform. He turned to Northmore and asked him whether he too thought that the men were unarmed. "Oui, mon Capitaine," replied Northmore, part perfect.

"So we have no call to be heroic. I think, sergeant, you should go for a hundred paces along this path and then swing left down the hillside. The lieutenant and I will follow you. Right? Off you go!"

Delancey had not exactly given an order, uncertain as to whether the sergeant would obey an officer from another regiment, but he had authority in his voice and the sergeant did as he was told, taking the corporal with him but with the lantern now extinguished. With more clattering and swearing, the patrol disappeared into the night and Delancey, with Northmore, followed at a more sedate pace. He feared that there would be a confused situation with friends attacking each other and foes escaping in the darkness. He felt tolerably certain, however, that Mr Xenophon would now be able to escape.

The eastern sky was turning pale and Delancey began to see the gunboat as an easy target for the French artillery. However, the immediate problem was to reach the shore, remembering that the sound of firing might bring more French soldiers into the area, and that further shots fired would bring them at the double. The path they were following was no sort of highway but it was flanked by rocks and bushes, enough to ensure that the French patrol would keep to the way they probably knew. Looking at the lie of the land and listening to the now audible sound of the breakers, Delancey knew that he was not far above the landing place. Below him and rather to his right he now heard voices raised, no doubt the challenge and reply. Then there followed a single shot and, after a pause, a ragged volley. Then there was silence broken by the hurried footsteps of the Frenchmen in retreat. They had run into Topley's men by whom they would have been considerably outnumbered. The likelihood was that several had fallen and that those on the run would number no more than three or four, the predestined prisoners included.

Delancey and Northmore drew their pistols and waited patiently on either side of the path. The first man to appear was a private soldier and Delancey shot him dead. The second, another private, lunged at Delancey with his bayonet. It was a clumsy attack, easily parried, and Delancey called on the young man to surrender. Surprisingly, the soldier threw himself again at Delancey with a fury which partly made up for his lack of skill. Slightly off balance, Delancey put the bayonet aside but found his opponent still ready to do or die. The butt of the musket swung upwards but missed and then the soldier, dropping that weapon, went straight for Delancey's throat. Delancey brought his knee up sharply but without much effect and he fell to the ground with his opponent on top of him. Pistol in hand, Northmore was afraid to fire for fear of hitting the wrong man, a danger made worse when Delancey rolled sideways to avoid being throttled. The struggle continued for a minute or two, the two opponents panting for breath but Delancey managed to free one leg and kick his opponent in the stomach. A minute later there was a shot and the Frenchman collapsed with a bullet through his head. Northmore dropped his smoking pistol and helped Delancey to his feet, asking anxiously whether he had been hurt. Recovering his sword, Delancey told the midshipman that he was unharmed and warned him to look out for the other Frenchmen. Having heard the shots and the voices, the other men approached at the double. First among them was the young Corporal Lazareff.

Telling Northmore to hold his fire, Delancey levelled his second pistol and told the young man that he was a prisoner. Lazareff obediently dropped his musket and raised his hands. His example was at once followed by the man behind him. No others appeared and Delancey concluded that the sergeant and another man had been killed at the outset. Northmore secured the two prisoners, using their own equipment to tie their hands, and both he and Delancey reloaded their pistols. Then they resumed their march.

"I think," said Delancey, "that the time has come to sing." Without further preamble he started on the first verse of a sea shanty, the one called "Spanish Ladies":

Farewell and adieu to you, fair Spanish ladies,
Farewell and adieu to you, ladies of Spain.
For we're off to find soundings in the Channel of
  Old England,
From Ushant to Scilly 'tis thirty-five leagues.

Unable to remember the second verse, he and Northmore sang the first verse again. Neither was particularly musical and the duet did them no credit at all. It served its purpose, however, for there was no firing as they scrambled down towards the shore. Topley's men would never fire on the singers of a shanty. Three minutes later Delancey was greeted by Topley himself, with evident relief.

"Thank God you're safe, sir!"

"Have you seen Mr Xenophon?"

"No, sir, he came in that lugger—" Topley pointed to a second craft drawn up near the gunboat, "—and went ashore with his two men. We have not seen him since."

"Two men are missing from that French patrol—do you know where they are?"

"One was killed, sir. His body lies to the left of the path. The other escaped, heading more in the other direction. I'm afraid our musketry was indifferent, sir."

"It was atrocious. It remains, however, to find Mr Xenophon. Have you a flare in the gunboat? I think we shipped two or three of them."

"Yes, sir."

"Light one. I want Mr Xenophon to see that the coast is clear."

"Even with a man unaccounted for, sir?"

"He is the sergeant, I think, and the man I wanted. Hurry up with that flare."

A minute or two later the whole landscape was lit as if in daylight. Low on the hillside to the right of the path three figures could be seen, two of them carrying a fourth. Delancey, now standing beside the gunboat, grabbed the speaking trumpet and shouted, "Come on, Mr Xenophon! The way is open but daybreak is near. Hurry!" Turning to Northmore, he added "Send a petty officer and two men to help carry the body—I think it is the sergeant's."

The next ten minutes seemed to last about a century with the sky growing lighter all the time. At long last, however, Mr Xenophon was on the beach, followed by two seamen carrying the sergeant. "He met with an accident," Mr Xenophon explained, regaining his breath. "He'll recover in an hour or two."

"All aboard!" ordered Delancey. "Hoist the tricolour and hoist a recognition signal—say, three lanterns in any pattern. Come with us in the gunboat, Mr Xenophon, but tell your men to get the lugger afloat and make sail after us. Now let's see how quickly we can have this gunboat afloat and under sail. Move, for God's sake!"

Within minutes the gunboat was through the breakers and Delancey, watching his men make sail, had time for a few words with Mr Xenophon.

"Well, sir," he said, "we can bring our government the news for which ministers have been waiting. All plans for invading England have clearly been cancelled."

"I agree," replied Mr Xenophon "and I hope that you will be given full credit for this exploit. You can surely expect the command of a larger frigate. After all, you have taken prisoners on French soil."

"Shall we learn anything from them?"

"I doubt it. They won't know anything."

"I am glad that we were able to save Jacquemard. He is a good man."

"Yes, but no longer of any use. He will be told to lie low until the war is over."

"Good. I hope they will be safe."

"My regret concerns that creature Fabius."

"Mine, too, Mr Xenophon, but don't grieve too much. His day of reckoning will come. I believe that somewhere, somehow, I shall meet that man again."

The sails filled, the gunboat gathered way, and Delancey stood by the helmsman, telling his men to man their guns and prepare for action. It was good to be at sea again and better to know that England—yes, and Guernsey—was safe from invasion for the time being. He would be given leave pending his next appointment and should be with Fiona in a matter of days or weeks. He had loved her as a child, loved her as an almost disreputable actress, and now loved her as a senior officer's wife and one who looked and behaved as if she had never been anything else. As a lover, at least, he knew himself to be the most fortunate of men. He also had the luck to be the bearer of good news for the Admiralty. He had fairly earned a better command.

It grew lighter every minute but the first hint of daybreak had been accompanied by a faint but freshening westerly breeze. The gunboat was under sail with creditable alacrity and the

lugger followed but Delancey presently made his men heave
to. When the lugger came ahead of the gunboat Delancey told
the men to keep their boat ahead of his and not worry if fired
upon. Mystified, the lugger's crew led the way on the course
that Delancey had given them. Soon afterwards the lugger was
fairly out of the bay where the landing had taken place and
plainly in view of the French artillerymen. The cannon boomed
on either side and French soldiers were already on the beach
from which they had sailed and from which they were now out
of small-arms range. But the scene was soon afterwards confused, from the French gunners' point of view, by the
appearance of a gunboat sailing in pursuit of the lugger. Not
only was the gunboat flying the tricolour, she was also engaging the lugger with her bow-chaser. Her broadside consisted of
mere swivel guns but she swung this way and that so as to
bring them into action. A lieutenant on the nearer battery of
the two in action cursed in fury: "If only that sacred gunboat
would take itself off we could sink the enemy!" It seemed to
him that the gunboat's practice was appalling, the shot splashing wide of the target, but the gunboat herself was too often
in his line of fire. Dancing with rage, he shouted to his sergeant
that the idiot, whoever he was, seemed to be doing it on purpose. "The imbecile!" he bawled. "The sacred and useless pig!"
As the swivel guns banged away the target was slowly passing
out of range from the shore batteries. It could not be doubted
that the gunboat would finally overtake her prey but without
choosing to share the credit with anyone else. It was obvious
that the gunboat, a far faster vessel, would have captured the
lugger already but for wasting time with her ridiculous pop-
guns. Seeing this, the lieutenant fairly shook his fist at the

gunboat and asked of an unresponsive heaven why the Emperor should waste money on his futile navy. In another hour the pursued and pursuer were hardly in sight. Leaving his men to scour out the cannon under his sergeant's direction, the lieutenant hurried to his tent and penned a letter of complaint. It was an eloquent letter, scribbled in the heat of the moment, and it led, inevitably, to the lieutenant's court martial.

Historical Fiction Published by McBooks Press

Available at bookstores. Call toll-free to order or request our free
book catalog: 1-888-BOOKS-11 (1-888-266-5711).
Visit the McBooks Press website: www.mcbooks.com

ALEXANDER KENT
The Bolitho Novels

___ 1 Midshipman Bolitho
0-935526-41-2 • 240 pp., $13.95

___ 2 Stand Into Danger
0-935526-42-0 • 288 pp., $13.95

___ 3 In Gallant Company
0-935526-43-9 • 320 pp., $14.95

___ 4 Sloop of War
0-935526-48-X • 352 pp., $14.95

___ 5 To Glory We Steer
0-935526-49-8 • 352 pp., $14.95

___ 6 Command a King's Ship
0-935526-50-1 • 352 pp., $14.95

___ 7 Passage to Mutiny
0-935526-58-7 • 352 pp., $15.95

___ 8 With All Despatch
0-935526-61-7 • 320 pp., $14.95

___ 9 Form Line of Battle!
0-935526-59-5 • 352 pp., $14.95

___ 10 Enemy in Sight!
0-935526-60-9 • 368 pp., $14.95

___ 11 The Flag Captain
0-935526-66-8 • 384 pp., $15.95

___ 12 Signal – Close Action!
0-935526-67-6 • 368 pp., $15.95

___ 13 The Inshore Squadron
0-935526-68-4 • 288 pp., $13.95

___ 14 A Tradition of Victory
0-935526-70-6 • 304 pp., $14.95

___ 15 Success to the Brave
0-935526-71-4 • 288 pp., $13.95

___ 16 Colours Aloft!
0-935526-72-2 • 304 pp., $14.95

___ 17 Honour This Day
0-935526-73-0 • 320 pp., $15.95

___ 18 The Only Victor
0-935526-74-9 • 384 pp., $15.95

___ 19 Beyond the Reef
0-935526-82-X • 352 pp., $14.95

___ 20 The Darkening Sea
0-935526-83-8 • 352 pp., $15.95

___ 21 For My Country's Freedom
0-935526-84-6 • 304 pp., $15.95

___ 22 Cross of St George
0-935526-92-7 • 320 pp., $16.95

___ 23 Sword of Honour
0-935526-93-5 • 320 pp., $15.95

___ 24 Second to None
0-935526-94-3 • 352 pp., $16.95

___ 25 Relentless Pursuit
1-59013-026-X • 368 pp., $16.95

___ 26 Man of War
1-59013-066-9 • 320 pp., $24.95 HC

DOUGLAS REEMAN
Royal Marines Saga

___ 1 Badge of Glory
1-59013-013-8 • 384 pp., $16.95

___ 2 The First to Land
1-59013-014-6 • 304 pp., $15.95

___ 3 The Horizon
1-59013-027-8 • 368 pp., $15.95

___ 4 Dust on the Sea
1-59013-028-6 • 384 pp., $15.95

Modern Naval Fiction Library

___ Twelve Seconds to Live
1-59013-044-8 • 368 pp., $15.95

___ Battlecruiser
1-59013-043-X • 320 pp., $15.95

___ The White Guns
1-59013-083-9 • 368 pp., $15.95

DEWEY LAMBDIN
Alan Lewie Naval Adventures

___ 2 The French Admiral
1-59013-021-9 • 448 pp., $17.95

___ 8 Jester's Fortune
1-59013-034-0 • 432 pp., $17.95

continues . . .

DUDLEY POPE
The Lord Ramage Novels
___ 1 Ramage
    0-935526-76-5 • 320 pp., $14.95
___ 2 Ramage & the Drumbeat
    0-935526-77-3 • 288 pp., $14.95
___ 3 Ramage & the Freebooters
    0-935526-78-1 • 384 pp., $15.95
___ 4 Governor Ramage R. N.
    0-935526-79-X • 384 pp., $15.95
___ 5 Ramage's Prize
    0-935526-80-3 • 320 pp., $15.95
___ 6 Ramage & the Guillotine
    0-935526-81-1• 320 pp., $14.95
___ 7 Ramage's Diamond
    0-935526-89-7 • 336 pp., $15.95
___ 8 Ramage's Mutiny
    0-935526-90-0 • 280 pp., $14.95
___ 9 Ramage & the Rebels
    0-935526-91-9 • 320 pp., $15.95
___ 10 The Ramage Touch
    1-59013-007-3 • 272 pp., $15.95
___ 11 Ramage's Signal
    1-59013-008-1 • 288 pp., $15.95
___ 12 Ramage & the Renegades
    1-59013-009-X • 320 pp., $15.95
___ 13 Ramage's Devil
    1-59013-010-3 • 320 pp., $15.95
___ 14 Ramage's Trial
    1-59013-011-1 • 320 pp., $15.95
___ 15 Ramage's Challenge
    1-59013-012-X, 352 pp., $15.95
___ 16 Ramage at Trafalgar
    1-59013-022-7 • 256 pp., $14.95
___ 17 Ramage & the Saracens
    1-59013-023-5 • 304 pp., $15.95
___ 18 Ramage & the Dido
    1-59013-024-3 • 272 pp., $15.95

DAVID DONACHIE
The Privateersman Mysteries
___ 1 The Devil's Own Luck
    1-59013-004-9 • 302 pp., $15.95
    1-59013-003-0 • 320 pp., $23.95 HC

___ 2 The Dying Trade
    1-59013-006-5 • 384 pp., $16.95
    1-59013-005-7 • 400 pp., $24.95 HC
___ 3 A Hanging Matter
    1-59013-016-2 • 416 pp., $16.95
___ 4 An Element of Chance
    1-59013-017-0 • 448 pp., $17.95
___ 5 The Scent of Betrayal
    1-59013-031-6 • 448 pp., $17.95
___ 6 A Game of Bones
    1-59013-032-4 • 352 pp., $15.95

The Nelson & Emma Trilogy
___ 1 On a Making Tide
    1-59013-041-3 • 416 pp., $17.95
___ 2 Tested by Fate
    1-59013-042-1 • 416 pp., $17.95

C. NORTHCOTE PARKINSON
The Richard Delancey Novels
___ 1 The Guernseyman
    1-59013-001-4 • 208 pp., $13.95
___ 2 Devil to Pay
    1-59013-002-2 • 288 pp., $14.95
___ 3 The Fireship
    1-59013-015-4 • 208 pp., $13.95
___ 4 Touch and Go
    1-59013-025-1 • 224 pp., $13.95
___ 5 So Near So Far
    1-59013-037-5 • 224 pp., $13.95
___ 6 Dead Reckoning
    1-59013-038-3 • 224 pp., $15.95

JAN NEEDLE
Sea Officer William Bentley Novels
___ 1 A Fine Boy for Killing
    0-935526-86-2 • 320 pp., $15.95
___ 2 The Wicked Trade
    0-935526-95-1 • 384 pp., $16.95
___ 3 The Spithead Nymph
    1-59013-040-5 • 288 pp., $14.95

PHILIP McCUTCHAN
Halfhyde Adventures
___ 1 Halfhyde at the Bight of
    Benin
    1-59013-078-2• 224 pp., $13.95
___ 2 Halfhyde's Island
    1-59013-079-0• 224 pp., $13.95

V.A. STUART
Alexander Sheridan Adventures
___ 1 Victors and Lords
    0-935526-98-6 • 272 pp., $13.95
___ 2 The Sepoy Mutiny
    0-935526-99-4 • 240 pp., $13.95
___ 3 Massacre at Cawnpore
    1-59013-019-7 • 240 pp., $13.95
___ 4 The Cannons of Lucknow
    1-59013-029-4 • 272 pp., $14.95
___ 5 The Heroic Garrison
    1-59013-030-8 • 256 pp., $13.95

The Phillip Hazard Novels
___ 1 The Valiant Sailors
    1-59013-039-1 • 272 pp., $14.95
___ 2 The Brave Captains
    1-59013-040-5 • 272 pp., $14.95
___ 3 Hazard's Command
    1-59013-081-2 • 256 pp., $13.95
___ 4 Hazard of Huntress
    1-59013-081-0 • 256 pp., $13.95

NICHOLAS NICASTRO
The John Paul Jones Trilogy
___ 1 The Eighteenth Captain
    0-935526-54-4 • 312 pp., $16.95
___ 2 Between Two Fires
    1-59013-033-2 • 384 pp., $16.95

IRV C. ROGERS
___ Motoo Eetee
    1-59013-018-9 • 400 pp., $24.95 HC

Classics of Nautical Fiction
RAFAEL SABATINI
___ Captain Blood
    0-935526-45-5 • 288 pp., $15.95
WILLIAM CLARK RUSSELL
___ The Yarn of Old Harbour
    Town
    0-935526-65-X • 256 pp., $14.95
___ The Wreck of the Grosvenor
    0-935526-52-8 • 320 pp., $13.95
A.D. HOWDEN SMITH
___ Porto Bello Gold
    0-935526-57-9 • 288 pp., $13.95
MICHAEL SCOTT
___ Tom Cringle's Log
    0-935526-51-X • 512 pp., $14.95

CAPTAIN FREDERICK MARRYAT
___ Frank Mildmay OR
    The Naval Officer
    0-935526-39-0 • 352 pp., $14.95
___ The King's Own
    0-935526-56-0 • 384 pp., $15.95
___ Mr Midshipman Easy
    0-935526-40-4 • 352 pp., $14.95
___ Newton Forster OR
    The Merchant Service
    0-935526-44-7 • 352 pp., $13.95
___ Snarleyyow OR
    The Dog Fiend
    0-935526-64-1 • 384 pp., $16.95
___ The Phantom Ship
    0-935526-85-4 • 320 pp., $14.95
___ The Privateersman
    0-935526-69-2 • 288 pp., $15.95

Military Fiction Classics
R.F. DELDERFIELD
___ Seven Men of Gascony
    0-935526-97-8 • 368 pp., $16.95
___ Too Few for Drums
    0-935526-96-X • 256 pp., $14.95